CALLING CHAOS

DEMON BOUND
BOOK 3

GRAE BRYAN

PROLOGUE

Chaos

Chaos was bored.

Bored, bored, bored, bored, bored.

If he'd known signing his powers into the Book would mean centuries in the Void with nothing to do... Well, he wasn't sure what he would have done, but fire probably would have been involved. Fire and screaming and maybe a dismemberment or two.

It had been bearable before, with the incubus to entertain him —or that big, fuddy-duddy warrior to annoy—but now Kai *and* Nix had been summoned, and it was just too much.

Or make that too little.

Especially because Nightmare was refusing to play.

"Come on," Chaos whined again. "Pretty please?"

Nightmare's white eyes flashed in the darkness of the cave, their eerie glow the only sign that he was getting truly annoyed. "No. I gave you what you wished for yesterday. Leave me alone, little demon."

Usually Chaos would have been pleased—he was one of the only demons capable of getting Nightmare to string more than two words together at a time, and that had been a whole sentence right there. But at the moment, he was too put out to glory in his triumph.

"But you're always alone!" he cried out instead, stamping his foot on the dry, dusty ground, his tail lashing furiously behind him. "And it's just the two of us, so that means *I'm* always alone! It's not fair."

"It has been a day," Nightmare pointed out in his low, creepy rasp. "One *day* since Nix was summoned."

That had Chaos pausing. "Really?" He nibbled on his lower lip, considering. "It feels like longer."

Nightmare let out a low growl. His growls weren't as rumbly grumbly as Kai's, more like the tumbling of rocks than the roar of a lion. But they still managed to put a shiver down the spine. "Leave, or suffer the consequences."

Oooh, consequences. Now he was talking. Maybe Nightmare would sic his shadow monsters on him and Chaos could try to set them on fire. It never worked—those things were barely corporeal —but it was fun to try, at least before they invaded his senses and tried to drive him to madness.

But suck it, shadow monsters—madness already ran in Chaos's veins. What was a little dollop more?

Chaos pushed forward into Nightmare's cave until the tall, lanky demon was visible beyond the glowing white eyes, his dark-gray skin blending in with the rock walls around him. Chaos put his hands on his hips, speaking deliberately. "I. Am. Bored."

Quick as a whip, Nightmare's hand lashed out, grabbing Chaos by the throat. Hard. Chaos grinned. See? Now they were having fun!

But then Nightmare's talons punctured Chaos's skin, and his grin fell.

Not the paralysis, damn it.

Nightmare used it to keep humans docile while he tormented them, which was hilarious to witness, but it wasn't so funny when Chaos was the one getting paralyzed.

He tried to jerk back, but he could already feel Nightmare's venom working through him.

No, no, no, no, no.

Nightmare pulled Chaos close by the throat until his gaunt face was looming over Chaos, his visage shifting back and forth between his usual demonic appearance and the skull-faced monstrosity he used when haunting humans' bad dreams. "I warned you, Chaos," he hissed. "I am not your friendly incubus, nor your ambivalent warrior. I am singular, and I tire of your antics."

Chaos tried to respond, but his vocal cords were already frozen. He wished he could stick his tongue out at least. Why did Nightmare have to be such a jerk? Just because Chaos had been hounding him for hours without letting up, ignoring his many requests for silence, Nightmare thought he had the right to chastise him?

Unfair. Unfair and *boring*, which was even worse.

Nightmare tossed Chaos's paralyzed body onto the cave floor —he didn't even do it gently either—and stalked off into the shadows of the deeper caves.

Chaos was left alone, stiff as a board, with only his stupid thoughts for company.

Nightmare hadn't even turned the portal on for Chaos to watch while he lay there.

Mean. Mean, mean, mean, mean.

Chaos spent some time entertaining himself by trying and failing to move different muscles, but that got old pretty fast and made him too aware that his wings and tail were crumpled underneath him. That was going to cramp later for sure.

He shifted to daydreaming, planning what he'd do first when he was summoned. Because he would be; he was sure of it. First Kai and now Nix? It was obvious their Book had been found, and now it was only a matter of time before Chaos got his turn in the human realm.

And then Chaos wouldn't be contained any longer, would he? No more boring Void. No more lazing around with only three lousy demons for company.

And while he couldn't *technically* hurt the human who summoned him—bound by the magical terms of their contract— there were ways around that. Always a loophole or two to be found, if need be.

Because Chaos refused to be leashed or muzzled any longer. He was finally going to be *free*, damn it. He would no longer bow to any master beyond the pandemonium that ruled his nature, and the poor, foolish human who summoned him was just going to have to deal with it.

So take that, boredom! Chaos would even be smirking right now, if his facial muscles were working properly.

It was all going to be so. Much. Fun.

1

Cooper

The upside of not showering for five days was just how amazingly *clean* Cooper felt now as he stepped outside of the steam-filled cubicle in his overly large bathroom.

The downside was, of course, the shame in remembering he'd just...forgotten to bathe for five days in a row. Not that it was the first time that had happened.

Nor would it be the last...

Cooper grabbed blindly for his towel, scrubbing at his hair and face first so he could snag his glasses from the counter and shove them on before he tackled the rest. He supposed it was a good thing Ivan had called, demanding Cooper's presence today. Cooper had gotten way too invested in this little challenge he was working on. He was close to breaking it, he knew, and it had been all too tempting to just keep at it until he cracked it.

But not tempting enough to risk Ivan's wrath; that was for sure —he may have been Cooper's cousin as well as his employer, but family ties didn't mean much to a man like Ivan when he was displeased.

Cooper made a point of *never* displeasing him.

Working as the main tech guy for a branch of the Russian Mafia wasn't the career path Cooper would have chosen if left to his own devices, he was pretty sure, but it was hard to know at this point. His dad had reluctantly signed him up to work for Dimitri —Ivan's late father and the old head of the family business— when Cooper was still a teenager.

Cooper hadn't had a chance to know anything else.

Luckily, now that Ivan was in charge, Cooper was able to do most of his work remotely. Gone were the days of him gofering between lieutenants at all hours, gut twisting as he tried to interact with hardened mobsters without drawing attention to himself.

But now Ivan wanted Cooper there in person.

It made Cooper's throat go all dry and tight, the thought of facing him in that cold office building, nothing between them except Ivan's admittedly massive desk.

Then again, leaving the house at all these days made Cooper feel all kinds of ways.

His dad would be so disappointed. Cooper could hear him now. *I don't want to see you become a recluse,* umnitsa.

Cooper frowned at the thought as he rifled through his dresser for clean clothes, his towel wrapped haphazardly around his hips. *Then you shouldn't have left me all alone, old man.*

He settled on a pair of jeans and a T-shirt he was mostly sure he'd washed recently, throwing one of his well-worn hoodies over it. He ignored his mirror—he wasn't going to be able to do anything with his not-sure-if-it's-wavy-or-straight tawny hair, anyway—and headed back to his workroom.

To get to his computer, he had to wade through the mess on the floor: a sea of empty energy drink cans and takeout containers.

It'd be embarrassing if there was ever another human over to see it.

Whatever. At least the takeout containers were a sign he hadn't been forgetting to eat. He'd clean when he got home from his meeting.

Cooper opened the encrypted chat he'd had minimized on his laptop. There was a message from RedRabbit waiting for him.

R: *You're close, aren't you? I can tell.*

Cooper nibbled on his thumbnail as he stared at the message, then realized what he was doing and shoved his hoodie string in his mouth to chew on instead.

Rabbit was the one who'd set up the challenge Cooper was working on: infiltrating the servers of what was supposedly a dummy corporation in Norway. It was most definitely something the guy—at least, Cooper was *mostly* sure at this point that Rabbit was a guy—had created to size up the competition in the hacker world.

It wasn't the sort of thing Cooper would have normally entertained, but he and Rabbit had gotten to chatting in various other forums a while ago. The guy was less awkward than most of the people Cooper connected with online, and he never tried to push or trick Cooper into giving away his secrets like some did. So Cooper hadn't minded giving Rabbit's little game a go. It was a way to pass the time, if nothing else.

But he left the message waiting for now. There wasn't any sense in bragging before the thing was done. Plus, if he waited until tonight to respond, when he wasn't about to run out the door, they could get a chat going, maybe connect in real time.

Just admit you're lonely as fuck.

Please. Like that was any sort of secret. Lonely and now getting to the point of being seriously touch-starved. How long had it been since he'd even had a hookup?

Maybe Cooper would venture into the apps tonight, see if he

could find someone to fuck him out of his head. But that would mean either inviting someone to his apartment—Cooper wrinkled his nose at the mess surrounding him—or going to some unknown location instead.

Cooper didn't have that in him after shutting himself off to the outside world for the past week. He'd need to do baby steps to get used to strange people and strange places again. He'd go to Ivan's office and get the meeting over with. Ivan always sent a driver, so Cooper wouldn't have to deal with the subway crowds or a chatty taxi driver. When he got home, he'd clean his apartment so it looked like an actual human lived there and not a garbage raccoon in a human suit. And tomorrow he'd make himself go out for a bagel.

Then he'd work his way up to getting fucked by a stranger.

In the meantime, there was always porn. Because, sure, porn was definitely a replacement for real human touch.

Cooper shook his head, annoyed at himself. He didn't *need* human touch to get off—that was what toys were for.

But first, he had to actually leave his apartment and see what Ivan wanted.

———

THE DRIVER IVAN sent didn't speak, beyond the initial mumbled greeting, for which Cooper was incredibly grateful. Same with the security guard that manned the entrance to Ivan's office building, who knew the sight of Cooper well enough to give him one of those manly nods as he passed by, but not well enough to attempt a conversation.

That was two hurdles passed. See? This was fine. Cooper was *fine*. So Ivan wanted to talk to him. So what? He wasn't going to *kill* Cooper or anything.

At least, probably not.

Cooper just hoped Sergei wasn't there today. Ivan's right-hand man was a mean, scary asshole in the same way Ivan's father, Dimitri, had been. Sergei seemed to think Cooper mainly played video games on the family's dime, and he loved to let him know how much that idea pissed him off.

Which was only half-true. Cooper *did* play a lot of video games, but he did work stuff too, when Ivan remembered to give him any to do. And part of the reason Cooper didn't want to catch sight of Sergei today was the work Ivan had asked him to do after Sascha's stabbing by a rival family two months ago: Cooper had been tasked to look into Sergei's finances. Finances that were definitely *not* on the up-and-up.

Sergei was taking money from someone who wasn't Ivan. He hid it well but not nearly well enough, given Cooper's skills. Ivan had shattered a full bottle of vodka by throwing it at the wall when Cooper had told him.

Cooper was hoping for less broken glass this visit.

He pressed the elevator button, fiddling with his hoodie strings and repeatedly reminding himself not to put them in his mouth when in public.

"Going up?"

Cooper didn't jump exactly, but it was a near thing. He shot a startled glance to the right, clocking the bearer of the smooth, flirty voice. No big deal. Just an inhumanly beautiful man with long, wavy red hair in a high ponytail now standing next to him. One who apparently moved like a ninja, since Cooper hadn't heard him coming.

He saw the guy do a double take as he caught sight of Cooper's eyes. Cooper was used to people staring. He'd been born with heterochromia, with one brown eye and one green. He didn't like the extra attention it brought him—hated it with a fucking passion, really. But it was hard to mind as much because this guy had freaky eyes too. They were purple.

"Well, aren't you lovely?" the guy crooned, like Cooper wasn't an out-of-shape nerd in desperate need of a haircut, wearing clothes that were only *probably* clean.

"Uh..." Cooper turned his gaze to his feet immediately. He was barely equipped for human interaction of any kind today, let alone beautiful men flirting with him. Especially because this seemed to be the kind of flirting attractive people like that did by habit. There wasn't any real intent behind it, and Cooper never knew how to respond.

What would it be like to be effortlessly charming like that? Cooper wouldn't have to be trawling through apps for dick; he knew that much.

They got into the elevator together, and Cooper did his best to breathe normally, trapped in the small space with a stranger. How *did* someone breathe normally? Like, two seconds in, two seconds out? He'd forgotten somehow, but he hoped he was doing it right.

What was a guy like this doing at Ivan's office, anyway? He was dressed in a flouncy blouse and extremely tight leather pants and had just been openly flirtatious with another man. Basically the opposite sort of presence Ivan usually allowed at his side. Cooper could see the guy being *Sascha's* friend—Cooper's other cousin had always ventured toward the flamboyant, those few instances he'd been able to get away with it—but not Ivan's.

There wasn't time to dwell on it, though, not when Cooper was about to face Ivan himself. He headed straight out of the elevator, toward Ivan's office, the only occupied room on the floor, glancing behind his shoulder every now and then to confirm the stranger really was going to the same destination.

At the last minute, the guy slid in front of him to enter the office first, announcing to Ivan, "You have a visitor."

Cooper stepped in after him, just in time to catch Ivan glaring at the guy from behind his desk. But as he caught sight of Cooper, his expression smoothed in an instant, back to his usual emotionless mask.

"Cooper."

Ivan looked the same as ever, in the brief glance Cooper caught before he looked to his own feet again. Handsome in a scary, icy way, all white-blond hair and pale-blue eyes. He looked just like his father, whereas Cooper was connected to him by his mother's side. She and Cooper's father had been siblings.

Now they were both dead and gone, and somehow Cooper was still here, working for mobsters.

"You needed me?"

"We have two people who need identification," Ivan told him, tapping at his desk.

"Fake IDs?" Cooper asked, a little disappointed. That was quick, boring work and could have easily been a phone call.

"Not enough. We need thorough documentation of their existence. Enough for travel, residency...whatever they might require. And it needs to come from nothing."

Now that was more interesting. A lot of paperwork was required to create a whole legal human out of nothing. Cooper looked up from his feet. "Social security cards, even?"

Ivan nodded at him. "Can you do it?"

"Uh...sure." Of course he could. Cooper nibbled at his lip, already going through the logistics in his head. "I need approximate ages," he told Ivan. "Photos."

"I can get you those." Ivan pushed a fat stack of old-fashioned ledgers on his desk toward Cooper. "And I need these digitized."

There was the boring busywork he'd feared. But Cooper didn't mind so much now—creating the false identities would be kind of fun, at least. And he needed to earn his spacious apartment and ample salary somehow. He stepped forward to the side of the desk and gathered the ledgers.

He was startled to find the pretty stranger at his side in the next instant, knocking his hip against an open desk drawer Cooper had missed, revealing another book. "You missed one."

"Oh. Um, thank you." Cooper grabbed for the thing blindly, trying not to flinch at the stranger's close proximity. He held all the ledgers close to his chest as Ivan cleared his throat, for some reason radiating disapproval.

"This is Nix, my new assistant. He's one of the ones needing ID."

Surprise had Cooper glancing up and meeting Nix's purple eyes. Assistant? Surely not. But Cooper wasn't going to go around contradicting Ivan. "You, um, have a preference for your birth-day?" he asked Nix instead.

Nix winked at him. Cooper had never met anyone who winked at people in real life. "Whatever you think best, Cooper, darling."

"Don't flirt with Coop," Ivan reprimanded. But it was weird, because even though his voice was harsh, he sounded almost... fond? "He can't handle your teasing."

Nix's voice lowered into a croon. "Not like you, Vanya."

Okay, so *that* was real flirting, not the flirting-on-automatic Nix had been doing with Cooper. Cooper's eyes widened as he glanced between the two of them. What the fuck was going on? Was Ivan *involved* with this guy? With a man?

It was the most unlikely thing Cooper had ever heard, considering Ivan's history, but then Ivan actually tugged Nix into his side, pulling him onto the arm of his chair. It was an act of intimacy if Cooper had ever seen one.

Everyone's getting laid but you, loser.

Thank you, brain, that's very helpful.

Ivan cocked his head pointedly toward the door. "That'll be all, Coop."

Nix waved at him. "Bye, Coop. So lovely to make your acquaintance."

If Cooper kept staring at them like this, Ivan was going to give him something to stare at, he was sure. Like a gun in his face. So Cooper pulled his hoodie up and walked out of the room quickly, the ledgers tucked against him, feeling more than a little dazed.

He'd thought he was going to be acclimating himself back into the real world slowly after a week locked in his apartment, but instead he felt like he'd just entered topsy-turvy land.

If Ivan—one of the most emotionally repressed representatives of toxic masculinity Cooper knew—was experimenting with bisexuality with what might just be a literal supermodel...

Well, what other strange things might the world have in store for Cooper today?

2

Cooper

Despite the strangeness Cooper had encountered at Ivan's office, there were no more acts of lunacy from the universe on the way home. No flying pigs (or flying monkeys, for that matter). No alien entities dropping from the sky.

Cooper wasn't sure whether to be relieved or disappointed.

Relieved, definitely. He wouldn't know what to do with a flying pig if he came across one. Take it to an animal rescue?

He summoned his boldness and asked the driver to stop at the corner of his block so he could head into the bodega. He gathered a few energy drinks and an armful of red licorice packages, plus a box of trash bags, since he was pretty sure he was out. He also ordered a chicken parm hero while he was at it, recognizing the need to eat something real for dinner. Or... lunch? Time was confusing when he'd been sleeping at odd hours, tucked in his workroom. He glanced at the clock—lunch it was.

So he'd eat half for lunch and save half for dinner, and bam, that was two square meals right there. Just like any old real, functioning human.

The guy manning the register knew him and knew Cooper wasn't much for chatting. He never commented on Cooper's eyes or said anything about the nutritional value of his purchases, so Cooper had an immense amount of fondness for him.

When the driver dropped him off at his apartment building—he'd insisted on waiting at the corner and dropping Cooper off directly at his building ("Boss's orders, Coop")—Cooper nodded to the doorman and headed up, ledgers in one hand and bags from the bodega in the other.

The building Ivan had set him up in was expensive as fuck, Cooper was pretty sure, but it wasn't fancy in a way that set Cooper's teeth on edge. The doorman and the guard at the desk were always polite but impersonal, and the other tenants all minded their own business. All in all, it was a pretty good deal for someone who didn't like leaving the house much.

Once Cooper had unlocked his ten different locks and reset them all behind him, he headed to his workroom, dropping the ledgers in the corner and eyeing the mess.

It was even worse with fresh eyes. His actual work area was fine—the large, L-shaped desk with its monitor, two desktops, and ergonomic keyboard, plus the laptop he kept to the side for convenience. There were a few half-empty energy drinks tucked here and there, but otherwise it was all clean enough.

It was the rest of the room that was the issue. Cooper hated when he got like this, or at least when he had to face the evidence of it. It reminded him too much of his father at the end, before Cooper had realized he needed to move in with him—when his dad had been too sick and drunk to look after himself but too ashamed to ask Cooper for help.

Not like this, umnitsa, his dad had pleaded one night, bleary-eyed and only half-conscious. *Don't—don't remember me like this.*

But what other way was there to remember him? Cooper blinked stinging eyes. He may not have been a drunk—he was too afraid to touch the stuff, considering how his dad had ended up— but he supposed he had his own ways of getting lost in his demons. Focusing too hard on projects and forgetting to take care of himself, for one.

He needed to watch himself, make sure he kept coming up for air. He couldn't lose it completely, not like that.

He got to work cleaning, which mostly involved stuffing garbage into trash bags and then taking them all to the chute. He did a cursory dusting and vacuum afterward and managed to make it look like a functioning person lived there by the end.

He settled in his cushy computer chair, eyeing his laptop and the message from Rabbit. It was tempting to respond now, but work came first, before he forgot about his tasks.

The false identities would have been fun to tackle, but Cooper needed to get in touch with a contact about social security numbers before he could really begin. He sent the message on a secure network, then swiveled his chair to face the corner, glaring at the ledgers he'd left there.

He really should get started on those. If he left them, he'd never want to tackle the chore. And he only needed to scan them in and send them back to Ivan—it wasn't like he actually needed to organize the data. Ivan would hire someone else for that part, probably a real accountant. A dirty one.

So Cooper gathered the ledgers and set them on his desk. They were all pretty much identical—big, old-fashioned, leather-bound things—barring the book Nix had reminded him to grab, which was much smaller.

Cooper pulled the scanning app up on his phone and got to work. It was—just as he'd expected—dull as all fuck.

He got through two ledgers, scarfing bites of his sandwich in between pages, before he had to stand and stretch the kinks out of his neck. Just the two books had taken him hours already—the stupid, thick things were full of stupid, thick data.

It was annoying—give him a good project and Cooper could go for more hours than this without even realizing he needed to pee. But give him a mindless task like this and he was painfully aware of every passing minute.

His gaze fell on the one outlier in the group. It wasn't just smaller than the other but also...pretty, kind of? Definitely designed with more in mind than just function. There were etchings on it, and it looked older than the rest. Cooper set it in front of him and—after making sure his hands were clean, no sandwich drippings to be found—began flipping through the pages, sipping on an energy drink as he did so.

There weren't any numbers in the thing, which was odd. And the writing wasn't in any language Cooper had ever seen before. It definitely wasn't Russian; he knew that much. The book was filled with intricate symbols set across from stanzas that were either ancient or...made up?

Why the fuck would Ivan want this thing digitized? Was this some black-market artifact he was hoping to sell? It wasn't like he needed the extra cash...

Either way, the symbols were cool to look at. At least it gave Cooper something different to stare at for a while. And it was, what, maybe a hundred pages? He could get through it fast, no problem.

Then he'd reward himself with a break. It wasn't like Ivan had given him a deadline with these things. It was only that Cooper knew if he didn't tackle them now, he'd forget they existed when more interesting tasks came along.

He got through the first fifty or so symbols without issue, but then he stopped. The symbol he'd just revealed was...interesting. They were all cool-looking, really, and Cooper wasn't exactly sure why this one was more entrancing than the others. Maybe the color? It was a bright, golden yellow, and the symbol was a mess of swirling loops, the kind of thing where the eye couldn't tell where one line ended and the next began.

The longer Cooper's gaze settled on it, the more it seemed to almost move.

Cooper side-eyed the energy drink in his hand, then set it aside. Maybe he should lay off for the rest of the day.

He traced the symbol lightly with his finger, even though he knew he probably shouldn't be touching it. But Ivan hadn't said anything about needing to be careful in preserving the thing, had he? And Cooper could swear there was heat coming off it too.

If Cooper were bolder—and if he had zero respect for the sanctity of books—he'd want to rip that page out and...what? Hang it up? Tuck it under his pillow? He wasn't sure. But he knew he'd want to keep it close, to pull it out and look at it whenever he wanted.

Well, whatever. He wasn't going to deface one of Ivan's books and run the risk of being defaced himself in retribution. After he scanned it, he could make the symbol the background image on his laptop if he really wanted.

But first, he needed to scan it in.

Cooper opened the app on his phone again and took a careful picture. The image took longer than the others to upload onto his computer, the lines seeming to swirl and pulse in and out of focus as the image resolution came through. Cooper rubbed his itchy nose and traced a finger over his laptop screen, the way he'd traced it over the book.

Red smeared on his screen, covering the now clear image of the symbol.

Damn it.

Cooper clapped a hand over his face, reaching for a tissue. A fucking nose bleed. Too little sleep and too much caffeine were finally catching up with him.

He stuffed the tissue into his nostrils, leaning forward so blood didn't start trickling down his throat. It would stop by itself in a minute, if past experience was any indicator. Cooper grabbed another tissue to wipe his screen while he was at it. *Gross.*

He really was a fucking gremlin today, wasn't he?

He stared at the pretty symbol as he waited for the bleeding to stop, but his perusal was interrupted by a chat box popping up.

Which was strange because it wasn't from any chat program Cooper recognized. Nothing he'd set up himself; that was for sure.

But there was a message anyway, in a bright-yellow font that hurt his eyes.

You summoned me?

———

BY THE TIME Cooper's nosebleed had stopped and he'd run to the bathroom to wash the blood off his face and fingers, his suspicion had only grown.

Where the fuck had the message come from?

He tried to look into the program, but there didn't seem to be one running. Just the little gray box with bright-yellow font, front and center. It had a close-out *x* in the corner of the box too, but Cooper wasn't dumb enough to click it. Not when the whole thing could be some phishing scam.

So the little box stayed up on his screen.

After another minute of Cooper poking around, a second message popped up below the first one in the box.

Well? Summoner? I don't have all day. And then, immediately after, *Well, I do. But it's very boring in here.*

That prompted a chuckle out of Cooper. He could relate well enough to mind-numbing boredom today.

He should leave it alone, but he was curious. And Cooper

wasn't stupid enough to click on any unfamiliar links, or to send any personal info, so what was the harm in replying?

How did I summon you? he asked.

Clumsily, the program replied.

Cooper let out another soft snort of laughter. This secret messenger was kind of funny. Was this an AI thing? They didn't usually have a sense of humor, but sometimes the comedy was accidental, as the programs tried to mimic human minds without any of the millions of layers of subtext real humans walked around with.

And what's the next step? he asked. *I give you my bank info?*

The next step is we make a deal.

Oh, of course. Something like...Cooper's social security number and birthday in exchange for the promise of a hundred grand, once the displaced prince he was talking to had secured his fortune?

Ridiculous.

What kind of deal? he asked anyway.

What do you need, human?

Human? Either this thing really *was* AI, or it was someone cosplaying a machine. Could this be a program one of his hacker acquaintances was demoing? Or just a new phishing scam? Either way, Cooper didn't like that it had managed to pop up on his computer. He had his own background programs running that were supposed to deal with these things.

He frowned at the screen. There was no reason to take it seriously, but...what *did* he need?

I'm lonely, he ended up replying.

Now he could only hope there wasn't a real human on the other end of this conversation. If this was any of the hackers in his circle messing with him, he'd just embarrassed himself horribly.

Although, it wasn't like any of those fuckers could claim they weren't lonely as hell too.

You wish for a bed servant? the program asked.

Cooper stared at the screen. Well, damn. He shifted in his chair. That was kind of a kinky reply for an AI bot, wasn't it? Was this about to turn into old-fashioned cybersex? He giggled, a touch of hysteria in the sound.

I don't think those are exactly legal these days, he typed.

I am not bound by the laws of man.

Okay, then. Cooper cocked his head, considering. He thought of some muscle-bound dude wearing...a jockstrap and a leather harness, maybe? Was that what a modern-day "bed servant" would wear? Anyway, some muscle-bound dude wearing something *revealing*, kneeling at Cooper's feet. Following his every order.

Cooper wrinkled his nose. That didn't really do it for him, did it?

I think I'd rather just have a friend.

He regretted it as soon as he typed it. It was too raw. Too real.

It wasn't like he was *completely* disconnected from humanity. He had friends on the internet—other hackers he'd connected with, although never in person. Some of them even lived in New York, he was pretty sure. But Cooper didn't have anyone in the real world these days. His last real-world friend had been...well, his dad. And he hadn't exactly been reliable.

Cooper swallowed through a thick throat as he watched the next reply pop up on the screen.

And what would be the ending terms of the deal? How would it be considered complete?

How the fuck was Cooper supposed to know? He considered, then typed, *I guess when I don't need you to be my friend anymore.*

Cooper stared at his computer, nibbling on his thumbnail. When he caught himself, he stuffed a licorice twist into his mouth instead, chewing absently. The program was taking a long time to respond now. Had Cooper broken its hard drive with his pathetic request?

But then a message popped up. The weirdest one yet.

I accept. I, Bracchus of the demon realm, will aid this computer human by being his friend, until that friendship is no longer needed, in exchange for a piece of his immortal soul.

Cooper's eyes widened. Demon realm? Piece of his immortal soul?

Had he stumbled into some underground marketing for a new video game?

He was kind of intrigued, honestly. Although, now he wished he'd thought of contract terms less lame-sounding than "please be my friend."

Hold your finger to the screen, the program prompted.

Cooper rolled his eyes. How the hell would the program know if he didn't comply? But he did it anyway. If he'd needed any further evidence that he was bored and lonely, this would have been it.

A shock ran through his body, like a bit of static electricity, and then another drop of red smeared his monitor.

Fuck. Was his nose bleeding again?

But no, Cooper's hand came away clean. And there was no time to wonder any more about it, because yellow-gold smoke was filling his room.

Cooper yelped, jumping up from his chair, the licorice dropping from his mouth. If his monitor was on fire, that was his whole life going up in flames.

But the smoke was coming from the floor, not his computer. And it wasn't the color of ordinary smoke, anyway. And Cooper could swear he could hear high-pitched giggling coming from somewhere.

So this was it—Cooper was losing his mind. It hadn't been an AI marketing thing at all. Cooper was just hallucinating nonsense.

The smoke began to clear, and Cooper nodded like a demented puppet at what it revealed.

Yep, he was definitely losing his marbles.

Because there was a man in Cooper's workroom. Or something vaguely resembling a man, if one was willing to discount the...accessories.

He was close to Cooper's height but leaner, with elfin features that included little pointed ears. Small, black feathered wings were extended behind him, and something resembling a lion's tail was flicking out from behind his legs. The hair curling around his ears was...blue? No, purple. Green? It kept changing.

And his eyes.

"You have a fox's eyes," Cooper said dumbly, the words coming out slurred as his vision dimmed around the edges. His knees were no longer doing what knees were supposed to do either—mainly, keep him standing.

And then everything went black.

3

Cooper

Cooper woke up on the hard ground. Or, not ground, but hardwood floor? Either way, it was unusual for him. Not that this would be the first time he'd fallen asleep out of his bed, but he usually at least managed to pass out in his computer chair.

He needed to take better care of himself, didn't he? This was definitely a sign.

He blinked up at the ceiling for another few moments, eyeing a water mark he'd never noticed before, then turned his head to the left.

There was a fox looking back at him.

Except that wasn't right. It was a man with fox eyes—yellow-gold irises and vertical black pupils—both of them rimmed by sooty lashes. So strange. But pretty, if Cooper ignored the uncanny aspect of them.

"You're awake."

With a bit of effort, Cooper managed to respond with a garbled "Guh."

The little man who'd appeared in Cooper's living room cocked his head. (Technically, Cooper wasn't sure he should be calling him little—he wasn't much smaller than Cooper himself. But Cooper's perspective on size had probably been skewed by spending so much time with mobsters.) "Not awake for long, though, I don't think."

Was that supposed to be some kind of threat? Cooper should be afraid, maybe, but he already knew what was going on here, so it was hard to be too alarmed.

The little man wasn't real. Neither were his freaky fox eyes.

Cooper was clearly having a psychotic break.

The sleeping at all hours, staring at screens for days on end, overdoing the caffeine and sugar—all the things his father had once warned him about—were catching up to him. He wasn't sure why they were catching up to him like *this*, exactly—an imaginary man (or maybe monster? What with the wings and the tail and all) whose face looked like a little elf but whose aura held an unmistakable air of "Beware! Danger here!"

But Cooper supposed one didn't get to choose one's hallucinations, did they? And maybe he should be more concerned that he was losing his mind, but it was an actionable thing. He didn't have any family history of mental illness he was aware of. He probably just needed to take himself to the hospital and let the doctors fix him. Maybe all it would take was some IV hydration and a short run on antipsychotics to tide him over until his brain rewired.

This was all fine. Totally fine.

"Your eyes are different colors," the little man-monster told him.

Oh, come on. Even his hallucinations had to comment on his heterochromia? Was his brain really that unoriginal?

"A very auspicious sign."

Cooper blinked. Well, okay, that was new. He'd never been called auspicious before.

He rose slowly onto his elbows, groaning at the stiffness in his muscles. The man-monster—or demon, if Cooper wanted to stick to the lore his mind had created before he'd passed out—was crouched on his haunches next to him. Like a gargoyle, or maybe one of the flying monkeys from *The Wizard of Oz*. He was staring at Cooper, unblinking, like *Cooper* was the strange sight in this room. His clothes were a loose brown matching set of pants and long-sleeved shirt that reminded Cooper of something a cult member would be given.

"You don't speak much, do you?" the demon asked, his tone making it unclear whether he felt any which way about that. He wasn't wearing shoes, Cooper noted.

Cooper shook his head, looking around the room to see if there were any other imaginary surprises. "How long was I out?"

Instead of answering, the demon shuffled closer, and Cooper held his breath, frozen there on his elbows, his legs sprawled out in front of him. He knew this demon wasn't real, but he couldn't help the feeling—the little raised hairs on the back of his neck—that said a predator was in his apartment and that he could pounce at any moment.

"Yes, lovely eyes," the demon murmured, peering closely at Cooper's face. "And so clever to cover them," he said, indicating Cooper's glasses. He held up two taloned fingers, bending them into claws. "So no one can poke them out?"

"Actually..." Cooper cleared his throat. The demon had never answered his question, but judging by the light coming through his window, Cooper hadn't been out for too long. He just felt kind of...wrecked for some reason. A side effect of breaking with reality, perhaps? "I need my glasses to see."

The demon lowered his clawed fingers. "To see what?"

"Um, everything?"

"Can you see under my skin?" the demon asked, leaning back on his haunches and sounding completely delighted by the idea. "To my very bones?"

What in the actual fuck was Cooper's brain coming up with right now?

He gave a nervous laugh. "No, not to your bones. Just...what everyone else sees."

"That's silly. No two people see exactly the same thing." The little demon sighed. "You're not very wise. And not very strong," he added, indicating Cooper's position on the floor. "What need do you even have for a demon?"

"Um...none? I didn't mean to summon one."

And as soon as I get the right medication, you'll be right back where you came from, Cooper didn't add. He didn't think the imaginary demon would appreciate it.

"Mm." The demon's lips pulled into a mischievous smirk. "I tricked you a bit, didn't I?" He tilted his chin at Cooper's desk and the computers there. "Being summoned into the machine was very strange. So many ones and zeros."

Cooper huffed out a laugh. Now that he wasn't holding his breath, he realized the demon smelled good, like a mellower, sweeter version of campfire smoke. His hallucination had an olfactory component too, apparently.

His brain had really gone all out.

"Do you have a name?" he asked. He supposed he could just make one up, but that seemed kind of rude, even if the demon was imaginary.

"All creatures have a name."

Cooper laughed again. "Yeah, but what's yours?"

"Most call me Chaos."

It wasn't a straightforward answer. "Because it's your name?" Cooper prodded.

"My name is..." The demon bit at his lip, in a way that made it seem like he was trying not to smile. "Beelzebub." At whatever he saw on Cooper's face, he stopped hiding the smile and cackled delightedly. "No, silly," he said between chortles. "Did you really think I'm the devil? That was a joke. It's Bracchus. That's my name."

"Which do you prefer? Chaos or Bracchus?"

The demon shrugged, his cackles dying down. "Try either. Or both. Or neither."

"How helpful."

The demon's eyes gleamed, and he shuffled even closer. His clawed foot was touching Cooper's hip now, and his smoky scent was making Cooper a little dizzy. Cooper didn't close his eyes though. He didn't even dare blink.

He'd stick with calling him Chaos for now. It seemed...fitting, somehow.

"What do they call *you*, computer human?" Chaos asked in a low murmur.

"Cooper. Or Coop," Cooper told him, giving him the nickname most of his family used.

Chaos made a face. "Like a chicken coop?"

"Um..."

Chaos shook his head, clucking his tongue. "I can't go around calling you Chicken Coop."

"I didn't ask you to?"

"I'll have to think on it." Chaos leaned forward, and then he was...sniffing Cooper? "Are you frightened of me?" he asked. And then said immediately, "Don't lie. I can smell it on you."

Then why did you even ask? Cooper wanted to say, but he held his tongue. He didn't think this little menace his mind had created would take kindly to sass. "A little," he admitted instead.

"Then maybe you are a little wise," Chaos said, holding his thumb and forefinger slightly apart to show just how *little* he thought Cooper's wisdom was. He started swiveling his head, finally looking around the room instead of focusing all that intense attention on Cooper.

Well, that was enough of that, wasn't it? Cooper dug his phone out of his pants pocket. He needed to call the hospital now. An ambulance might be overkill, but he wasn't sure he could make it there on his own at the moment, given how vivid this hallucination was.

But before he could dial, his phone rang in his hand.

Chaos's eyes darted to it immediately. "Your cellular telephone is yelling at you."

"It's ringing, yes."

And it was Jace calling. Cooper's stomach twisted. Jace was one of the more tolerable of Ivan's lieutenants, but he didn't usually just call Cooper up out of the blue. This wasn't a good sign.

Or was this part of the hallucination?

Losing his mind was confusing.

Cooper picked up anyway. "Hello?"

"Cooper?" Jace sounded harried. "You at home?"

"Yeah."

Jace let out what sounded like a sigh of relief. "Okay. Stay there. Boss has been shot at."

Ivan had been shot? Cooper couldn't imagine it. The guy was paranoid as all hell, never letting an enemy weapon within a hundred feet of him. "Is he okay?"

"Yeah, it hit his new, um...assistant."

The pretty man with the purple eyes.

"*Nix* was shot?"

Chaos let out a strange little growl. When Cooper looked at him, his eyes were... Well, they had, like, flames dancing in them.

Holy fuck, that was unsettling.

Jace made a sound, and Cooper turned his attention back to his phone. He should focus on reality, not imaginary demons and their imaginary fire eyes. "Is Nix okay, then?"

"Yeah, just a graze. Stay put. If you see Sergei, shoot him in the head." At the strangled noise Cooper made, Jace let out a laugh. "Kidding. No one expects you to shoot anyone. Don't let him in though. If he shows up, he's probably there to kill you."

There was nothing to say to that except "Okay."

"Good. Bye, Coop."

Cooper lowered the phone to find he had Chaos's full attention again. "Nix was injured with a human weapon?" the demon asked.

If he wasn't a figment of Cooper's imagination, Cooper would be questioning why Chaos even knew who Nix was. "Not seriously, it doesn't sound like."

Chaos plucked the phone out of Cooper's fingers. "I'll take this."

Cooper blinked at him. "Um. I need that, actually. To call the hospital."

"For Nix?" Chaos asked absently, stowing the phone somewhere in his loose brown pants with the deft fingers of a pickpocket. Cooper supposed he *was* a pickpocket. He'd just stolen Cooper's phone. "That would be useless."

"For *me*," Cooper told him. "The hospital's for me. Because you're not real?" He wasn't sure why it came out like a question.

"I'm not?" Chaos looked down at his hands. "Well, that would be a surprise." He reached up, placing one of his hands on Cooper's cheek. Heat. So much heat. The warmth of his touch was almost shocking. His wings fluttered, filling Cooper's head even more with the sweet smell of campfire smoke. "Do I not feel real?"

"I don't know," Cooper murmured, his eyelids suddenly feeling heavy. "I haven't been touched in a while."

"Yes, your soul piece tastes of it."

Right. Cooper had given a piece of his soul in exchange for... friendship? "Tastes of what?" he asked, his head full of cotton.

"Loneliness."

Cooper couldn't exactly argue with that. He found himself leaning into the touch on his cheek. It was...intimate, this hand on his face. He could even feel Chaos's breath puffing gently against his lips. Was this hallucination about to turn into some kind of sex dream? Cooper wasn't sure how he felt about that.

It would be embarrassing to admit to the doctors later.

But apparently that wasn't something he needed to worry about. Chaos withdrew his hand after a moment. "Would this help convince you?" he asked.

And then Cooper's computer monitor was on fire.

Even with his certainty that none of this was real, and the ample backups he kept of his work, Cooper couldn't help jumping to his feet in alarm. He wasn't sure where he got the strength, but maybe it was one of those weird adrenaline things, like how mothers lifted cars off their babies. "No! Fuck! That's my whole life!"

"That thing?" Chaos frowned at the flaming computer. "That can't be right."

But the flames disappeared in the next moment, as quickly as they'd appeared in the first place, and there was no sign of damage. Cooper ran his hands all along his monitor, checking anyway. It didn't even feel warm.

It kind of had the opposite effect of convincing him this was all real, actually.

"Puppy."

Cooper turned to look back at Chaos with a frown. "What?"

"That's the animal humans get," Chaos said, his eerie fox eyes latched onto Cooper's face. "To keep and to care for?"

Cooper ran a hand through his hair before pressing it hard against his forehead. "Sometimes, sure. Some do. What—"

"Okay. Puppy." Chaos grinned, the picture of delight as his tail swished behind him. "That's what I'll call you."

"You think I'm a pet? Didn't I— If I summoned you and made a contract for my soul and everything...aren't I supposed to be the one in charge of *you*?"

Chaos's tail stopped its rhythmic movement. His whole body went still, and that air of danger Cooper had almost forgotten about—even with the flames—returned in an instant. "You think to order me about?" Chaos asked softly. "Command me? *Contain* me?"

"Um... No." Cooper shook his head vehemently, resisting the urge to back away. There wasn't anywhere to go anyway. He was already pressed up against the desk. It was tempting to crawl *under* the desk, his hindbrain recognizing there was danger in the air. "No, no. No commanding. Puppy's fine. Call me whatever the fuck you want."

Chaos brightened, that eerie stillness dissipating in an instant. "Perfect! Because you're about to pass out again, and I'll be going exploring. So you be a good puppy and stay here when you wake. No running off without me to protect you. It sounds like you have enemies. I approve. Enemies are very exciting."

Cooper could only focus on the part that made any sort of sense. "I'm about to pass out again?"

"Yes." Chaos nodded eagerly. "A contract takes it out of a human, and like I said, I don't believe you were in peak physical condition to start with."

Well, ouch. It wasn't like Cooper thought he was the finest specimen of man out there, but...

He swayed on his feet. Maybe the passing-out part was right. Still...

"You don't have to be rude about it."

"Was that rude?" Chaos cocked his head, considering. "I don't think it was. I didn't say you were displeasing. I like your features. They are in fact *quite* pleasing to the eyes. And your scent pleases the nose." He shuffled forward on his haunches. "I think I'd like to nibble your fingers, even, but I might accidentally take one off, so I'll refrain."

Come to think of it, Chaos did have awfully sharp teeth.

Standing straight was suddenly an extreme challenge. "I'm going to pass out now," Cooper confirmed.

"I'll catch you."

Cooper's brow furrowed as his vision once again went dim around the edges. "You're kind of...dainty though."

Chaos kept up his strange, shuffling approach. "I'm stronger than I look. Go to sleep, puppy. I'll do my best to be back before you wake."

Cooper wanted to tell him that when he woke up, this whole imagined scenario would probably be over, but his eyes were already falling shut, the world falling dark. Again.

4

***

Chaos

Chaos stared down at the human who'd summoned him.

He had lowered him oh so very gently onto the floor after he'd collapsed. Chaos hadn't even dropped the human's head to hear the crack.

He was already taking such good care of his puppy.

The slumbering human wasn't at all like Chaos's usual summoners, who were more often than not wild, brutish men hungry for power or mayhem. Or both.

Why else would one summon a chaos demon? The reward had to be worth the risk.

This summoner, though, was slight and fearful, with a quiet voice and soft hands. His delicacy was actually a bit...disturbing. Chaos would need to pay attention to keep him protected. From the sound of the telephone call his puppy had accepted, there were enemies in the area. Enemies with projectile weapons.

But protected Cooper would be, enemies or not. Chaos had decided so.

He'd been all ready to snap his teeth and threaten to bite his summoner's face off—show them who the real boss of this arrangement would be—but Cooper clearly wasn't the megalomaniac Chaos had been prepared to subdue.

His soul piece was…soft. And sad. And tired.

Chaos couldn't stop prodding at the little niblet in his chest, wishing he could take the piece out and study it. How did one so young become so sad and lonely? Humans, like much of this realm's creatures, seemed to roam in packs, even the modern-day ones. Chaos had spent quite a bit of time watching them through the portal in the Void, so he knew. So…where was this Cooper's pack? Why weren't they taking care of him?

Chaos couldn't see any obvious reason Cooper would be cast out. He hadn't lied before—Cooper's looks were quite pleasing. His lips were plush, and he had that pretty reddish-blond hair, like a fox's fur. And those mismatched eyes? Wonderful. He had skinny limbs and a soft tummy, one Chaos wouldn't mind laying his head against. Slender, clever fingers too. Ones Chaos would *not* bite off, no matter how nibbly they might look.

Yes, quite pleasing. A sad, yummy soul piece and a pleasing meat suit. So why all alone?

It would have to be a mystery for later. For now, Chaos wanted to explore. He wasn't going to stick in one place while he waited for this new puppy of his to rouse. Who knew how long that would take? His summoner had clearly been running on fumes even before the summoning, and a contract took it out of a human.

Although, before he left… Chaos stopped in the doorway of the room, looking back at Cooper, sprawled out on the floor. If this human was to be Chaos's puppy to care for and tend to, he should make sure he was comfortable as well as safe, yes?

Chaos scurried into the hallway, checking the rooms until he found one with a bed, before grabbing the blanket off it and bringing it back to place over the unconscious human.

There.

Chaos whirled away, only to pause again.

A pillow. Humans used pillows when they slumbered.

He didn't want to go all the way back to the bedroom—been there, done that—so he grabbed one of the large tomes off the desk and shoved it under his puppy's head.

It was the right shape for a pillow, even if it was a bit firm.

Perfect. All tucked in.

Should Chaos take Cooper's glasses off? But no. Chaos couldn't have anyone poking out those delightful eyes while he was away. He straightened them on Cooper's face instead, then left the room for good.

He took a cursory look around the dwelling, scoping out the rooms he'd missed. There wasn't much—it was just a typical, boring human home. There was a living area with couches and a television. A gleaming kitchen Chaos had no use for. A bathing room and the aforementioned bedroom. Plus the room with the machines where Cooper lay unconscious.

It was all spacious and clean enough, but only the machine room really *felt* like Cooper, with his sweet candy scent and aura of nervousness permeating the air.

Chaos switched over to his preferred human form, one that was similar in build and face to his demon presentation but with brown hair and ordinary brown eyes. It was funny to be so ordinary, wasn't it? No wings or tail, not even a little stubby one poking out of the back of his pants.

Speaking of clothes...

The modern world had too many to choose from, and Chaos wasn't interested in human fashions the way Nix was. So he copied what his summoner was wearing, dressing in sweatpants and a matching hoodie. If he wanted, he could scrunch the hoodie strings tight, tight, tight so only the tip of his nose was poking out of the little circle the hood made.

Hilarious.

Chaos headed out the front door to find himself in another hallway, one with doors with little numbers hanging off them. He knew what this was—an apartment building. Those doors were other apartments, with other humans living in them.

Were they all the same? Maybe. Or maybe one of Cooper's neighbors had a disco ballroom and a creepy clown fun house.

Wouldn't that be interesting?

Now Chaos was curious, and he was never one to ignore a curiosity.

There were four doors on this floor, including Cooper's. The first two Chaos knocked on—how polite was he, knocking on the door?—no one answered. Rude.

But at the last door, a woman opened up. She had artificially light hair and lovely wrinkles. On her face, at least. There wasn't a wrinkle to be found on her clothes, stiff and starched as they were. Did she not move in them? Perhaps she stood there, as still as a doll on the other side of the door all day to keep them pristine.

She looked down her nose at Chaos, keeping the door open only a crack. "Can I help you?"

Chaos tried to peer around her, standing on his toes when he wasn't able to see much. She had shoes on her feet with pointy bottoms that gave her added height. "I want to see inside," he finally told her, pushing at her arm so she'd move aside.

"Who the hell—"

Chaos was bored of the doorway now. He ducked under her arm and went inside. The lady started yelling, following after him, so Chaos waved a hand, securing her inside a ring of fire to keep her contained.

That made her yell louder, which was kind of fun.

The apartment, though, was less fun. There was no disco ballroom. No creepy fun house with a murderous clown. The rooms were the same as Cooper's, just with more...stuff.

There were things on the walls and things on shelves. Why didn't Cooper have more things? Not that he should emulate *this* exactly. These specific things were ugly and boring—why was every item either white or beige?—but surely there were more exciting things to decorate with.

Oops. Now Chaos had thought "things" too many times, and the word had lost all meaning.

Things, things, things, things, things.

He left the apartment and the yelling woman behind, releasing her from the fire at the last minute. She yelled after him some more, something about calling the police.

He hadn't even singed her, so he wasn't sure what she was so annoyed about. Maybe she'd wrinkled her clothes trying to escape the fire.

The police could be interesting though. He'd never been attacked with modern weapons before—it sounded exciting. Apparently Nix had been shot, and Chaos was a little jealous.

If the police came...

Well, maybe later. Chaos wanted out of this apartment building first. If he hurried, maybe he would be back from exploring before his puppy woke up.

Then he could be the very first thing those mismatched eyes saw when they roused from slumber.

How lovely.

———

THE AIR OUTSIDE was cool but not freezing. Not that it would have mattered to Chaos if it was—he didn't have a human's sensitivity to heat or cold.

But still, it was nice to have a different flavor of air rushing through his lungs, something other than the stuffy, still air of the Void.

He breathed it in deeply, walking against the rush on the crowded sidewalk. The humans abounded, all different ages, shapes, and genders. Some dressed elegantly, some slovenly, most somewhere in between. A wonderful mix. Chaos could smell their different scents as well as food, and gasoline, and the not-so-faint scent of urine coming from an alleyway.

Delightful.

He was pleased to have been summoned into a city—there was an inherent chaos in the makeup of them, wherever they fell in humanity's timeline. The modernity was a nice change, though, from the last time he'd been summoned. He could hear the beeping of a truck backing up to make a delivery, the buzz of one-sided conversation from people talking into their phones, the honking of cars and the drone of construction across the street.

It was much better than watching through the portal only. Chaos could *feel* it—the mess and disorder of it all, filling him up.

He walked through the crowd, bumping people on purpose just to see how they'd react. Most ignored him and continued on their way—boring—but a few cussed him out viciously as they walked by, which was fun.

He spent some time doing a sort of circuit, not going too far in any one direction. He didn't want to stray too great a distance from the apartment where his puppy slumbered. Not just yet, at least.

But after a while, after the thrill of the hum and buzz of humanity wore off a little, there really wasn't much for Chaos to do. The shops in the area seemed to center around food, and Chaos didn't eat human fare. The rest were apartment buildings, and Chaos had already established those were quite boring.

Why wasn't this more fun?

Perhaps because he *had* seen it all through the portal before. And perhaps because he was doing it all alone. He had no one to talk to, no one to spill his twisty, bendy thoughts to. He'd been stuck with the same three demons for so long, and now he was finally *here*, but he didn't even have those fuddy-duddies to chat with.

Maybe he should have brought his summoner with him. It would have required waiting for him to wake up, though, which would have been a drag. But then Chaos would have had him here, and he could ask his questions.

Questions such as, Why pee in the alley when buildings had toilets? Why have lights that told people when to walk across the street only for everyone to ignore them? Why did men yell come-hithers to the women walking by when not a single one so much as smiled back at them?

Yes, it would be nice to ask his questions.

Chaos sighed, stopping in the middle of the sidewalk with his hands on his hips and looking around. It made the people walking by him give him dirty looks, which was amusing. He threw his head back and cackled loudly, and the dirty looks were now given to him from a bit of a distance. Like he was a large rock in a river, and the water was rushing all around him, forced to part around his steady presence.

Did his puppy like to laugh? Cooper hadn't looked very jovial. More timid, like if he laughed, it might be a quiet sort of giggle. Still, it could be nice to hear. He had a pleasant voice, to match his pleasant looks.

Maybe Chaos should go back and see if he was awake.

He could always set a building on fire to pass the time, but using his power like that might draw attention to himself sooner than he'd like. Nix was clearly in the area, which meant Kai might be as well, and Chaos didn't want that big, old warrior raining on his parade just yet.

It would be a gamble: Kai might try to fight Chaos, which would be hilarious. But he also might try to lecture him ("Grr!

Argh! We do not set human dwellings on fire for no reason!"), which would be decidedly *less* hilarious.

Although...Chaos had felt Kai's energy leave the Void completely not long before he himself had been summoned. Which meant either Kai had completed his contract and been sent back to the demon realm permanently, or he'd found a mate bond to keep him here in the human realm.

It was an interesting thought. This wasn't Chaos's last contract —not even close. Summoners were wary to call chaos demons because they were harder to control than most, which meant he had fewer summonings under his belt than the other demons.

So if Chaos completed this contract with Cooper, he'd maybe have to wait ages and ages for someone to brave the Book and call him again.

But if he had a mate...

Yes, yes, an intriguing thought. Chaos demons didn't mate often. Apparently, from what Chaos had been told, they were, if one roughly translated the demon sentiments into human jargon, "annoying" and "too much for anyone with more than two brain cells to shackle themselves to." Chaos would need to find someone desperate. Someone...lonely.

He brightened, cackling again for good measure. His puppy was desperate and lonely, wasn't he? Maybe *he'd* be willing to mate with Chaos.

It would probably be unwise to mate with the first human he saw—that was a long and binding arrangement to jump into—but acting wisely was boring.

Plus, Chaos liked the little soul piece he'd acquired. Its sadness had a heft to it. Like it grounded Chaos in some way, just by being in his chest. And while Chaos normally didn't like being held down, this wasn't some forceful holding back. It was more like...sinking under the weight of water in a warm bathing pool.

What would the entirety of Cooper's soul feel like, if this little piece held such comfort?

"Christ on the cross. Go lose your mind somewhere you're not in everyone's way."

Chaos focused in on the stern, bearded face frowning over him. Right. He was still standing in the middle of the sidewalk, laughing. Chaos quieted his cackling, grinning at the scowling man instead, then flashed back to his demon form, quick as a blink, flapping his wings and showing sharp teeth.

He switched back to human form immediately.

The man blinked at him, mouth gaping open. He looked around nervously, perhaps hoping for someone else to confirm what he'd just seen, but no one else was watching them. Chaos had been too quick for that.

"Careful who you scold, little man," Chaos purred, even though technically the man was much bigger than him. Chaos was using poetic license, okay? The man was small in *spirit*. "You never know whose mind is going to go next."

The man scurried off with a few more muttered curses.

What a silly bean.

Ah, well. Chaos twirled, blending into the flow of the sidewalk. It was time to return to the apartment.

If Cooper was still asleep, perhaps Chaos would try nibbling at one of those elegant fingers after all. He'd be very careful though.

It wouldn't do to damage his future mate.

5

Cooper

Cooper woke up on the floor. Again.

At least this time, he was covered by a blanket. And was that a...book under his head? How the hell had he gotten a blanket and a book pillow?

Slowly, with every muscle heavy and leaden, Cooper used his hands to sit himself up. By the light coming through the window, he'd guess it was early evening. He craned his neck, peering into every corner, but he didn't see any signs of his hallucination from before.

So that was it—it was all over? Just a super temporary psychotic break, nothing to worry about?

He should probably still get checked out. For all he knew, there was a gas leak in his apartment, and this was just a symptom of it. But when he tried searching for his phone so he could call someone—nothing.

Where the hell was his phone?

Cooper stood carefully and checked around his computer, only to see another message from RedRabbit.

R: *I'm waiting.*

Cooper wrinkled his nose as he stared at the message. The guy was getting pushy, and Cooper didn't have time at the moment for a throwaway hacker project. He was going insane, for one. He'd lost his phone, for two. And he hadn't finished either of Ivan's jobs, for three.

The phone thing would have to be taken care of. Ivan had been shot at, and Sergei was on the loose—Cooper needed to be available if anyone called, if only to be told of his own impending doom. It also meant none of Ivan's gofers were going to be free for something as unimportant as getting Cooper a new phone.

So he'd need to go get one himself. He could stop at an urgent care clinic along the way, see what they had to say about his... extremely vivid break with reality. After the day he'd had, he would have preferred to stay in the comfort of his own apartment, but he'd already gone outside into the world once today, and all that had happened was a shooting and a visit from an imaginary demon. What was one more errand?

At least Cooper's normal underlying buzz of anxiety about leaving the house seemed kind of insignificant compared to the bigger issues at hand. He should maybe find his newfound levity alarming, but maybe it was a side effect of the psychosis.

After making sure he still had his wallet and keys, Cooper headed down to the ground floor.

As soon as the elevator doors opened, he heard a commotion coming from the apartment entrance around the corner.

The sound of raised voices had Cooper's hackles rising, along with a looming sense of foreboding. Because Cooper recognized that voice. His mind had made *up* that voice.

Except how could it all have been in his head, when the voice was talking to the guard at the front desk, who was very much a real person?

Shit.

"I *am* allowed," Cooper heard his imaginary demon say crossly. "I was expressly summoned here. Into this apartment."

"You're not on Cooper Zaitsev's list of guests," Sam, one of the front desk guards, rebutted. "And I can't get him on the phone to verify."

"That's because I *stole* his phone."

A third voice joined in. "I told you he's a thief. He broke into my apartment!"

Cooper rounded the corner, his chest increasingly tight. There was Sam, standing in front of his desk. And there, to Cooper's immense dismay, was the demon—Bracchus or Chaos or whichever—except he didn't have any of his demon accessories. And his hair was brown. And his eyes weren't creepy fox eyes.

He looked human, basically.

And for some reason, Cooper's neighbor Mrs. Cross was also there, saying stuff about how Chaos had broken into her apartment.

Double shit.

Cooper knew the only reason Sam hadn't already called the cops was because this whole building was owned by Ivan, and employees of mobsters didn't fuck with police. The residents knew not to either. Things were handled in-house, or Ivan's wrath would sometimes work as its own deterrent.

Cooper's gut churned as three pairs of eyes landed on him. His mind was battered with countless memories of his father making some sort of scene, a too-young Cooper trying his best to smooth it over before someone took it in their head to investigate his living situation.

I'm not a child anymore, he reminded himself. *This isn't one of Dad's messes. This is* my *mess.*

And while, just like his father, he hadn't meant to make it, *unlike* his father, he'd fix it himself.

Cooper squared his shoulders and met the demon's now brown eyes. "Bracchus?" he asked, as calm and casual as he could.

Chaos's face lit up like Cooper's very presence was some sort of delight. Nobody looked at Cooper like that these days. It was kind of...sweet, actually. "Puppy!" he exclaimed.

Cooper's cheeks went hot. Jesus. Now everyone was going to think he had some sort of kink arrangement with this guy. He could practically see Mrs. Cross filing the info away for later. Most of Cooper's neighbors minded their own business, but that one didn't have anything better to do than gossip. Too much money and not enough real responsibility.

Cooper cleared his throat with an embarrassed laugh, looking to the guard now. "Sorry, Sam. I, um, forgot to put my friend on the list."

"This *deviant* is your friend?" Mrs. Cross asked, her voice full of accusation, like the information was damning.

"Um. Yes?"

"He forced his way into my home."

Of fucking course he did. "Did he take anything?" Cooper asked, reaching for his wallet. "I'll pay for any damages."

"No. He— There was a—" Mrs. Cross trailed off, suddenly at a loss for words.

Oh boy. What exactly had Chaos done to her?

Cooper startled when a warm hand landed on his arm. He hadn't even realized Chaos had sidled up to him.

"I only wanted a peek." Chaos made a little pout, like a child who'd been caught sneaking candy, as he grasped Cooper's bicep. "To check for fun-house clowns."

As Cooper tried to process what that could possibly mean, Sam spoke up. "Cooper, your friend can't go breaking into other apartments. We'll have to ban him from the building."

Shame. Embarrassment. Defeat. Cooper was used to those feelings when dealing with the general public.

But what exactly was shameful about this situation? It was a mess, sure, but...assuming Chaos was real—and he certainly seemed to be—then he was a demon, presumably from some other dimension, maybe not used to their world at all. He didn't know any better.

And Cooper was the one who'd brought him here, even if he'd done it unintentionally.

Cooper ignored his hot cheeks and roiling belly, raising his gaze to meet Sam's. "He's helping me with something for Ivan," he said firmly, watching Sam's eyes widen at the mention of Cooper's intimidating cousin. "Do you want to be the one to explain to him why we were delayed?"

Cooper had never once invoked his relationship with Ivan when dealing with the guards here, so he could only hope Sam would take the exception seriously.

And Sam did, holding up his hands as if to ward off an attack. "No. No. He can stay." He raised an apologetic brow to Cooper's neighbor. "I'm sorry, Mrs. Cross, my hands are tied."

With one last scowl at Chaos, Mrs. Cross stalked off in a huff back to the elevators. She might not have liked it, but she knew the order of things around here, same as everyone else.

Cooper lifted Chaos's hand off his arm and tugged him gently to the side. He tried to release him afterward, but Chaos kept a tight hold, bringing Cooper's fingers up to his face and stroking them slowly. It was...weird but not as freaky as it might have been if he still had all his sharp teeth.

"You've been getting into trouble," Cooper murmured, too quietly for Sam to overhear, his spine tingling with a strange shiver at the way Chaos's exploratory touch was tickling his fingers.

"Me?" Chaos widened his eyes with faux innocence. Their

plain brown color was less unsettling than before, but Cooper kind of missed the fox-like pair. They'd been so strange. Pretty, kind of.

Cooper almost laughed at Chaos's completely unsuccessful attempt to look guileless, but he was interrupted by the loud growl of his stomach rumbling.

Chaos's gaze zeroed in on Cooper's belly, his eyes narrowing. "You're hungry," he accused.

"You're real," Cooper countered.

Chaos straightened to his full height, pinching the tip of one of Cooper's fingers in reprimand. "Of course I am."

The thought of it made Cooper lightheaded again. He'd summoned a demon. An actual, real-life demon.

Now would have been a nice time to dive into his bed and hide under the covers. Maybe stay inside for a whole week this time.

But if Cooper hid his head in the sand, what other kinds of trouble would Chaos get into?

Chaos stole back Cooper's attention by pressing his teeth lightly into Cooper's knuckle, holding Cooper's finger in his mouth. "There are a lot of food establishments in the area," he mumbled around Cooper's digit.

Demons were fucking weird. Cooper gently—but firmly—tugged his hand away from Chaos's mouth. "You want to go out again?"

"If you'll come with me." Chaos directed a frown to the front entrance, like the outside world had offended him. "It's boring by myself."

It was a bad idea, surely. Cooper should be hiding Chaos away until he could figure out the scope of what he'd accidentally brought into his life.

But his apartment, usually so spacious, seemed way too small to hold all Chaos's energy inside it. The walls that had always been so comforting to Cooper were suddenly confining. Could he really keep Chaos inside for any extended length of time?

And there was one place Cooper liked. A diner nearby where everyone minded their own business.

"All right," he said, hoping against hope he wasn't going to regret this. "Let's go out."

Chaos gave him a dazzling smile, a dimple appearing in his left cheek.

He kept hold of Cooper's hand as they left the building.

———

THE EVENING AIR was a little too cold to be wearing just a sweatshirt, but Cooper didn't want to deal with herding Chaos back into the apartment and out again to get a coat, so he dealt with the discomfort. The diner wasn't too far, anyway.

Plus, Chaos's hand was warm in his, enough so that the heat seemed to spread, seeping up Cooper's arm.

"You have pleasing hands," Chaos told him brightly as they walked, echoing Cooper's thoughts eerily.

"Um, thank you?"

Chaos did a little test swing of their joined hands. "It makes it quite agreeable to clasp one together with mine."

"That's...good?" All Cooper's statements were coming out like questions, but he'd summoned a literal demon today, so he was cutting himself some slack.

"It *is* good," Chaos agreed. Then, "Tell me, puppy—"

Okay, here it was. They were going to get into it now, right? Cooper had apparently sold his soul to a demon, even if he hadn't meant to. What exactly were the terms? When this contract was done, did Cooper have to, like, go to hell with him?

But Chaos didn't get into any of that. Instead, he asked,

apropos of nothing, "Why would someone urinate in an alley, when humans went to all the trouble of inventing bathrooms?"

It took Cooper a moment to realize they really weren't going to discuss demonic contracts, and another moment to answer. "Um. Well, not everyone has easy access to indoor bathrooms. Not everyone has easy access to the indoors, period." He thought of his father and added, "And some people are...altered. Drunk or using drugs. They might not be totally aware of what they're doing."

"Ah. I see." Chaos started to swing their hands with abandon, enthusiastically enough that they almost hit a man coming from the other direction. He gave what sounded like a happy sigh. "I was right, this is all much better with a companion."

Cooper took the opening. "You didn't come from here? From...Earth?"

"I came from the Void," Chaos said easily. "And before that, the demon realm. You summoned me with the Book, we made a contract, and now I'm here."

Jesus. Somehow hearing it out loud was more intimidating than imagining it. Cooper swallowed, his throat dry. "And when our contract is done, do I...go back with you? To the demon realm?"

Chaos giggled with delight, like Cooper was spouting adorable nonsense. "Not *you*, silly. Just a little niblet of your soul. You won't miss it. Humans never do." His giggling quieted, and he muttered, seemingly to himself, "*If* I go back, that is."

"You might stay?" Cooper asked, trying to keep the note of panic out of his voice. What the fuck was he going to do if this demon decided to never leave?

"I might," Chaos said cagily, smiling to himself.

And then he was pulling them to a window of a restaurant, pressing their joined hands as well as his face against it to peer inside. "Oh! Pancakes! I've never seen them in real life."

Cooper tried to tug their hands away, and when Chaos gave a

little growl instead of moving, Cooper—his cheeks once again flushed with embarrassment—made an apologetic face to the people inside, who'd raised their brows and then their middle fingers at Chaos's blatant inspection.

Fuck. If Chaos *did* stay, it was going to end up being some sort of social anxiety exposure therapy: extreme edition, wasn't it?

Although, it was hard to worry too much about what other people were thinking when Cooper had to focus all his attention on the loose cannon that was this little demon.

"Bracchus," he said quietly, when it was clear tugging wasn't going to work. "This is the diner I was telling you about." He'd almost missed it, distracted as he'd been with the thought of Chaos staying. "Will you come eat with me?"

Chaos turned from the window immediately. "Will you order pancakes?"

Cooper nodded. It was an easy concession. "I can, if you like."

"If *I* like," Chaos repeated, his eyes laser-focused on Cooper, like he'd said something fascinating.

They went inside and were seated across from each other at a booth, this one in the interior of the diner and not at a window. Chaos didn't seem to mind the lack of a view—he was fascinated by the menu itself. He apparently didn't eat human food, but he had strong opinions on what Cooper needed to order. French fries. Pancakes. A milkshake. Meatloaf, for some reason.

When the waitress had taken their large and varied order, they sat staring at each other, Chaos still holding Cooper's hand across the table. For a noisy, chaotic thing, Chaos had a way of sitting unnervingly still when he wanted to, every fiber of his being seemingly intent on Cooper.

"I don't really know what's happening," Cooper finally admitted, breaking the silence.

Chaos grinned at him, revealing his dimple again. "Isn't it wonderful?"

"Um, well..." Cooper pushed at the table's ketchup bottle with his free hand, needing something to do that wasn't staring into Chaos's unblinking eyes. "I usually like to know, actually. It makes me feel better."

"Better than what?"

It was hard to tell if Chaos was fucking with him or if he genuinely didn't understand Cooper's way of speaking. "It makes me less...anxious," Cooper clarified.

Chaos cocked his head. "Are you afraid of me, Cooper?"

Cooper could almost have lied. At the moment, Chaos looked human. Like a cute human, even. And even though he was keeping Cooper's hand captive, his touch felt nice. Warm and soothing.

But Cooper could remember how it had felt in the apartment, when he'd dared to ask if he was the one in control of Chaos. And he could see it in the way Chaos watched him now, with eerie stillness.

Not human after all. A creature, and a predatory one at that.

"You *are* scared of me." Chaos was pouting again, his lower lip jutting out in a way that should have been ridiculous but somehow came off as adorable.

"I'm sorry. I can't help it." Cooper slipped his fingers under his glasses to rub at his eyes. He didn't want to offend Chaos, but he wasn't a very good liar. "You can set things on fire with, like, your mind."

The pouting intensified. "This won't be very fun if you're frightened of me all the time."

Against all odds, Cooper found himself wanting to reassure the demon. Chaos was just so...cute, even in all his otherworldly terribleness.

Could I be any more of a pushover?

Cooper tried to figure out how to word his thoughts in a way Chaos would understand. "I'm scared of a lot of things, to varying degrees," he explained. "Part of coping with that is just...powering through. I'm used to it. I can be a little scared of you and still be your friend."

"Really?" Chaos brightened immediately. "How interesting." He leaned forward across the table. "What else are you afraid of? Your enemies? The ones with the guns?"

"My enemies, yeah," Cooper agreed. They weren't exactly *his* enemies. He was Ivan's hacker, not a leader of the Mafia himself. But Sergei certainly scared the shit out of him. "But also just...I don't know." How the hell did he explain to a powerful demon that sometimes he got nervous just running errands? He pushed the ketchup bottle around some more. "People can make me uncomfortable. Interacting with strangers. Trying to make small talk and getting lost in what they think of me. I get anxious. I don't have it as bad as some—I'm not stuck in the house or anything. But it's like a muscle you have to exercise. When I leave it too long, it atrophies. I have to build it back up."

"Fascinating," Chaos murmured. It didn't sound like he was taunting Cooper, but his response didn't exactly make sense either.

"Not really," Cooper hedged. He didn't want to, like, trick this demon into thinking he was something special. "It's common enough."

"Laugh for me," Chaos ordered, like that was a normal thing to request of someone for no reason.

Cooper gave a nervous chuckle, darting his eyes reflexively to see if anyone was looking at him making a fool of himself. But everyone near them was minding their own business.

Chaos made a face. "That's not a real laugh."

"It's hard to do on command."

"Well, I can't mate with you if I've never heard you laugh."

Cooper froze in his seat as their waitress appeared, placing an inhuman amount of food on the table. He stayed frozen long after she'd left.

Eventually, he found his voice, although it came out thready and strange. "I'm sorry, you can't *what* with me?"

"Mate with you," Chaos said absently, studying the plates in front of them. "Bind our souls and our bodies for eternity, keeping me here in the human realm and giving you an unnaturally long and youthful life." He looked hopefully at Cooper's plate, as if he hadn't just said the most insane thing Cooper had ever heard. "Now can I watch you eat a french fry?"

6

_____

Chaos

Even though Chaos had asked very nicely, Cooper didn't start eating a french fry for Chaos's entertainment.

To speed things along, Chaos selected one and held it to his puppy's lips. Brow furrowed and gaze distant, Cooper opened obediently before chewing on the fry absently. After only a moment, he opened his mouth again and let the half-chewed fry fall out.

"Hot," he explained, keeping his mouth open, as if to cool it with the diner's air.

Chaos nodded. "Fascinating."

The fries had barely been warm to the touch, as far as he could tell—humans were such delicate things. Chaos would need to be careful with Cooper's fragile body when it came time to mate.

Speaking of. "Do you think we should get to it today, or would you like an—" Chaos paused as he thought of the human term. "Extended engagement?"

It took Cooper a moment to respond, even after his mouth had seemingly recovered from the scorching heat of the innocent french fry. His gaze kept darting to the table, to the side, to somewhere beyond Chaos's shoulder. "Can I ask why you'd want to, um, mate with me?"

"To stay here beyond the terms of our contract, I must bind myself to a human permanently." Chaos grinned, wishing he had his lovely sharp teeth to display. "I choose you."

At some point, Cooper's hoodie string had migrated to his mouth, and he was nibbling on it nervously. Perhaps it was tastier than the molten french fry. "Is that because I'm the first person you saw?"

Chaos had a feeling the question was a trap. He put on his most innocent face. "No..."

Cooper's lips twitched, and then he let out a sigh, dropping his hoodie string out of his mouth. "I don't think I'm actually the mate you want."

"You're not?" Chaos looked him over. He *seemed* like a perfectly acceptable specimen. Chaos liked looking at him, and he liked all the varied emotions that ran through him at any given moment: the curiosity and the dread, the embarrassment Cooper was so prone to, the one that turned his cheeks and ears red. Chaos had never had need to feel embarrassed before, so it was delightfully novel to feel it through the soul piece in his chest. Uncomfortable and tickly.

And as for Cooper's physical form...

Well, Chaos thought he would be quite nice to touch some more. His hand was already incredibly pleasant to hold, cool and firm in Chaos's grasp. And despite Cooper's slender limbs and nimble fingers, he had a wonderful softness to his middle and his rump. Squishy and fine.

"I'm boring," Cooper told him, almost gently.

That stopped Chaos's daydreams short. He cocked his head, frowning. "I'm not a fan of boring."

He felt a surge of relief run through Cooper as the human smiled. "Of course you're not. You're a powerful, fascinating demon."

Chaos liked the sound of that. It was a simple truth, of course, but it was nice to know Cooper was aware of the facts. Chaos *did* have a sense he was being played, however.

But Chaos didn't mind a game or two.

Cooper popped a french fry into his mouth, this time keeping it inside to chew. Apparently they weren't too hot anymore. "We can, um, work together to find you someone else."

Chaos narrowed his eyes, little hot licks of fire running through his veins. "I'll choose my own mate, summoner."

Cooper missed a beat before he resumed chewing. "Of course. I wouldn't—I'll just...keep an eye out. You're in a city of millions. You'll find someone better in no time."

Chaos peered around the diner. It was mostly full, with lots of humans eating their various nonsense, but none that drew him in the way Cooper did. *They* were boring, he could already tell, these strangers that weren't his puppy. "I don't see anyone better here," he pointed out, tightening his grip on Cooper's fingers.

That little thrill of anxiety pulsed from Cooper's soul piece again. "Well, yeah, maybe not right this second."

Chaos plopped his chin onto his free hand, studying his puppy. "I'm not known for my patience," he warned. He didn't usually give warnings. Why let an enemy know his next steps? But Cooper had been so polite up until now. He'd earned it.

"Right." Cooper swallowed hard, the acrid scent of nervousness wafting off him again. He *was* a fearful creature, wasn't he? "We'll...find you someone soon, then."

Chaos let it go for the moment, gesturing for Cooper to try more of the strange plates they'd been given. Why make meat into the shape of a loaf when one could rip it straight from the haunch of the animal in question? But maybe humans didn't have the strength for haunch-ripping anymore, in these modern times. Or had they ever? Chaos couldn't remember.

Anyway, it was displeasing that Cooper was not eager to mate with him. But his puppy had already told Chaos he was easily frightened. And Chaos could be...intimidating; it was true. Cooper had been right to say Chaos was a powerful and fascinating demon.

And while Chaos wasn't patient, he didn't really have to be. Cooper was right here in front of him, bound to him for the moment by their contract. He was even still holding Chaos's hand, working his way around his meal one-handed so as not to let go.

So accommodating. It pleased Chaos. Immensely.

Just like the way Cooper had said, "If you like," when Chaos had requested he order pancakes.

It had never been about what Chaos liked before, when he was summoned to this realm. It was all about what the summoner wanted, with Chaos having to find a way around his orders to explore the delights the world had to offer.

It could be fun, the sneakiness, make no mistake. But it was occasionally...tiring.

Yet sweet Cooper wanted to please Chaos, not the other way around.

Possibly because Cooper was afraid of Chaos, but still.

Chaos swung his feet happily under the booth, pleased with the general state of things. This might prove to be his best summoning yet, even without blood and mayhem to attend to. Although, who knew? Blood and mayhem could still make their way onto his plate, like a half-eaten french fry dropped from Cooper's mouth.

Wouldn't that be lovely?

"Why are you frightened of people?" Chaos asked, poking his finger into the meatloaf now that Cooper had taken a bite. It was...

squishy. Very strange. "You said you were, but people are generally inconsequential. Did you not know that?"

"Oh." Cooper swallowed, his gaze darting around the diner again. "Um...I don't know. It's not exactly logical, most of the time."

Chaos nodded. That was good. Logic was boring.

"My dad was...erratic, growing up. He tried, but he was an alcoholic, and he wasn't...in control, a lot of the time. I had to be on top of things if I didn't want to get taken away from him. I just got used to a certain hypervigilance after a while. It's so ingrained it's hard to shake off, even if it's...inconsequential."

"*You're* not inconsequential," Chaos told him with a frown. Had Cooper misunderstood him? "*People* are."

"Well, thank you."

"Your father didn't take good care of you," Chaos surmised. He wasn't very familiar with the concepts of parents or family—demons didn't stay with their young, and those humans inclined to summon a chaos demon tended not to be family men—but he had a general idea parents were supposed to protect their young, not the other way around.

"He tried," Cooper protested, a certain bite to his words. "He loved me. He just...well, he was already prone to depression, and then my mom died, and I think he was just...self-medicating for most of his adult life. Alcoholism is a disease," he said, like it was a mantra he'd repeated before. "I can't blame him for succumbing to it."

"But you were a child," Chaos countered. "Children should be protected."

"You like children?" Cooper asked, sounding surprised.

"Left to their own devices, children are the embodiment of chaos. Of course I like them."

And then Chaos was treated to a real, genuine smile from his summoner. There was no repressed anxiety, no subtle quirk of his lips. His pretty, mismatched eyes crinkled at the corners, and his teeth were on display.

It was kind of wonderful. Lovely, even.

Chaos grinned back.

This really could be his very best summoning yet.

———

AFTER COOPER HAD EATEN his fill—which had only been maybe a third of what Chaos had asked him to order, much to Chaos's disappointment—they walked around for a while, at Chaos's eager request. (Once again, his puppy was so very accommodating.)

This was much better than before, when Chaos had been wandering on his own.

Now Chaos was able to spill all his many thoughts to his companion, their joined hands swinging between them, and Cooper didn't get bored or frustrated or sassy with him. He answered all Chaos's other questions too: people ignored the traffic lights because "this city is always in a hurry—they've got places to be" and the men called out to the women because they were "acting like misogynist douchebags."

In turn, Chaos explained more about the Book, his many centuries waiting in the Void, and how Cooper had managed to summon him. Chaos found it *very* funny that his puppy had accomplished it with a nosebleed and not a ceremonial knife.

How times had changed.

Eventually, many hours after the sun had set, Cooper grew tired—again—and they had to return to the apartment so he could rest.

Humans required a lot of care, didn't they? Chaos maybe should have known that already, but he'd never bothered to pay much attention before.

There was Cooper's need for regular food, for one. And regular sleep. And the way his feet seemed to get tired after miles of walking. There was also the teeth chattering he was succumbing to—apparently a light sweatshirt was not enough to protect Cooper's fragile human skin from the cold night air.

So many things to keep track of.

Back in the apartment building, they walked past the guard at the desk, and Chaos stuck his tongue out at the man. The guard should consider himself lucky Chaos hadn't set him on fire. The only reason Chaos had attempted to *reason* with him—ugh—was because Cooper had been so upset about the flames on his machines. For all Chaos knew, Cooper would be *equally* upset over flames on the people in the building.

Chaos had been acting out of amazing, thoughtful consideration, and the guard hadn't even appreciated his efforts.

Chaos should bite off all his fingers in retribution.

But the guard's fingers didn't look nearly as tasty as Cooper's, which sort of lessened the appeal right now. Chaos refrained. For the moment.

Cooper led Chaos up the elevator and back to his apartment. He said he was going to get ready for bed, so Chaos followed him to his room, where he finally released his hold on Cooper's hand and watched him select sleeping clothes that weren't much different from what he was already wearing.

They stood staring at each other for a moment, and then Cooper held up the clothes in his arms. "Um. I'm going to get changed now."

Chaos nodded. "Yes. I see." In solidarity, he changed back to his demon form, although he kept on the comfortable sweatpants and sweatshirt. His magic adjusted the sweatshirt for his wings, creating little slits in the back for them to escape from.

Cooper gestured to the bedroom door with a nervous smile. "Would you like to give me some privacy, maybe?"

Chaos settled down on his haunches, stretching his wings out. "No, thank you."

See? Chaos was very polite when he wanted to be. The guard downstairs hadn't appreciated it, but Chaos had a feeling Cooper would.

Cooper seemed stuck for a moment. Was Chaos's puppy malfunctioning? But then he let out a heavy breath, tossing his bedclothes on the foot of the bed. "I guess I probably won't be the first naked man you've seen."

"Nope," Chaos told him cheerily. He'd seen many a nude man in his time. Usually when they were fleeing for their lives from his terrible destruction.

Somehow this was better.

Cooper started getting undressed, and Chaos stared, unblinking. He liked not blinking sometimes, even if it made his eyeballs itchy. It unsettled people. It definitely unsettled Cooper. But even more than that, Chaos was curious about his summoner, and he didn't want to miss a detail.

And oh, he *was* pretty, wasn't he? Cooper didn't have much hair on his chest, but the down under his arms was the same reddish blond as his hair, which Chaos found delightful. And the soft swell of his belly was even nicer unclothed. Chaos wanted to butt his head against it, to breathe in Cooper's sugary-sweet candy smell. But he refrained. For now.

Once bared, Cooper tugged his sleeping clothes on with haste, and Chaos rose from his crouch in indignation. "You weren't *nude*," he accused. "You kept your underwear on."

Cooper made a surprised sound, glancing down at himself, then gave Chaos a sympathetic nod, almost as if he was teasing. "False advertising?"

"Incredibly false," Chaos agreed with a pout.

And Cooper laughed.

Chaos had been right—it was a very pretty sound. It wasn't

bright or boisterous like Chaos's cackling tended to be. Instead it was soft and gentle, like a happy little babbling brook.

Chaos let it fill his head, a pleasing chime he'd replay when he was feeling restless.

When his soft laughter had trailed off, Cooper asked, "What will you do while I sleep?"

"I don't know." Chaos's tail swished in agitation. "It's bound to be dull though." He cocked his head. "Perhaps if you slept just a very little amount."

Cooper rubbed at the back of his neck with a sigh. "I know I've passed out, like, twice already, but I really am exhausted. I don't think a couple hours is gonna cut it. I could set you up with a movie?"

"No," Chaos said immediately, not caring if he sounded petulant. "I've spent centuries *watching*. No more."

Cooper looked around, as if to search for ideas. After a moment, his face brightened. "Hey, have you ever played a video game?" He immediately shook his head, not waiting for Chaos's answer. "Of course you haven't. Do you want to try?"

Chaos would try anything once.

Not too many minutes later, Chaos was in front of one of the machines in the machine room, and Cooper was showing him how to use the "mouse" and the "keys" to play something called *World of Warcraft*.

As lovely as his puppy's attention to his needs was, Chaos was a little skeptical. "I've watched humans playing video games through the Void," he whined. "It's very dull."

Cooper shrugged. He was leaning over Chaos to help him with the keyboard, and that part of it was very nice. Cooper smelled good and sweet, and his arm brushed against Chaos's face every now and again. "Yeah, it can be boring to watch someone else play, but... I think you might like playing yourself. You get to create a character, be someone else for a while. Follow quests. Kill things."

"Really?" Chaos leaned forward, studying the screen. He didn't usually yearn to be anything other than himself, but he *had* been stuck in the Void with only his own thoughts for a very long time. And killing things was always fun.

He examined the character options and wrinkled his nose. "I don't want to be a warrior."

Warriors were boring. Just ask Kai.

"You don't have to be," Cooper reassured him. "You'd probably fit well as a rogue...or maybe a demon slayer." Cooper bit at his lip, smiling to himself at his little joke. It was very endearing. "If you hate it, we'll try something else tomorrow."

He had set up a video on the laptop next to Chaos, one that had a man explaining how the game worked, just in case Chaos got stuck or confused. Overall, it didn't seem like a terrible way to spend the time Cooper would be sleeping. It was something new, at least. Chaos had been *inside* the machine, but what was showing on the screen now was nothing like the ones and zeros he'd been surrounded by. It was sort of like the animated movies humans watched, except Chaos would be controlling the action this time.

"Yes, this will do nicely." Chaos gave Cooper's arm a fond pat. "You may sleep now, puppy."

Cooper straightened, raising a brow. "How very generous of you," he drawled.

He was getting more comfortable with Chaos already. And Chaos didn't mind a little sass, if it meant his puppy would be less nervous around him.

So he only nodded sagely. "Yes. I know."

Cooper padded off to bed, and Chaos was left with the machines.

7

Cooper

This time, Cooper woke up in his bed. That was great, right? Waking up in a bed like a normal person. Things were getting back on the right track.

Except he also woke up with an inhuman screech leaving his throat, because there was a pair of fox eyes a hair's breadth away from his face, staring, unblinking, at him.

Without his glasses on, they were kind of a fuzzy blur in the dim, curtained-off room, but it was still fucking startling.

"That was loud," Chaos told him, not exactly sounding put off by having scared the bejesus out of Cooper, or by getting an earful for it. He didn't move any further away either. "And your heart's beating quite fast."

Cooper sat up, putting some distance between their faces. Chaos was squatting on his heels by the head of Cooper's bed, his wings flared behind him, as if to help him keep his balance.

Cooper had almost managed to get weirdly used to the little demon yesterday. It had been hard to maintain his fear and anxiety when Chaos was marching him around the block, swinging their hands together and asking question after question, like an overinquisitive child.

It didn't make it any less unsettling to have him looming over Cooper while he was sleeping though.

Cooper grabbed his glasses from the bedside table and turned back to Chaos with clear eyes. The demon's hair was a violently bright purple this morning. It suited him. He also had small, stubby black horns, short enough that Cooper had missed them in the nest of his hair yesterday.

Cooper cleared his throat. Was Chaos still waiting for him to respond? "Yeah, well, my heart beats fast when someone scares the shit out of me first thing in the morning."

Instead of taking it as a rebuke, Chaos seemed to take it as an invitation, crawling up onto Cooper's bed and sitting cross-legged on the covers, facing him. He held Cooper's laptop in his hand.

"Did you like the game?" Cooper asked.

"It was quite tolerable," Chaos told him. "I have advanced many levels." He looked almost thoughtful as he said, "It's a strange sort of chaos to feed off of. Kind of faint in flavor. But also novel." He gave Cooper's knee a pat over the covers. "You did well."

"Great." Cooper was weirdly proud he'd managed to find something entertaining for the demon to do. He hadn't even considered Chaos could feed off chaotic energy through a video game.

It had been such a long time since Cooper had had anyone in his space, let alone a strange creature from another realm. He'd half expected Chaos to have run off and found someone better by now.

He can't, stupid, he reminded himself. *He's bound to you by the contract.*

Chaos's continued presence didn't have anything to do with Cooper at all, or his talents as a host.

"I found something else," Chaos said, a sly cant to his voice.

Cooper stuck his fingers under his glasses to rub some of the sleep from his eyes. "Oh yeah?" He could only hope Chaos hadn't downloaded some horrible virus onto his computer. That would be just his luck.

Chaos opened the laptop, and the sound of moans and wet slapping filled the room before Cooper's eyes managed to focus on the writhing bodies on the screen.

Sweet, holy fuck.

Chaos had found Cooper's porn stash.

Cooper's cheeks heated, and his heartbeat, which had slowed down to a normal rate, ramped up again. "Um..."

That was all he could come up with. A big, fat "Um."

He cleared his throat. Came up with nothing. Cleared his throat again. "So that's... Well, pornography is—"

"I know about pornography," Chaos told him dismissively, even as his eyes gleamed at Cooper's blush. "Nix liked to watch the shoots through the portal."

There was so much to process in that statement.

"Nix?" Cooper asked dazedly, his gaze still stuck in horror on the porn Chaos had decided to show him. His *own* porn. "Ivan's Nix?"

"Mm-hmm."

"How—how do you know Nix?" Had Nix summoned Chaos first? But Chaos had said he'd been in the Void for centuries before Cooper found him, so that wouldn't make sense.

"Nix is a demon." Chaos fast-forwarded the video, pressing play again when the two men on-screen had changed positions. "An incubus. Your boss summoned him, I think."

Of course. Sure. Ivan had summoned a sex demon. A *male* sex demon. That made perfect sense.

What the fuck was Cooper's life turning into?

"Anyway, you have a splendid variety here," Chaos told him. "I approve."

He clicked on another video, one Cooper had found in the "Groups" tag on his favorite site. Now there was an entire chorus of moans filling the hole left by Cooper's awkward silence.

"You like orgies?" Chaos asked him, cocking his head. At some point he'd shuffled closer so his bent knee was touching Cooper's leg, his tail swishing over Cooper's calf.

Cooper supposed there was no use giving in to the embarrassment crawling over his skin. Chaos was immune. Or maybe oblivious to it. Either way, the only thing to do was answer his questions and pretend like getting interviewed about his porn taste first thing in the morning was par for the course. "Um. I like watching them?" Cooper told him. "On video. I don't...participate." It seemed only polite to ask, "Do *you* like orgies?"

Chaos hummed a little tune, considering. "You wouldn't be in this orgy?" he clarified.

Cooper shook his head. "Not really my scene. People make me anxious, remember? I wouldn't know what to do."

Chaos's lower lip pushed into a pout, like Cooper was disappointing him with his answer. "Then no."

A strange warmth ran through Cooper at that. Chaos wanted him in his hypothetical orgy? Why was that so fucking cute?

Or maybe Cooper was just having a hot flash from the shame of Chaos displaying his saved porn in some sort of private screening.

"And what about this one?" Chaos asked, pulling up another video.

Oh yeah. Cooper knew this one well. It was a slow, sensual fuck, with lots of kissing and whispered encouragements. Cooper kind of had a thing for it in his porn. He was no virgin, but he'd only had one boyfriend in his life, and the guy hadn't been very nice.

Everyone else he'd slept with since then had been more of a casual hookup. So he liked to watch couples that seemed super into each other, even if he knew they were probably acting for the camera.

"They're being very gentle," Chaos said quietly, stroking a taloned finger over the screen.

"Yeah," Cooper rasped, his throat dry. He couldn't meet Chaos's eyes at the moment, so he kept staring at the video. It was probably the worst place to look—arousal was pooling in his belly now, and he was willing himself not to get hard.

"Cooper?" Chaos asked.

Somewhere in the back of his mind, Cooper was vaguely aware it was Chaos's first time using his real name. "Yeah?"

"Have you kissed someone before?"

"I have..." And again, since it seemed polite to reciprocate Chaos's interest, he asked, "Have you?"

"I've mated," Chaos told him, sounding adorably proud. "But I've never kissed. That's more of a human thing. I'm not at all accustomed to...gentle mating."

Cooper glanced up at the admission, only to find a specific sort of sly look on Chaos's face. It was the kind of look Cooper was beginning to realize meant trouble was imminent.

"If I'm to find a human to mate with," Chaos mused, his voice full of false innocence, even as his eyes began to sort of...glow, "I *should* become accustomed, don't you think?"

"Um...yeah?" Cooper didn't know where was safe to focus anymore, but the screen grabbed his attention as the couple flipped over, one man riding the other. "Sure..."

"I don't wish to hurt my future mate," Chaos said, just barely loud enough to be heard over the moans. "To become...overzealous."

"Right," Cooper said absently. Now he was distracted by the thought of what an overzealous Chaos might look like. Sharp teeth and grasping hands, probably. Would the tail come into play? Or the wings?

"So you'll help me?"

"Sure," Cooper agreed, completely on automatic.

He froze, taking his eyes off the laptop to meet Chaos's gaze once more. What had he just agreed to? And were those *flames* reflecting in Chaos's slit pupils? "Wait, what?"

Chaos moved closer with alarming speed, abandoning the laptop to crouch over Cooper's torso. Cooper had to lean back on the bed so their heads didn't bump.

"You'll teach me to be gentle? A good mate for a human?"

"Oh. I'm not—" Cooper sucked in a breath, almost choking on the smell of sweet smoke. "You wouldn't—"

"You haven't mated before?"

"I have." Cooper's brow furrowed. "I'm not a virgin," he clarified. Maybe that was a demon thing, going off for human virgins?

But Chaos didn't seem put off by his answer. "Then what's the difficulty?" he asked, gesturing to the laptop. "These are all videos of men. You find the male form pleasing, yes?"

"Yeah, I'm gay. It's just—"

"You don't find *my* form pleasing?" Chaos's tail swung, closing the laptop with a thump.

"No, you're—you're very pleasing. I just—" Cooper didn't know what to say. He wasn't even exactly sure how they'd gotten here. He found himself blurting out, "I prefer to bottom! So I can't—you know—depending on which way you—"

He trailed off as, in answer, Chaos swung a leg over him, straddling Cooper's torso fully and leaning down until their faces were barely an inch apart. "Oh, puppy," he crooned, his voice full of sympathy even as his eyes gleamed with some sort of sinister intent. "Here I've only been discussing kissing. But if you wish me to penetrate you...that can be arranged."

———

COOPER RINSED the toothpaste out of his mouth, avoiding his own eyes in the mirror.

He'd shouted something about not being able to kiss with morning breath and run off into the bathroom. Chaos had mercifully let him flee.

Cooper had just...needed a moment.

He eyed himself in the mirror now, wondering what the strength of his appeal might be for someone like Chaos. He supposed he was attractive enough. He definitely needed a haircut, but the overlong mess kind of suited him. He had a nice face and an okay smile, and people were always intrigued by his eyes. And yeah, maybe he could benefit from going to the gym every now and then, but...it wasn't like no one had been interested before.

Cooper had been fucked. Quite a bit for a semirecluse. But never by a literal demon. A strangely cute one who held Cooper's hand when they walked and looked at him like he was something fascinating and not a boring, nerdy shut-in.

But if Cooper ignored that last dig about penetration—and he *would* ignore it, so as not to court a full-blown panic attack—then Chaos was just talking about a little making out.

Cooper could handle that.

Who was he fucking kidding? Nervousness aside, Cooper was *dying* to handle that. He hadn't been on the apps in a while, and he hadn't been kissed in forever. Or touched in any significant way. In terms of a sex life, he was basically crawling through the desert, and Chaos's offer was a straight-up pitcher of ice-cold water. Like Cooper was really going to refuse?

And if Chaos didn't like kissing Cooper—if he didn't like *Cooper*, in the end—well, that was to be expected, right? Cooper wouldn't get hurt by it, because he wasn't holding out for anything anyway. Chaos was going to find some other human to bond and mate with, most likely some jacked supermodel type who liked skydiving and going to raves and participating in every single orgy they came across.

This was just...practice.

And yeah, maybe Cooper should have more self-respect than agreeing to be someone's practice hookup, but the truth was that he really, really didn't.

He blew out a breath, narrowing his mismatched eyes at himself in the mirror. *Let's fucking do this.*

Bolstered by the shortest pep talk of all time, Cooper walked back into his bedroom, only to halt in the doorway, frozen in horror.

He'd thought the porn was bad. He'd thought it couldn't get any more embarrassing.

He'd been wrong.

Chaos had found Cooper's sex toys.

The drawer to Cooper's bedside table was open, and the demon had a dildo—a squishy purple monstrosity Cooper hardly ever used, one that by some disturbing luck matched Chaos's hair perfectly—in one hand and a string of anal beads in the other. There was a Fleshlight and a vibrator beside him on the bed, where he was still sitting cross-legged.

Chaos held the items up like he was showing them off, grinning brightly. "You have accessories!"

"Oh my fucking God."

Chaos stroked the dildo. "So nice to play with, yes? Is this what you do instead of going to orgies?"

No. No, no, no. That was not happening.

Cooper stepped up to the bed. After a moment of initial reluctance from the demon, he was able to gather the toys from Chaos's hands. But when he tried to place them back in the drawer, Chaos's tail whipped out, slamming it shut before he could.

Cooper let out a frustrated breath. Forbidding Chaos outright from something didn't seem to work well, but distraction...

"Bracchus," Cooper said gently, abandoning his battle for the drawer handle. "You want to kiss me, right?"

Chaos perked up immediately, his tail abandoning its hold on the drawer to curl up behind him. "Yes, please."

Well, that was...polite. "Okay. So let's put the toys away."

"Why?"

"Because I'm not ready for those yet."

Fuck. Why had Cooper phrased it like that? Why the fuck would he say "yet"?

But Chaos was nodding sagely. "Of course, puppy. You're very nervous. And embarrassed. I should go slowly with you."

"You—" Cooper was stopped short as he shut the toys away. He'd assumed Chaos was oblivious to his emotional roller coasters. The demon definitely hadn't said anything about them until now. "You know I get embarrassed?"

"Of course." Chaos cocked his head, widening his eyes in that way he did when he wanted to seem innocent. "Did I forget to tell you? I can feel your emotions through your soul piece. And scent them on you besides. Your embarrassment's strange but tasty. Kind of sour and tingly on the tongue."

"You can feel my emotions," Cooper repeated woodenly.

"Just bits and pieces." Chaos grinned, flashing his dimple. "Right now, you're embarrassed again."

Of course he was. He was a fucking mess, and apparently Chaos knew every bit of it.

Although...Chaos didn't seem to mind Cooper's nervousness or his embarrassment. He'd even just said it was...tasty?

Still, Cooper *was* embarrassed and also felt sort of...flayed open, in a strange way. He spent so much time worrying about what other people were thinking, worrying about trying to seem normal and less anxious than he really was. And apparently, with this demon, it was a lost cause.

Cooper didn't have to pretend or worry or fret. Chaos already had his number.

Holy shit.

Chaos was going to turn Cooper's life upside down, wasn't he?

Whether Chaos was here for a few days or...longer, Cooper was just now realizing he wasn't going to come out of this the same as he'd started. It didn't seem possible to remain unchanged by someone like Chaos.

It was scary but also...intriguing. Cooper's life had become so small. So contained. Maybe it wouldn't be the worst thing in the world to have it blown wide open.

Whatever Chaos was feeling from Cooper's soul piece now, it made his grin drop and his eyes go heavy-lidded. He scooted to the edge of the bed until his legs hit the ground, widening them invitingly. "Come here, puppy," he crooned.

Cooper went, standing between Chaos's knees. It made him taller than Chaos, the demon gazing up at him through dark lashes.

Chaos placed his hands on Cooper's hips, and the warmth burned through Cooper's clothes, straight to his skin.

Right. Kissing lessons. Cooper licked dry lips. "You know the basics?" he asked.

Chaos nodded. "We press our mouths together. We stroke our tongues."

"Yeah." Cooper pressed his thumb to Chaos's lower lip, studying the row of sharp fangs that was revealed. "I'm a little worried about your teeth," he admitted.

"Because I might bite off one of your fingers?" Chaos opened his mouth, capturing Cooper's thumb and holding it in place between his fangs.

"No, I— Wait, do you *want* to bite off one of my fingers?" Carefully—so fucking carefully—Cooper withdrew his thumb from Chaos's mouth.

Instead of answering that extremely important question, Chaos bared his teeth, which were suddenly of the blunt human variety. "So I don't accidentally take your tongue," he said in a way that was maybe supposed to be reassuring.

"Cool. Great." After a beat, Cooper added, "Thank you."

The insanity of this moment aside, Cooper was grateful for the training wheels. He'd had some bad kisses in his life, but he'd never lost his tongue for his troubles. That seemed too high a cost for one kiss, even from an adorable demon.

Cooper had kind of expected Chaos to just go for it. To jump on him with the same giddy glee he approached everything else. But instead, Chaos kept sitting there with his unnatural, predatory stillness, his hands steady on Cooper's hips.

Waiting for Cooper.

Luring him in.

Cooper lowered his head slowly, pressing his mouth against Chaos's lips. Like his hands, Chaos's mouth was uncommonly warm. It made Cooper's lips tingle.

He hummed, licking the sensation away, only to press another kiss against Chaos's top lip, then the bottom lip. He kept it gentle. Soft. Sweet.

He leaned back after a moment. "See?"

Chaos's eyes were on Cooper's mouth. "More," he demanded, his voice as soft as Cooper's touch.

Cooper pressed in again. This time, Chaos's lips parted against his, so Cooper gently—slowly—swiped in his tongue. Chaos tasted smoky and sweet, just like his scent.

Chaos's fingers tightened on Cooper's hips, and after a moment, Chaos's tongue met his, following Cooper's lead and stroking against him slowly.

Cooper shuddered, biting back a moan. The slow pace of

things was making everything feel unbelievably intimate. In some ways it was familiar, like kissing anyone, but also...

He leaned back again, ignoring Chaos's pout at his retreat. "Let me see your tongue."

Chaos opened his mouth obediently, like it was a normal question to be asked mid-make-out session.

Yeah, that thing was longer than a human's for sure. And... pointier. Cooper blinked, and suddenly it was forked.

"What—?"

"More," Chaos rasped instead of letting Cooper finish his question. He didn't wait for Cooper this time—he released his hold on Cooper's hips and grabbed his cheeks, pulling Cooper's face down to his. He surged up and captured Cooper's mouth, his now forked tongue swiping in to claim and plunder.

Cooper groaned, his eyes falling closed as he gave in to the newly demanding kiss. Chaos's hands were somehow everywhere, like he had more than the normal amount. On Cooper's hips again but also in his hair, stroking his arms, teasing under his shirt. Cooper's muscles went limp, and he relied on Chaos's body to hold him up.

When Chaos let him up for air—probably some time after he should have, judging by how lightheaded Cooper was feeling—Cooper gasped the question, "Are you sure you haven't kissed befo—"

"More," Chaos growled, tugging Cooper's hips closer and kissing him again.

Cooper had gotten hard at some point. Could Chaos feel his arousal, like he'd felt Cooper's embarrassment? Although, the point was probably moot, since no doubt Chaos could feel Cooper's fucking erection against his stomach.

Cooper should put a stop to this now, right? Practice was one thing, but this was...

Cooper wasn't going to let this demon actually *fuck* him, was he?

But then Cooper's shirt was being tugged over his head, and Chaos was leaning forward, butting his head against Cooper's belly like some kind of cat.

Cooper stroked Chaos's purple hair, trying to catch his breath now that his mouth was his own again. "Do you think you—you have a handle on it now? The kissing?"

In answer, Chaos's hands wandered from Cooper's hips to his ass, grabbing and kneading the flesh there. It felt good.

Too good.

"Um, maybe I should add to the lesson," Cooper said frantically as more blood rushed to his dick. "You need a human's permission to mate with them. You know that, right?"

Chaos's hot breath huffed against Cooper's bare belly. "Of course." He raised his head, peering up at Cooper beseechingly through his lashes. "Do I have your permission, Cooper?"

Well, that was Cooper's fault, for setting that one up. Because he was in no way actually ready for that question.

Luckily, just then, Cooper's phone rang.

His phone that was in Chaos's pocket.

And judging by the growl Chaos let out at the interruption, the demon didn't seem very inclined to give it back to him.

8

Chaos

C haos pushed his lower lip into a pout as his puppy held out a hand for the phone. "No telephone," Chaos insisted. "More kissing."

He'd very much been enjoying the kissing. Cooper tasted minty and fresh, and his mouth was warm and wet and welcoming. His body would be the same; Chaos just knew it. He could tell by the lovely, soft give of Cooper's belly, and the delightfully fleshy handfuls of his bottom.

Chaos had enjoyed the way Cooper went limp in his hold, the way he let Chaos's hands roam over him while he kissed him feverishly. The human's arousal wasn't a violent, possessive wave, like some men Chaos had known. It was a slow, burning sweetness, and it smelled like charred caramel.

Tasty, tasty, tasty.

But it was melting on the air now, as Cooper was distracted by the ringing telephone. "I can't ignore it," he was saying. "It might be work. If it's Ivan, I need to answer it."

Chaos held the phone up to see what name was displayed. He scowled at the screen.

Ivan.

Cooper kept reaching for the phone. "I need to answer, Bracchus."

Chaos held the phone behind him, out of Cooper's reach. He wasn't going to be swayed by his true name leaving Cooper's sweet, soft lips. "Why?" he asked petulantly.

"He might need me."

No, no, no. Chaos didn't like that. Cooper had been taking care of *Chaos's* needs, taking him out and giving him games to play and practicing kissing with him. What did Ivan's mortal needs matter? The other human had Nix for those things. He didn't require Chaos's puppy too.

"What happens if you don't pick up?"

Cooper sucked in a harsh breath. "Um, Ivan kills me?"

Chaos let out an enraged growl, his wings stretching out behind him as his tail lashed against the mattress. Ivan would dare *harm* Chaos's summoner?

Cooper shrank into himself, away from Chaos, the scent of his arousal extinguished completely, replaced by the acrid bite of fear now. "Oh damn. You don't like that." He smiled awkwardly, holding his hands out in supplication. "Okay, he's not going to literally kill me. That was an exaggeration. He'll probably start by leaving an angry voicemail."

The ruffled feathers on Chaos's wings smoothed back down. And oops—the bedspread was smoking. Chaos put out the small, smoldering flame. He hadn't meant to do that.

He gave a delicate cough, trying to push back the growl that still seemed to want to come out. "We'll wait for the voice message, then," he said primly.

Cooper only nodded, eyeing the charred circle on his bedspread.

They waited together. Cooper's legs were still bracketed by Chaos's knees—he hadn't retreated that far—but he wasn't leaning on Chaos anymore. There was...distance.

It was irritating.

"You don't have to be afraid of me," Chaos reminded his puppy. He usually found humanity's fear of him funny, but he wasn't even slightly tempted to cackle right now. "I'm your friend."

He was, by contract and now by choice. And also potentially his future mate, but Chaos kept that part to himself for the moment.

Cooper gave him a smile that looked a little more genuine than before. "I told you, I'm just...going to be, sometimes. I'm not used to demons, you know. To growling and wings going all crazy and my bed catching on fire."

Chaos frowned down at the phone in his hand. "You're not going to want to kiss me anymore," he said in a quiet voice. Quiet and pathetic. Cooper should really take pity on him.

Chaos was counting on it.

Cooper let out another one of those funny breaths. "I'm not worried you'll hurt me."

"So we can kiss again?" Chaos asked immediately, pressing his advantage.

"You want to?" Cooper's cheeks flushed a lovely pink. "That wasn't enough, um, practice?"

"Of course not. I set the bed on fire, didn't I? I'll need lots of practice." Chaos gave Cooper a stern look. "*Lots*."

"But the bed thing was about—"

"Lots," Chaos repeated firmly.

The flush on Cooper's cheeks deepened. His fear was dissipating, giving way to more nervous embarrassment. That was much better. "Okay. We'll...practice again," Cooper agreed.

Chaos's lovely, agreeable summoner.

The phone dinged, and Cooper told Chaos it was a sign that the voice message was ready.

Chaos handed him the phone, only to pull it back at the last second. "Play it out loud," he demanded.

Cooper pressed play, then the little speaker button, and they listened to Ivan and his frustrated words. "*Cooper.*"

Chaos frowned. He didn't like the way Ivan said Cooper's name. Like he was angry. Like Cooper had done something wrong.

"Why the hell aren't you picking up? You have something of mine. Something you never should have taken. I need it back. Right the *fuck* now. I'm coming over. Be ready."

Ivan was obviously talking about the Book. He wanted it back? Was he trying to bond with Nix? That was hilarious, but it didn't really matter—Chaos wasn't ready to give the Book back to the man with the mean voice.

What if Chaos got very good at kissing in the next few hours, and Cooper agreed to mate with him after all? He'd need it then.

At the diner, Cooper had insisted he wasn't the right human for Chaos, but Chaos wasn't convinced at all. With each passing moment, he was getting fonder and fonder of his puppy.

"He's talking about your Book," Cooper muttered, echoing the less fun half of Chaos's thoughts. "If he wants it, I have to give it to him."

Chaos grabbed the phone back, shoving it into his pocket. "No."

"Bracchus..."

"If he tries to take it, I'll slash him with my claws. Right across the belly." Chaos held up taloned fingers in demonstration. He would too. Ivan's belly would deserve it, for not being Cooper's belly.

Cooper pressed his fingers to his forehead, like he was thinking very hard. "Okay. Right. So if this day is to have a nonviolent end, we need to leave and, um, take the Book with us."

Chaos beamed at him. "You're more than a little wise, after all. I was wrong to say otherwise before."

Cooper rolled his pretty eyes. It was a bit sassy of him, but Chaos didn't mind, if it meant Cooper's fear of him was dwindling even smaller. Soon it would be a tiny pea, too inconsequential to matter. *Then* Cooper might not mind bonding him.

And they were going out again! That was delightful. The computer game had been fun, but Chaos had played for hours already. He wasn't sure he wanted to return to it, when there was the whole outside world to explore.

"Where will you take me?" he asked eagerly.

Cooper still had his fingers pressed to his forehead. "I guess a hotel?"

"A love hotel?" Nix had told Chaos all about those. He'd liked to watch them through the portal, just like the porn shoots.

Cooper's ears turned the same pink as his cheeks. "We don't really have those here. Just—just a regular hotel."

"That's fine," Chaos told him agreeably, magnanimous now that he was getting his way. "I've never stayed at one."

He hopped off the bed, ready to start their adventure. So many new experiences his puppy was giving him already.

———

Not too much later, they were at a hotel bar. It was just like a regular bar but at a hotel.

Apparently Cooper had a few "secret bank accounts" with "stealth credit cards" so he could check them into the hotel under a different name, in case Ivan came looking.

It seemed like an awful lot of trouble just to hide from a regular human, but maybe it was like the numerous locks Cooper had on his apartment door.

Chaos's puppy liked to feel secure.

Cooper had waited patiently while Chaos inspected the hotel room on their arrival, delighted at the novelty. Cooper had gotten them two beds, for some reason. Chaos *was* due to sleep soon, but he didn't see why he had to do it in his own bed. He was going to curl up with Cooper, obviously. Friends snuggled, didn't they?

The room had smelled like sterile cleaning supplies but not strongly enough to mask the layers of human emotions that had built in over the years. Lust, sorrow, and boredom were the strongest, although there were little pockets of other things, like a bit of rage and disgust.

The bar was a little more Chaos's cup of tea. It was quieter than a tavern of old, but the people were still a mix, as they tended to be in establishments like this. Everyone here had come from different places for different purposes, and their conflicting goals and emotions stirred up a mild bit of disorder in the air. It was a calm sort of chaos, but it was still something.

Chaos had always been partial to the flavor of violent mayhem above all—spicy and sharp and metallic—but now, with Cooper, he was getting a taste for many different types of disarray.

It was oddly pleasing. After all, variety was the spice of life. Chaos had read that on a tea towel through the portal once.

Cooper was beside Chaos on a stool at the bar, studying the menu with a furrowed brow. The bartender—an annoyingly handsome man with very stupid facial hair—returned, and Chaos did *not* like the interested gleam in his eye as he looked Cooper over.

Yes, Chaos's puppy was aesthetically pleasing, but that was for Chaos to know and others to...not know.

"I'll just have a seltzer with lime, please," Cooper told the bartender, his eyes remaining lowered on his menu. He might have been too shy to look up and notice the man's interest, but Chaos certainly saw it.

The bartender hesitated, then placed his hand on Cooper's

menu in a way that had Cooper looking up at him. The man's eyes widened when he took stock of Cooper's mismatched pair, then gleamed anew. Like he thought Cooper was exceptionally pretty. Like he thought he might have a chance.

I will bite your hand off at the wrist, Chaos threatened in his mind, sensing Cooper might not like him saying the words out loud. *There will be fountains and fountains of blood.*

"If you're interested," the bartender drawled, oblivious to the murder and mayhem Chaos had planned for him, "we've got some good mocktails here, on the back page. There's one with guava that's my favorite."

Cooper's cheeks flushed with embarrassed pleasure at the suggestion, and Chaos let out a low growl from somewhere deep in his throat.

The growl was too quiet for the bartender to hear, but Cooper's gaze darted to Chaos, and whatever he saw on Chaos's face had him blanching.

Cooper nodded frantically at the bartender. "Guava mocktail sounds good," he said quickly, pushing the menu away. "And a water for my friend, please."

Chaos didn't need any water, and good thing too, since requiring the consumption of a tasteless liquid to live sounded as boring as anything could be. But he was pleased his puppy was thinking of him. He cut the growl off and lowered his head onto Cooper's shoulder, snuggling his face into Cooper's cool neck.

When the movement garnered the bartender's attention, Chaos flashed his true demon eyes at the man, grinning when confusion washed over his face.

"That'll be all," Chaos crooned, just as sweet and polite as his puppy.

When the man had scurried away, Chaos lifted his head. "You *like* him," he accused, something strange and bitter swirling in his belly.

"What?" Cooper seemed genuinely confused by the allegation. "I don't even know him."

Chaos pressed a finger to Cooper's cheek. "You blushed."

"I blush when strangers are nice to me. It's embarrassing in, like, a nice way."

Chaos considered that. "Am *I* nice to you?" He thought he was, at least by his own standards, but he wasn't sure Cooper felt the same way. Chaos didn't know how he could be much different, though, if Cooper disagreed. He was what he was.

Cooper seemed to consider the question, his brow furrowing thoughtfully. "You are," he said after a moment. "In a bossy sort of way."

"And you like bossy?" Chaos pressed.

"I don't mind it," Cooper said with a shrug. "I'm pretty easygoing."

"Even though lots of things make you nervous?"

"It's easier to deal with that stuff when I'm doing it for someone else. Like, I wouldn't necessarily be hanging out at a hotel bar by myself. But with you here, it's not so bad."

Oh, that was a lovely thing to say. Chaos lowered his head onto Cooper's shoulder again, suddenly pleased with the general state of things.

The bartender approached with their drinks, and this time, Chaos flashed his fangs at the man. He backed away with a start, then held a hand to his forehead, as if checking for a fever. He eyed Chaos warily as he headed to the opposite end of the bar, leaving them in peace.

Cooper shot Chaos a suspicious glance as he tasted his mocktail. "What did you just do?"

Chaos grinned innocently, his blunt human teeth back in order. "I smiled at him."

Speaking of mouths. And teeth that were sharp and then not sharp.

Chaos took out Cooper's phone. Cooper had given him his password, and Chaos had done some research while they were in the rented car on the way to the hotel, when Cooper had been distracted by his cards and accounts.

Just because Ivan had interrupted them didn't mean Chaos was letting go of his advantage.

"Puppy?" Chaos asked sweetly.

Cooper looked up from his drink. "Yeah?"

Chaos pushed the phone toward him, showing Cooper the video he'd pulled up. "Can we practice this next?"

Cooper yelped, flipping the phone over and shoving it down onto the bar top, glancing around like he'd just committed a crime. His cheeks were *much* redder now than they'd been with the bartender.

"Chaos," he said in a low voice, as if afraid for his words to carry. "You can't pull up *porn* at the bar."

"Why not?" Chaos asked with a pout. "I kept the sound off."

Chaos had thought Cooper would appreciate the courtesy—his puppy didn't like too much attention being drawn to him—but perhaps Chaos had been mistaken.

Cooper took some slow, deep breaths, his chest rising and falling noticeably with each one. He sipped his drink once. Then again.

Chaos waited him out. See how patient he could be?

"You want me to blow you?" Cooper finally asked, his voice just as low and quiet as before, not even looking at Chaos for some reason.

"No, silly," Chaos told him, at his usual volume. "*I* want to blow *you*." In case Cooper didn't fully understand, he clarified, "I want to put my mouth on your cock and suck on it."

He'd wanted to do it since he'd seen the first video of it in Cooper's porn stash. There were just so many ways for humans to mate with each other, almost none of which Chaos had ever had a chance to explore, too busy following orders and unleashing mayhem.

But now he was here, with his agreeable puppy, and he wanted to try all of them.

Cooper lowered his head onto his hand, his ears now the same red as his cheeks. "Oh my fucking God."

Chaos patted Cooper's pretty hair and winked at the bartender, who was gaping at them. Chaos didn't mind the man and his stupid facial hair so much, now that everyone knew where everyone else stood.

The hotel bar was pretty fun after all.

9

Cooper

Cooper sat on the edge of the hotel bed in his underwear, nibbling on his thumbnail as he tried to get the storm of butterflies in his belly to calm its rioting. Chaos was standing in front of him, fox eyes narrowed and gleaming in anticipation.

They'd finished their drinks at the bar with Cooper in a sort of daze. (Or at least Cooper had finished *his* drink—Chaos had just dipped his fingers in his water and flicked them at the bartender when Cooper wasn't looking, until Cooper had caught him and asked him to stop.) Cooper was pretty sure he'd paid his bill. Or maybe he'd charged it to the room? Hopefully he'd tipped that poor bartender. Jesus.

Why had Cooper agreed to this again?

Except he knew why, didn't he? He'd agreed because there was something about Chaos that pulled him in, something Cooper didn't have it in him to resist. It was...all of it. The whole package. Chaos's delight in everything Cooper had to offer. The warm weight of his head on Cooper's shoulder. The firm grip of his hand as they walked. The intensity of his attention and the dangerous aura he emanated without care.

It was all so...compelling. Cooper would probably never come across anything or anyone as compelling ever again in his life. And he might be a little cowardly by nature, but he still wanted to take advantage while he could, before he had to go back to the small, contained existence he'd been living before.

And even though it should have been horribly awkward—Cooper sitting in his underwear while Chaos stared at him, back in his demon form but still fully clothed—Cooper was already half-hard, nervous embarrassment mixing gleefully with arousal in his belly in some sort of strange, internal cocktail.

He cleared his throat, dropping his hand from his mouth. They couldn't stare at each other forever, as much as Chaos seemed willing to. "You said you've mated before. Was that with...humans?"

Chaos shook his head, his gaze laser-focused on Cooper's underwear-clad cock in a way that should have been ridiculous but was for some reason making Cooper's dick twitch. "Demons, mostly. There were a few in the Void in the very beginning who were agreeable." He cocked his head in thought, although his eyes never left Cooper's dick. "One human, long ago. A madman. Vicious and wild."

He said it almost fondly, and something bitter clenched in Cooper's gut. Which was stupid, plain and simple. What right did Cooper have to be jealous, especially of some random hookup from centuries ago?

Still, he found himself warning, in case Chaos was expecting more of the same, "I'm not generally, like, some sort of wildcat in the bedroom."

"No, you aren't, are you?" Chaos said with a sly smile, his golden eyes finally darting up to meet Cooper's gaze again. "You're sweet." He reached out a taloned hand to stroke Cooper's bare knee. "Pliant." His thumb swept up the sensitive skin of Cooper's inner thigh. "Agreeable."

Cooper squirmed. Should he be offended right now? And Chaos tightened his hold. He'd said those things—sweet, pliant, agreeable—like they were positives. Like they got him hot or something.

Cooper cleared his throat again, trying for a smile. "I guess I'm the right person to teach you to be gentle with humans, then, huh?"

Flames danced in Chaos's vertical pupils. "Yes. Exactly the right person." He stepped closer, his hand sliding up Cooper's leg to tug on his boxer briefs. "Off," he demanded, somewhere between insistent and petulant. "They're covering what I want to see."

Jesus. Cooper sucked in a breath, but he supposed *agreeable* might be the right adjective after all because he shimmied his underwear down and off as ordered, revealing his half-hard cock to Chaos's intent gaze.

He was aware he was painfully average in that department— even on the smaller side—but Chaos made a quiet, intrigued noise, his lips curling in delight. His fingertip brushed against the head of Cooper's cock, and Cooper held back a shiver at the light touch.

"I don't have this," Chaos mused, stroking again.

For a second, Cooper thought Chaos was telling him he didn't have a cock at all, but then he realized. "Foreskin?"

"Mm. I like it." Chaos continued to stare, unblinking, as Cooper started hardening fully under his touch. He licked his lips as Cooper's cockhead started peeking out, his foreskin retracting, and then Chaos pushed it back fully, his touch gentle as anything, despite what he'd said about needing to learn. "Pretty," he whispered, more to himself than to Cooper. "Very pretty."

He knelt in front of Cooper's spread legs then, licking his lips like he was seating himself at some lecherous buffet. His wings were tucked behind him, his tail suspiciously docile. His hair was electric blue today, and Cooper brushed it back from Chaos's eyes.

"Show me, please. Before we get started."

Chaos knew what Cooper was asking for—he bared his teeth, displaying their blunt human ends, as opposed to his usual sharp fangs.

"You know the basics?" Cooper asked, an echo of his earlier question, before their first kiss.

"I don't bite down," Chaos told him somberly, then bared his teeth again in a quick snap. "No chomping."

He was clearly teasing, but it was still a little nerve-racking, having such a volatile creature eye level with Cooper's vulnerable dick. But something about that little bite of fear, of uncertainty, was doing it for Cooper in a weird way. He hadn't thought he worked like that. He'd never even been particularly kinky. But messing around with unpredictable Chaos was....exciting. Strange.

"You don't bite down," he repeated, really hoping that mantra stuck in Chaos's brain. "Or I'm never gonna want to do this again."

Chaos grinned at him. "So stern, puppy."

"Yeah, well, I have strong feelings about my dick getting bitten off."

"I would never bite off something so lovely," Chaos murmured, stroking a finger along the head of Cooper's cock again. A drop of precum beaded at the slit as Cooper sucked in another sharp breath, and Chaos hummed happily. "You only have the one, after all."

"Do you—" Cooper was struck by a daunting thought, and his eyes dropped to Chaos's crotch. "You don't have more than one, do you?"

"Would you like to see?" Chaos didn't wait for an answer—he

stopped caressing Cooper and hopped to his feet immediately, his clothes disappearing in a flash, leaving him naked.

He was...

Wow.

The skin Cooper had seen until now—the skin on Chaos's arms and feet and face—had always looked mostly human, even in Chaos's demon form, like he had a tan that was a touch more golden than natural. But naked, Chaos's skin gave way to a light, downy fur on his chest, fur that traveled down to his belly, hips, and thighs. It matched the light, golden brown of the tuft of his tail.

It looked soft. And strange. And kind of beautiful.

But that wasn't what Chaos had been wanting to show off when he stripped, apparently. He grabbed hold of his now bare cock, opening his fingers so it lay on his palm, like he was offering it up to Cooper's perusal.

So Cooper perused, if only to be *agreeable*.

Chaos's cock was already hard—Cooper took a moment to be flattered—and *almost* human-looking, much like the skin on his arms and face. It was larger than what Cooper was used to taking but tapered at the tip. And it had...bumps going along the top and bottom. They almost looked like subdermal piercings, if those were a thing that demons had. The veins running along it were black and weirdly plentiful.

Overall, it was more intimidating than what Cooper had been expecting. But what the fuck did he know about demon dicks? He guessed it was just a good thing he wasn't the one giving head this time around.

"What do you think?" Chaos asked eagerly, lifting his cock higher, as if to give Cooper a better look.

"Um..." Cooper had to bite back a laugh. Nothing was even funny—he was just a nervous laugher sometimes. "Very nice."

"Yes, I think so." Chaos's gaze dipped down, as if to confirm the niceness of his own dick, and then he was dropping to his knees again, and suddenly Cooper didn't feel like laughing at all.

Chaos sat there for a long moment, just staring again, his breath hot against Cooper's sensitive skin. He wasn't making a move, but he also wasn't asking for pointers, so Cooper didn't give any. Instead, he gave in to an urge that had been bubbling within him and started petting those electric-blue strands of hair.

They were surprisingly thick and a little coarse. As Cooper brushed through them gently, his fingers ran over one of Chaos's short, stubby horns. It was hard to the touch, like an antler. Warm though. Cooper rubbed his thumb over it, and Chaos pressed into the touch.

His ears were slightly furred at their pointed tips, Cooper realized, like the fur on his belly and tail.

What a strange creature to have come into Cooper's life.

Maybe Chaos thought the same of him.

Cooper was so caught up in his exploration that he was taken by surprise at the feel of Chaos's tongue dipping to his slit, licking up the precum that had gathered there. Cooper sucked in a strangled breath—Chaos's tongue was rough and pointed again. Hot to the touch.

Chaos swirled it around Cooper's tip, and Cooper shuddered, his lower belly tightening.

"Fuck," he hissed when Chaos did it again, Cooper's hands still caught in his hair.

Chaos started licking him in earnest then, slow but thorough. Along the sides of his cock, down at the base, only to come back up and slowly trace the folded ridges of his foreskin.

Cooper hardly breathed through it, this careful exploration. It should have been a miserable tease, but it had been so long since he'd been touched properly...

His legs were shaking in no time.

After he'd covered every bit of Cooper's dick with his saliva,

Chaos leaned back with a happy hum. "You taste nice. Salty."
Cooper could only nod, still barely breathing, and Chaos smiled at
him. "I'm going to take you in my mouth now, and I'm going to
watch my teeth."

"Okay," Cooper managed to say, nodding again. "Yes."

"And you'll keep petting my hair."

It wasn't a suggestion, and Cooper let out a breathless laugh.
"Yeah, okay."

In contrast to his exploratory licking, Chaos didn't hesitate
when it came to sucking Cooper down. He enveloped Cooper's
entire cock in his mouth, taking him in like he didn't have a gag
reflex. Maybe he didn't—he didn't eat; what need did he have for
one? His mouth was almost unbearably hot, and Cooper gasped at
the sensation, his thighs tensing and his toes curling. "F-Fuck."

Chaos held him in his mouth, his tongue exploring again, and
it took everything in Cooper to keep his hips still, to let Chaos run
the show without any interference.

Chaos butted his head into Cooper's hand, and Cooper realized he was slacking on his orders. He tried to focus, petting
Chaos's hair again.

And then Chaos started sucking, the tight, hot pressure almost
painfully good. Cooper let out a weird, inhuman noise he'd never
made before—half strangled moan, half plea. He couldn't find his
breath again, too busy choking on air as Chaos shoved his cock
deeper before coming back up and doing it all over again.

Chaos hummed happily at Cooper's frantic noises, and the
vibrations from it did nothing to help Cooper's composure. It had
been barely any time at all, and Cooper's balls were already drawn
tight against him, his spine and face and ears too hot. He'd never
been sucked like this. So fiercely. So mercilessly.

He tried to focus on his hands, on petting Chaos's hair like the
demon had demanded, but he kept forgetting, his mind going
blank as Chaos sucked and bobbed.

He wasn't prepared when Chaos popped off suddenly, the rush of cold hotel air on Cooper's dick making him cry out.

Chaos grinned at him, sly and pleased. "Is that gentle enough, puppy?"

Cooper wouldn't in any realm call what Chaos was doing to him "gentle," but it wasn't violent either, so he just nodded dumbly, taking panting gasps of air while he could.

Chaos gave him another sly, pleased look and then took him in his mouth again, peering up at Cooper now as he sucked him down.

Cooper could only stare back, his fingers clenching and unclenching in Chaos's hair as his lower body tightened, something hot and almost frightening building in him. "Bracchus," he moaned, either in supplication or warning. "I'm gonna—gonna—"

Something broke within him, and he hunched over again with a pained groan, shooting into Chaos's mouth as the world went dim around the edges. Chaos hummed around him as he came, and Cooper could barely handle the tightness of the demon's throat as he swallowed. He wanted to get closer. He wanted to push away. He wanted to pull Chaos into him so tightly it hurt.

He was left weak and trembling, but he managed to pull out, hissing with oversensitivity when Chaos's rough tongue kept scraping against him even after he'd come.

Chaos licked his lips with a smack, although there was no trace of Cooper's cum on them. Chaos had swallowed it all, greedy as anything. "I didn't bite," he said proudly.

"But—but you swallowed." Cooper's brow furrowed as his chest heaved. "Can you—I mean, you don't eat or drink."

"It won't harm me." Chaos lay his head on Cooper's knee, peering up at him. "It's human essence—demons thrive off of that. Cum. Blood. Sweat. Tears."

Well, that was only slightly terrifying.

Chaos stood abruptly, his cock still hard, still intimidating as it jutted out, black-veined and studded. "Will you touch me, puppy?" he asked with disarming sweetness.

And even though Cooper had just come, that nervous edge of excitement bubbled in his belly again as he was faced with Chaos's hard demon cock. "Yeah," he breathed. "I'll touch you."

He wrapped a hand around Chaos. His cock was just as hot as his mouth, the skin softer than Cooper might have expected. Chaos was oozing something thick and viscous now, and Cooper used it to ease the glide of his fist. The studs were rigid, not at all pliable, but Chaos seemed to like having them touched, making small, pleased noises when Cooper ran his thumb over them.

Cooper had always been a little self-conscious when it came to sex, overthinking what was normal or hot or whatever. But he didn't really have to worry about that with Chaos, did he? Nothing was normal here, not by any standard Cooper was aware of. Who knew what was hot to a chaos demon? The thought of biting off Cooper's fingers, apparently, so what did it matter what Cooper did? All he *could* do was give in to what felt natural and trust that Chaos would tell him what he liked.

And Chaos, being who he was, did exactly that. "I like your touch, puppy."

Cooper smiled up at him, still stroking with one hand, petting the soft fur of Chaos's lower belly with the other. "I'm glad."

"I want to release my spend right here," Chaos told him, touching Cooper's chest, right over his heart.

"Okay," Cooper said easily. "Wherever you want."

"Yes," Chaos hissed, his hips moving with Cooper's touch now. His wings were twitching and rolling behind him, his tail lashing out to thump against Cooper's leg. "Wherever I want. *Whatever* I want." He placed his hands on Cooper's shoulders, steadying himself. "Faster, puppy," he urged.

Cooper followed his lead, stroking faster, tightening his grip the way he liked it when he wanted to jerk off speedily in the shower. He fixed his eyes on Chaos's cock, watching the way the head grew fatter as Chaos approached his release, but he could feel the heavy weight of Chaos's stare on his head.

Watching Cooper, as he always seemed to be.

Chaos came with a surprisingly soft breath, splashing Cooper's chest with cum that was hot and thick. Cooper felt weirdly proud and pleased, in a way he never had after a hookup. He'd made his demon feel good. Made him happy. And it had been easy and natural and perfect.

Chaos immediately clambered into Cooper's lap, straddling his legs. Cooper's sticky hands fell to Chaos's thighs, and he stroked the fur there. It was just as soft as the fur on his belly. He kind of wanted to rub his cheek against it.

"You came very quickly," Chaos told him brightly, wrapping his arms around Cooper's neck, not sounding nearly as winded as Cooper felt. "When I had my mouth on you."

"It's been a while," Cooper admitted, too content to feel even slightly embarrassed. For some reason, he added, "I've been really lonely."

"I know, puppy," Chaos told him, running his talons gently through Cooper's hair. "I know." After a moment, he said quietly, "I think I was lonely too."

Cooper gave in to his urges and dropped his head to Chaos's chest, rubbing along the fur there. He was tired all of a sudden and yet felt too good to want to move. "Didn't you have your demon friends?"

"They were there, but they weren't mine. Not like you." Chaos twisted Cooper's earlobe, tugging gently. "The four of us were just...thrown together. Except maybe Nix. I would call him a friend, I think."

Nix, the gorgeous, purple-eyed demon. Was he one of the ones who'd been agreeable to Chaos's advances? Cooper didn't want to think about it, not when he was feeling so nice. "If we'd waited for Ivan, you could've seen him again."

Chaos didn't respond to that. Instead, he said, his voice serious and almost sad, "I was in the Void for a very, very long time." He paused, and Cooper thought that might be it, but then he continued, "I thought a lot about what I wanted when I finally escaped. How I wanted to be summoned back to the human realm but didn't want to be ordered about, following some summoner's pathetic whims. I wanted to explore. To play. But then you came along..." Chaos leaned back, pushing Cooper's head up from his chest. He stroked Cooper's cheek. "You summoned me, but I think I summoned you too."

Cooper didn't know what to say to that. So he told the truth. "I'm glad you did."

Chaos beamed at him, hopping off his lap in the next instant. Before Cooper could mourn the loss of their closeness, Chaos was tugging his hand, pulling him into bed and under the covers. He draped himself over Cooper's chest, his wings tucked tight against his back, like he was going to sleep with him there. Cooper saw for the first time that he had a tattoo on his back, in between his wings, swirling and chaotic and golden.

"I'll sleep beside you now," Chaos murmured. "And when I wake before you, I'll play more of your game. In the morning, you'll teach me new games to play so I don't get bored and destructive when you're busy. And after we feed you..."

He was warm and soft, and his smoky scent was becoming addictive. Cooper sighed, tucking his chin over Chaos's head, listening to his plans and sweet demands.

The sex part had been...unreal. Amazing. But this—having someone curled against him, someone for Cooper to hold and be held by—*this* was what was going to be hard to lose, when Chaos found his human mate.

Cooper could only hope he'd survive it.

10

Chaos

Chaos batted at the thick, soft hotel pillows with his tail. He was happily curled up on the bed next to his puppy, each of them with their own laptop. Cooper had brought two to the hotel, one for each of them. Thoughtful as always.

After that first night in the hotel—when Cooper had so agreeably let Chaos practice being gentle with his mouth—they'd spent all day yesterday and last night switching off between exploring outside (for Chaos) and "work time" (for Cooper), where Cooper attended to Ivan's tasks for him and Chaos played video games while wishing various deaths upon Ivan for taking up so much of his puppy's precious time.

So far Chaos had been many different characters, had shot and exploded things with abandon, and had even been a little goose with a knife, causing a delightful amount of mayhem. It was all surprisingly entertaining, considering he'd been in bed for all of it.

Much, much more entertaining, however, were the four other blow jobs Chaos had given Cooper, each as titillating as the first.

Who had known sucking on an appendage and *not* biting down could be so delightful?

Chaos hadn't exactly been lying when he'd told Cooper he needed to practice being gentle with a human mate. Mating for him had always been some furious clash of bodies, each partner searching for their own release with no thought to the other's welfare or pleasure. It also hadn't been something Chaos had participated in often—sex wasn't one of his primary drives, not like Nix. Chaos could go for a long, long time without finding the urge particularly overwhelming.

But he also hadn't realized just how intriguing it could be, to have someone like Cooper gasping and trembling under his touch, yearning under Chaos's searching mouth. Chaos found himself thinking about it even when it wasn't happening, his cock filling at the funniest times. Aching for more.

Aching for his mate.

Chaos had officially decided after that very first time with his mouth around Cooper's cock—Cooper was the human for him. It was part of why it was so fun to mark Cooper in his spend afterward, which Cooper always agreed to eagerly, whether it be on his belly, chest, or face. Chaos didn't tell Cooper, but every time he coated Cooper with his cum, he was secretly saying, *Mine. My human. Marked and claimed.*

He giggled to himself at the thought.

Cooper glanced over with a little smile. "Having fun over there?"

He looked fond, which he did more and more these past few days when looking at Chaos. It turned out sex and close proximity were very good for bonding. Chaos couldn't have planned this little interlude better if he'd tried. It almost made him want to thank Ivan for making Cooper run away. Almost.

Except there was one teeny, little problem: the longer they stayed in this hotel, the more anxious Cooper was becoming. Orgasms didn't seem to be enough to fix it, nor did Chaos politely playing video games while Cooper worked.

Chaos let his giggle trail off, narrowing his eyes at Cooper instead. It was time to get to the bottom of this. "Why are you afraid right now?" he asked.

Cooper's eyes widened in surprise at the shift in tone. "What?"

"Every hour we stay here, you become a little more afraid. It's not because of me." Chaos pouted a little at the thought. It wasn't that he *wanted* Cooper to be terrified of him. That would have ruined their fun. But he didn't want anyone else to have that power over his dear puppy either.

"Well..." Cooper pushed his glasses up the bridge of his nose, clicking something on his computer and then shutting the laptop to focus on Chaos. "I guess it's knowing that the longer I avoid Ivan, the more pissed he's gonna be when I see him again."

Ugh. Ivan.

Cooper was afraid of this human—his cousin and his employer—and Chaos didn't *like* it. It was okay when Cooper was a little nervous around Chaos, because Chaos knew *he* wasn't going to do anything to hurt Cooper. Not really. But this Ivan...

Chaos flexed his talons. He could feel his eyes changing colors as he battled his rage. It wouldn't do to have a fit. Not now. "Why do you work for mobsters when they scare you?"

He'd been wondering. Cooper wasn't the type, as far as Chaos could tell. His soul piece didn't contain any greed or bloodlust inside it, and his technological skill set could surely have been used elsewhere, considering how much the modern world seemed to run on computers.

Something soft and sad pulsed from Cooper as he cleared his throat. "My dad," he said quietly. "We came here from Russia when I was a baby. He and my mom wanted a fresh start, but my mom died when I was little, and after that he..." Cooper rubbed at his arm, as if to soothe himself. "Well, he had trouble holding on to a job. When he heard that his brother-in-law, Dimitri, had made a name for himself in the mob..."

Cooper shrugged, but the sadness wafting from him didn't ease. "He offered himself up. But he was too much of a mess, and Dimitri asked for me instead. Someone small and unassuming to run errands without drawing attention. My dad was going to refuse, but I knew we needed the money. So I started working for Dimitri when I was still a teenager, and then when Ivan took over, he started using me for what I actually do best."

Chaos frowned, trying to sift through the emotions roiling around the room. He couldn't tell if Cooper was sad because he was thinking about his dad or sad about the circumstances surrounding him coming to work for Ivan. This was where Nix would have come in handy. He knew humans better than Chaos did.

But Cooper was *Chaos's* human, so Chaos would have to muddle through.

"You could leave," Chaos offered. "I'd protect you."

Cooper didn't say anything. Maybe he didn't believe that Chaos *could* protect him. At least not forever.

Because he still thought Chaos was leaving one day.

Chaos pouted, shoving the laptop off his lap with a huff. He turned to Cooper. "If we were to give the Book back to him, would you be less afraid?"

Cooper scratched at his neck sheepishly. "It would be one problem solved, sure."

Chaos considered as he stared at his human, amused at the way even that little bit of attention turned Cooper's cheeks pink.

Cooper wasn't ready to commit to a bond yet; even Chaos knew enough to know that. And when he *was* ready, it would be easy enough to get the Book back from this Ivan fellow. And

Chaos would most likely get to see Nix in the process. It would be good to see his friend. Plus, if Nix had convinced the human he was with to bond...

Maybe it wouldn't be a bad idea to see what that looked like in person.

Chaos dug Cooper's cell phone out of his pocket, offering it over. "You may call him. Ivan."

After a moment of hesitation, Cooper reached for the phone. "Yeah?"

"But if he tries to harm you...," Chaos warned, miming swiping at Ivan with his claws.

He was oddly pleased when, instead of cowering in fear, Cooper rolled his pretty eyes. "Please don't disembowel my cousin."

Chaos decided to pretend he hadn't heard. He couldn't make any promises, anyway. It was all up to Ivan, really.

Cooper stared down at the phone in his hand for a moment, then sighed, sliding it into his sweatpants pocket. "We should head back to the apartment first. He'll want it right away." He glanced at Chaos, nibbling at his lower lip. "Ivan is very...possessive of his things. If he summoned his own demon, he's not going to be happy that I did the same."

As if summoning Nix was anything akin to summoning Chaos. Silly humans. Still...Chaos rose onto his knees. He'd had an exciting thought. "I could pretend to be human! That would be fun, wouldn't it?"

Cooper eyed him, his gaze darting first to Chaos's spread wings, then to his tail, then somewhere around his hairline, where his horns peeked out. "I think that's probably a...bad idea?"

Chaos ignored that too, leaning forward to nuzzle his head into Cooper's neck instead. He placed a kiss there—he liked the way Cooper shivered when he did. He'd like to suck him again, since it had already been hours since the last time. But it would be more satisfying when Cooper wasn't distracted by worry over his cousin.

And if Ivan caused any problems...

Well, then it wouldn't matter what Ivan did anymore, because Chaos would burn him down to a crisp.

———

CHAOS HAD an ongoing list of things that were *not* fun, and waiting for things to happen went right toward the top.

A little anticipation was one thing, but after too long, it became boring.

Boring, boring, boring, boring.

Like right now, waiting for Ivan in Cooper's apartment. Because Cooper had been wrong about needing the Book on hand right away—his cousin hadn't come running the second he'd called after all. They'd been waiting for *hours* now.

They didn't know why either. The phone call between Cooper and Ivan certainly hadn't been very informative. From what Chaos had overheard, it had been mostly awkward and strange, with Cooper acting a bit like a loon. Chaos would have found it funny if Cooper hadn't been so nervous talking to the man.

And now Cooper was pacing, nibbling on his fingers like he never allowed Chaos to do, getting more anxious by the minute. He wouldn't even let Chaos soothe him with his touch and his mouth, muttering something about, "If I'm interrupted by Ivan mid-blow-job, it'll ruin sex for me forever."

Rude.

That was what it came down to. Rudeness. This Ivan was rude and annoying, and not in the good, fun way Chaos was. Having Nix at his side had clearly done nothing to teach the man about the importance of respecting a demon's time.

Not that Ivan knew Chaos was here. Still. Who said Chaos had to be logical about it?

Would Ivan bring Nix with him, when he came to ruin all Chaos's fun? Chaos had a feeling he would. If Ivan and Nix were looking to bond, they wouldn't want to be apart while the mortal half of their duo was still vulnerable.

Speaking of...

"Don't go thinking any lusty thoughts while Nix is here," Chaos warned Cooper from his cross-legged position on the coffee table. "He can smell them."

His words stopped Cooper's pacing in its tracks. "Why would I—"

"He'll meddle if he scents anything," Chaos muttered darkly, annoyed at the very thought of it. "He's an incubus, he can't help it."

Chaos would be shutting that part of himself—the part that looked at Cooper even now and wished to see him writhing and whining underneath him—right off the very moment Nix arrived. In that sense, it was probably good Cooper wasn't letting Chaos use his mouth to soothe him. The place would reek of sex if they were interrupted. It wouldn't take an incubus to scent it.

Chaos and Nix were friends, it was true, but Nix also had a soft spot for humans. He'd see someone like Cooper and assume he needed protection from Chaos. With the contract in place between Cooper and Chaos, there wasn't much Nix could actually *do* about it, but it would be...tiresome to have someone try to keep Cooper from him.

And again, *not* in the fun way.

"I want your sweatshirt," Chaos said suddenly.

Cooper paused the pacing he'd resumed, his fingers falling from his mouth. He looked down at his chest. "The one I'm wearing?"

"Yes." Chaos reached out a hand for it. "Maybe if I smell like a human, I can fool Nix. That would be entertaining."

Nix hadn't seen *all* Chaos's human forms, after all. Who was to say Nix would recognize him?

"Um." Cooper pushed up his glasses as he looked Chaos over. "You know your face looks the same, right? Whether you're in your demon or human form—it's identical, either way."

Chaos waved his outstretched hand, dismissing Cooper's concerns. "Details, details."

Chaos didn't actually care how unlikely fooling Nix was. That was part of the fun of playing any game—there was inherent thrill in the possibility of losing, just as much as in the possibility of winning. Anyone who felt otherwise was playing for the wrong reasons.

Cooper handed the sweatshirt over with a sigh, and Chaos grinned, tugging it on before cocking his head, listening closely. He could hear footsteps in the apartment hallway, followed by the murmuring of voices, one of them very familiar.

Sure enough, there was a knock on Cooper's door the next moment.

Cooper made a sad, strangled sound and headed toward the door to undo all his many locks.

Chaos stayed right where he was. He was fast enough to interrupt any danger if Ivan tried something against Cooper. And he could see the door from where he was, although at the moment any sight of what was on the other side was blocked by Cooper.

"Ivan," Cooper greeted.

A cold voice answered him. "Cooper. Where's the demon?"

Oh no, no. Chaos didn't like that tone. And not even a hello? No hug for Ivan's lonely, touch-starved cousin? (Never mind that Chaos would have thrown him off the moment he tried.)

Rude, just as Chaos had thought.

"No demons here!" Chaos called out from his perch on the

coffee table. He was pleased when Cooper laughed, even if it was an awkward, nervous sound.

Cooper opened the front door wider, stepping to the side to reveal both Ivan and Nix, who was beaming at Chaos. Maybe he wasn't fooled by the sweatshirt after all. It didn't matter at the moment—Chaos was distracted by his own perusal of Cooper's mean cousin.

They looked nothing alike.

Ivan had none of Cooper's shy mannerisms or interesting features. He was maybe handsome, if someone was looking for a block of ice made sentient. He had white-blond hair, pale skin, and an expressionless face.

Boring, boring, boring.

Chaos cocked his head at Cooper, who was standing to the side now and nibbling at his fingers again, and Cooper drew closer to Chaos, anxiety wafting off him.

Ivan scared Chaos's puppy, even with Chaos here to protect him. It wasn't life-or-death fear, but Cooper clearly didn't want to disappoint the man.

"Ivan, meet our chaos demon," Nix announced.

Chaos shot him a pout. "No demons here," he insisted. "I'm just a mortal, human friend of Cooper's here."

If Cooper hadn't summoned any demons with the Book, then Ivan would have no need to be angry with him. And if Ivan wasn't angry at Cooper, Chaos wouldn't have to kill the man for scaring his puppy.

Chaos was saving lives with his little game here, and no one was appreciating it.

Ivan pinched the bridge of his nose. "How—"

And then Cooper spilled the beans before Chaos could say anything at all, his words coming out in a rush. "I was uploading the ledgers you gave me. I wasn't quite sure why you wanted that old, weird book with them, but I didn't want to miss it if you needed it, so I did it anyway, and then it just kind of...happened."

Whatever Ivan felt about that didn't show on his face. "You summoning a demon just kind of happened," he repeated.

"Yes?"

"And where is the Book now?"

"I still have it."

"I should fucking hope so," Ivan snapped.

No. Nope. Nuh-uh. Chaos didn't like it. Not the tone, not the language, not the look in Ivan's icy eyes. Chaos hopped up, standing in front of Ivan in an instant. He felt Nix edge closer, and Chaos shot him a warning glance, stopping his dear friend in his tracks. *Ivan* might not realize he wasn't the biggest predator in the room, but Nix did.

"Hi," Chaos said to Ivan because he could be polite for Cooper's sake, even when the other person was a rude icicle creep. "You're scaring Cooper."

"Chaos," Nix warned.

Chaos ignored him.

"I didn't intend to scare him," Ivan said slowly. "I'm simply...irritated."

How funny Ivan should use that word. *Irritated.* What did this man—this *human*—know of irritation? He thought he had some idea because he'd lost his Book for a few measly days? *Chaos* was the one who was irritated. Locked in the Void for centuries, nothing to do but watch and wait. Stuck there as demon after demon completed their contracts and were set free. Finally summoned again, graced to find his perfect puppy, only to have his bonding time interrupted by this mean. Cold. Man.

"Irritated...," Chaos repeated. He cocked his head, imagining the perfect slice of his talons through Ivan's mortal belly. Or better yet... "If I set that suit of yours on fire with you inside it," he asked, the flames' pull already tingling at his fingertips, "do you think you'd be more or less irritated?"

"Chaos," Nix tried warning again. And then, "Bracchus."

It was strange, the way Chaos's true name sounded wrong now coming from the lips of anyone but Cooper. He turned to look at Nix—his friend's eyes were beseeching. "I'm rather fond of this one," Nix said, none of his usual teasing or flirting or sly little innuendos. "I'd like to keep him in top condition."

And there was something in his words, something true and genuine that not even Chaos could ignore. Nix wasn't looking for a bond just to free himself. He *liked* this human. Enough to stay with him forever.

That was...unexpected.

Chaos loved unexpected.

"Oh." Chaos released some of his rage, allowing his inner flames to bank and cool. "Why didn't you say so?"

He felt a rush of fondness for his friend, who'd tried his very best to entertain and distract Chaos through the painful boredom of the last centuries. The two of them may have been thrown together by circumstance, but their bond was real.

Chaos had maybe gotten a bit of Cooper-focused tunnel vision and forgotten to be a good friend to Nix.

Oopsies.

He smiled brightly. "Hello, Nix. You could tell it was me?"

And then he threw himself into Nix's arms for a hug, his last, lingering irritation soothed away by Nix's quiet "Hello, sweets."

Chaos would let the mean cousin live. At least for now.

11

Cooper

Cooper stood awkwardly by while Nix and Chaos embraced in his living room.

Something bitter was churning in Cooper's gut, something beyond just his nerves about Ivan's anger. Nix was so beautiful, and Chaos seemed so fond of him. It had only taken one word from Nix for Chaos to back off of Ivan.

Cooper hadn't known Chaos could be so obedient.

He cleared his throat, wanting an excuse to get out of the room. "Let me just grab that book for you." He hurried into the computer room and grabbed the Book off his desk before coming back quickly to hand it back to Ivan.

Ivan.

Cooper had never seen his cousin actually cautious of another being before, at least not since Dimitri had died. Ivan was usually the scariest person in the room, and he knew it. But apparently now Cooper's demon—the one he'd been holed up in a hotel room playing faux honeymoon with—was scarier.

It almost made Cooper smile, but Nix and Chaos were *still* hugging, so he couldn't quite manage the curl of his lips.

"There's a meeting the day after tomorrow," Ivan said after staring at the Book in his hands for a long moment. "If you and your demon would like to attend."

That was the politest request for a work event Cooper had ever gotten from his cousin. Come to think of it, Cooper was pretty sure he'd never gotten a *request* at all before. He received orders, curt and cold and nonnegotiable.

It was so far from the norm that Cooper didn't even know how to respond. "Um...what about?"

Ivan didn't glare at him or snap at him for asking unnecessary questions. "We're making some changes," he answered instead, side-eyeing Chaos, who'd finally released Nix. "Getting rid of the rest of Sergei's men, for one."

The *rest of* Sergei's men. "Does that mean you found him?" Cooper couldn't quite keep the relief out of his voice. An angry Sergei wasn't someone he'd ever wanted to run into. Not after he'd been the one to spot the inconsistencies in Sergei's finances.

"He's in the trunk of our car," Ivan said, matter-of-fact.

Of course he was. Of course Ivan had been running around with his right-hand man in the trunk of his car. Alive or dead, he hadn't specified, and Cooper wasn't going to ask. If Sergei *was* still alive, it wouldn't be for long.

"Will it be fun?" Chaos asked Nix—not Cooper—tugging at the other demon's arm like a little kid. "The meeting?"

"You might get to kill someone," Nix told him, his voice full of fondness.

He said it like it was a reassurance. And it probably was because, unlike Cooper, Chaos *liked* violence. Thrived on it, it seemed. Vicious and wild—that was how he liked his humans. And his fellow demons, apparently. No doubt Nix had a vicious side, if he was spending this much time with Ivan unscathed.

Cooper could almost picture the two of them together: Nix and Chaos, wrapped around each other in that Void of theirs. But he stopped himself before the image could crystallize. Chaos had told him no sex thoughts. Because Nix could smell them.

Nix, who was so beautiful, and probably looked even more beautiful naked...

Had Chaos seen him naked? He must have. They'd been together for centuries.

"Fuck," Cooper swore, unable to find a way out of his circling thoughts.

All three of his guests turned to look at him, and Cooper could feel the blood drain from his face. That was three people's very intense attention to have on himself.

As if summoned by Cooper's discomfort, Chaos finally left Nix's side, bounced over to perch on the coffee table again, and tugged Cooper into him with an arm around his hip.

Despite his embarrassment, Cooper let out an inaudible sigh of relief at the touch. Chaos might have been wild and vicious by nature, but he'd also become a comfort to Cooper these last few days. His touch was as reassuring as it was sometimes...stimulating.

No sex thoughts, Cooper reminded himself. *No thinking about Chaos on his knees, his mouth around your dick. Bad brain. Bad, bad brain.*

Luckily, Ivan seemed to attribute Cooper's outburst to its most likely cause: the thought of the impending "meeting," which would no doubt end in bloodshed.

"Cooper doesn't involve himself in the violence, usually," Ivan explained to Nix, like it was a funny character quirk.

"He won't have to, though, if I'm there," Chaos said immediately, patting Cooper's hip.

That was actually kind of nice to think about. Cooper had never had anyone to protect him before, when it came to these things. He'd been to plenty of Mafia meetings, and...his heart jumped at the thought of it. Bloodshed. Betrayal.

"Cooper will let you know," Chaos told them suddenly, his hand tightening on Cooper's hip as he seemed to register Cooper's anxiety. "Or he won't. But you two can go now. You're still scaring him."

Was he really dismissing Ivan, just like that?

It seemed to piss Ivan off as much as Cooper might expect. His cousin lost the tense air he'd been holding, a vein in his temple jumping as his jaw clenched—never a good sign. "Are you sure *you're* not scaring Cooper?" he asked Chaos in a voice as cold as ice.

But of course Chaos wasn't intimidated. "It's different when it's me," he said haughtily. "I'm afraid your tiny human brain wouldn't understand."

Jesus. A fight could *not* break out between the two of them. Chaos hadn't seemed opposed to killing Ivan, and having a murdered mob boss in his apartment was the last thing Cooper needed.

Besides, Ivan might have been kind of terrifying, but it wasn't like Cooper actually wanted to end his life. Ivan wasn't nearly the monster Dimitri had been. He was just...scary. But that wasn't an execution-worthy offense in Cooper's opinion, no matter what Chaos might think.

"Um, you can send me the details," Cooper managed to say, trying to keep an eye on both of them at the same time. Now it sounded like *he* was the one dismissing Ivan from his presence. But he couldn't figure out how else to break this tension.

Ivan didn't respond, and it was Nix who asked, "You sure you two will be all right?"

Cooper felt the sharp, bitter sting of jealousy again. Did Nix want to stay here, with Chaos?

But Chaos only said, "Go away, Nix." Bright and cheerful and just as dismissive as he'd been with Ivan.

When Nix's gaze swung to him, Cooper only shrugged. He didn't need protection from Chaos. Whatever happened would happen. Cooper had already decided to lean into the uncertainty his demon had brought into his life. It may have made his stomach flip, but Cooper was used to that. And he was learning that maybe it was a good thing every now and then, to be uncomfortable in that way. Cooper had spent too long shying away from discomfort, caging himself in.

It was a safer way to live, maybe, but it had also made his life lonely and small.

With another glare at Chaos from Ivan, Ivan and Nix finally left. Cooper ran after them to lock the doors behind them—just because he was giving in to the uncertainty didn't mean he had to let go of safety altogether—and then pressed his forehead to the door, taking in deep, soothing breaths.

Chaos stood next to him, cocking his head like he was listening. A mischievous grin graced his lips. "Your Ivan's annoyed. He thinks they can't control me." His grin widened, his golden eyes twinkling. "He's right. They can't."

Cooper let out a breathless laugh. At least he wasn't the only one out of his depth when it came to this demon.

————

Cooper sat cross-legged on the couch, stewing in his own nervousness as he clenched his hands in his lap, trying to stop chewing on his fingers. Chaos was perched next to him, their knees just touching. His head was cocked again, like he was studying Cooper.

He'd been quiet a surprisingly long time, but now he spoke, "We won't go if you're so scared, puppy."

To the meeting, Chaos meant. He was offering to skip it. For Cooper.

Cooper shoved his glasses up his nose as he tilted his head to glance at the demon. "But Nix said it would be...fun for you."

Nix had actually said Chaos might get to kill someone, but Cooper wasn't up for repeating that at the moment. The thought of his new friend murdering some mobster, even with Cooper's awareness of who and what Chaos was, would still take some adjusting to.

Chaos suddenly grabbed Cooper's hand, coaxing it out of its clenched fist to examine his bitten-down nails. "Staying with *you* is fun for me," he muttered.

Cooper sighed. "Bracchus."

Chaos pouted at him, pinching Cooper's knuckle. "What?"

"When you do find your human mate, you can't go pushing aside your own needs for them like that all the time," Cooper chastised. "It's not healthy."

Cooper knew a little bit about that, from his one disastrous relationship. He'd made himself small and unobtrusive and ignored his every inner instinct, and his boyfriend had *still* been a massive dickhead to him in the end. Cooper didn't want anything like that for Chaos. The demon was too...sweet, for all that he was dangerous and maybe a little feral.

Chaos's pout deepened. "You think I'm lying."

"I think you need more excitement than holing up with me in my apartment," Cooper told him, arching a brow.

"We *have* done more than that," Chaos argued, his tone petulant all of a sudden. "The hotel. Sex. Geese with knives."

Cooper bit back a smile. Chaos was trying to be thoughtful, in his own way. He didn't want to push Cooper into something he didn't want. Something that scared him. But Cooper had been to dozens of meetings like this before, and he'd always survived. They might make him a bit nervous, but he could push through the discomfort. And he'd have Chaos there, watching his back. Cooper had never had that before.

"We'll go," he said firmly, curling his fingers around Chaos's hand, and before Chaos could protest, he added, "Would you like to practice kissing with me some more?"

Chaos blinked back at him, mouth half-open. Cooper had actually caught him off guard for once. Cooper had never been the one to suggest they start their "practice" before—he always let Chaos take the lead when it came to that.

But right now, Cooper wanted it—needed it—and he didn't want to wait for it to happen. He'd been forced to watch Chaos snuggle up to beautiful Nix, and now Chaos was being so unbearably sweet, offering to give up exciting bloodshed just to make Cooper more comfortable.

Cooper wanted to touch him. To be touched by him. He hoped Chaos wanted the same.

Chaos's hesitation didn't last long. "Yes." He nodded eagerly, wild strands of hair flopping in his face. "Yes, puppy. Good idea. Let's *practice*."

He said the last word with a wicked bite of humor, like it was some sort of inside joke. And then he was tugging Cooper onto his lap, arranging Cooper's legs until he was straddling the demon. Chaos was still in his human form, though his hair had stayed purple, and his eyes were a golden yellow instead of brown. But he had no wings to contend with as he leaned back on the couch, his hands settling on Cooper's hips.

Chaos had gotten very familiar with the process of kissing during their sessions, and he slid his hand easily into Cooper's hair now, tugging Cooper's mouth to his.

Cooper moaned into the kiss as he slid his tongue into Chaos's waiting mouth—he loved how warm Chaos was, in whatever form he took. Loved the way he met Cooper with such greedy intent, like Cooper was a meal he'd been starving for. Cooper's cock filled rapidly, his body associating Chaos's touch with incoming pleasure after the way Chaos had been tossing him blow jobs like candy the past few days.

He ground his hips against Chaos shamelessly as Chaos licked and nibbled and murmured approvingly at him. Cooper's own movements were artless and sloppy, his arousal coming on too fast, but Chaos liked that just fine, Cooper had learned. As long as Cooper was enthusiastically into whatever they were doing, Chaos was delighted.

When oxygen became a scarce commodity, Cooper leaned back, trying to catch his breath. He couldn't help asking the question that had been plaguing him, the words coming out between pants. "Did you and Nix ever..." When Chaos only cocked his head with a frown, Cooper gestured between them. "Like this? Together?"

"Oh! Practice?"

Cooper bit back another surge of bitterness at Chaos using *their* word to describe what he'd done with Nix, but Chaos was already shaking his head. "No. Nix prefers human prey. And I prefer..." He bit at his lower lip mischievously, thumbs stroking the soft skin of Cooper's hips. "Something different."

"Oh." Cooper fiddled with the hoodie strings on Chaos's sweatshirt. Cooper's sweatshirt, really, that Chaos had taken. "Bracchus?"

"Yes, puppy?"

Cooper didn't know quite how to ask what he wanted to. He had gotten too used to the apps, too used to walking into a room and already knowing what was expected.

Would you like to fuck me? Will you fuck me? Please, God, just go ahead and fuck me?

He cleared his throat, grinding down just a touch, reassuring himself that Chaos was hard too. Cooper wasn't the only one. "Do you want to...see my toys again?"

Flames lit up in Chaos's pupils. "Just to see?" he asked coyly, thumbs pressing hard into Cooper's skin now.

"No. You can—" Cooper's breath hitched as Chaos's fingers dipped below his waistband. "You can play with them. With me. If you—if you want."

Chaos's gaze dropped to Cooper's sweatpants and the erection tenting them. It was obvious what *Cooper* wanted, no matter how roundabout his request. But it was hard for embarrassment to linger when Chaos stroked a finger over the fabric, humming appreciatively when Cooper's cock jerked under his touch.

"But, puppy," he murmured, a sly edge to his voice. "What if I put one of those toys inside you and I get all jealous?"

Cooper swallowed with a dry throat, trying to stop himself from rocking into Chaos's touch and focus. Cooper hadn't said anything about putting the toys *inside* him, but he wasn't going to correct Chaos. Not when that was exactly what he'd been looking for. "What do you mean, jealous?"

"What if *I* want to be inside you instead?" Chaos asked, his lower lip pushing out as he teased Cooper's cock. "What if I want to fill you up?"

"Then...then..." Cooper's face felt hot, his body strung tight with tension. "Then I guess you could...you could do that. If you—if you end up feeling jealous."

Chaos grinned at him, no longer coy but triumphant, and then he was standing, Cooper in his arms. Cooper didn't know how that was possible—they were the same fucking size—but he supposed that was the demon strength coming in handy.

Chaos walked them to the bedroom, tossing Cooper onto the bed like a sack of potatoes when they got there. Cooper giggled as he bounced on the mattress, the sound trailing off as he felt a strange flash of warmth. He yelped.

Holy shit—his clothes were on fucking *fire*.

But the fear only lasted a moment. His clothes disintegrated around him in an instant, his skin untouched and unharmed by the flames, his bed not even smoking. Cooper was left nude, his heart racing with residual adrenaline. He gaped at Chaos, who was naked now as well, that intimidating cock bobbing in front of him as he opened Cooper's bedside drawer.

Chaos ignored Cooper's shock, humming in thought as he stared inside the drawer, then pulled out Cooper's anal beads. "Like eggs," he murmured. "Hatchlings." He grinned at Cooper, waving the beads in front of him. "Our hatchlings would be so cute, don't you think? Should we try to make some?"

A new sort of anxiety coursed through Cooper. Chaos couldn't mean...

"Right. But. Wait." Cooper shook his head. "That can't actually —*we* can't actually—"

Chaos cackled, setting the beads and a bottle of lube beside Cooper on the bed. He knelt between Cooper's thighs, pushing Cooper's legs apart to give himself more room, stroking Cooper's hip. "Silly puppy," he soothed. "Don't fret. I'm going to take such good care of you."

It wasn't nearly as reassuring as Chaos seemed to think—not when Cooper didn't have an answer to what the fuck "hatchlings" were—but apparently Cooper's body didn't care about any of that. He was still hard as a rock, precum dripping from his tip, waiting for whatever would come next.

Whatever Chaos wanted.

12

―――――

Chaos

Chaos knelt between Cooper's spread legs, practically vibrating with giddy excitement.

After the extreme terribleness that had been Ivan's visit, Chaos was being rewarded for his restraint. He hadn't maimed the cousin, or set him on fire even a little bit, and now he was going to play with Cooper in new, exciting ways, and it had all been *Cooper's* suggestion.

Splendid. Splendid, splendid, splendid.

Chaos licked his lips, sliding his taloned hands up and down the soft skin of Cooper's inner thighs, watching the way the swell of Cooper's lower belly clenched at the touch. Cooper's muscles were trembling, and his hard, flushed cock was bobbing in the air like a tasty treat.

A tasty treat just for Chaos.

Still, Cooper's nerves permeated the air as he licked his lips and muttered, "You'll need to use, um, lots of lube. And—and prep me. Don't just jam the beads in."

Chaos grinned. He knew that much from all the human porn sets Nix had made him watch through the portal. But he didn't mind Cooper's nerves. They were like a delicious delicacy, wrapped up as they were in his trust in Chaos. Trust that, by all rights, Chaos shouldn't have deserved.

"You're such a good teacher, puppy," Chaos crooned, pushing Cooper's legs back, purring his approval when Cooper grabbed the backs of his own thighs helpfully. He tugged a pillow from the head of the bed and placed it under Cooper's rump, then leaned forward and removed Cooper's glasses, carefully setting them on the side table. "I could just eat you up."

"No teeth," Cooper reminded him, his face flushing pink as he held himself open for Chaos.

"No teeth," Chaos repeated. "Only fingers and lips and cock and tongue and toy."

He thumbed at Cooper's exposed crease, that little hole he was about to play with winking at him. Speaking of lips and tongues...

Chaos dropped down onto his hands and shoved his face into that furrow, mouthing at Cooper's entrance.

"*Oh!*" Cooper cried, his hands falling from his thighs as his lower body jerked off the bed. "Oh fuck! What—"

Chaos lifted his head, grabbing Cooper's hands and putting them back where they'd been. He stroked Cooper's hole, now wet with his spit, as he asked, "This is something humans do with their lovers, yes?"

"Um, yes?" Cooper said, sounding unsure as Chaos leaned down to lick at him again. "Oh my *God*."

Chaos settled into place, wiggling his pointed tongue right into that waiting hole, delighted by how easily it slid in. Cooper tasted musky and secret there, and he made the most interesting noises as Chaos's tongue split into a fork, twisting inside him.

Oh, this was *wonderful*. Chaos didn't need to nibble off fingers or break any skin—he could devour Cooper just like this, in a way they both enjoyed.

And by the sounds of it, Cooper was enjoying it very much.

Chaos got lost in the pleasure of it, humming and giggling and taking turns licking and sucking and kissing, until he was brought back to the present by a sharp tug at his hair. "Bracchus!"

Oh. Had Cooper been calling him long? Chaos lifted his head, licking at his spit-soaked lips. "Yes, puppy?"

Cooper's beautiful, mismatched eyes were half-lidded and glassy. "I'm going to come if you keep doing that."

"That's good," Chaos soothed, stroking his hands up Cooper's thighs in approval.

"Didn't you want...?" Cooper cocked his chin to the beads that were still laid out on the bed.

Oh. Right. Chaos had maybe forgotten about those. Oops. He started bobbing his head, pretending otherwise. "Yes, yes. Right, right, right."

He grabbed blindly for the lube before plopping a generous amount onto Cooper's hole, no matter that it was already dripping with Chaos's saliva. He used his finger to push it all inside, grinning at the way Cooper's inner muscles sucked his digit in. Just like they had with his tongue. Just like they would with his cock.

Next Chaos covered the beads dutifully. Then he looked down at the soaked bedspread. "Very messy," he commented mildly.

There was laughter hidden in Cooper's voice as he said, "Well, you used, um, quite a lot."

"You told me to." Chaos shuffled closer on his knees. "Turn onto your stomach now, puppy. It's time to play."

Cooper rolled over for him. He still had the pillow under his hips, which put his perfect bottom right in Chaos's face.

Splendid.

Chaos held the beads in front of him, studying them. They weren't like a necklace, all laid out on a string. They were firmer than that but still a little bendy. Silicone, Nix had told him once about a toy like this.

"Ready, puppy?"

Cooper made a vague sound of confirmation, his head pillowed on his folded arms. The nervous energy that had disappeared when Chaos was eating him out was back again, but Chaos was sure it would disappear again in no time.

He was going to take such good care of his puppy.

He went slowly with the beads, watching his progress so very closely. Cooper would bear down with each new bead, his rim stretching to take the width before swallowing it inside him. He'd make a little breathy groan, like he was relieved and turned on at the same time. Until the next one came along and the whole process started again.

It was fascinating, especially when Chaos tried to hold the bead there at its widest point, his finger tracing the stretched skin of Cooper's rim, Cooper whining at him to "hurry up, please."

When Chaos had pushed all but the last two beads inside him, Cooper was shiny with sweat, his muscles trembling again.

"How do you feel?" Chaos asked curiously.

"Full."

Cooper made it sound like a good thing. Chaos slid his hand under his puppy to check. Yes, his cock was still hard, all slick with precum too. Cooper ground against Chaos's palm, making a little gasping sound as his hips moved.

"How does it feel inside you, when you move like that?" Chaos asked.

"Strange." Cooper moved again, and he made a funny, mewling sound. "Oh fuck. Feels—feels good. They press against —" He let out a gasping breath. "Jesus."

Chaos laughed. This was just as much fun as putting them in had been. He palmed Cooper's ass cheek, kind of massaging the muscle around, loving the way Cooper moaned at his touch. "Rub yourself against my hand more," he ordered.

Cooper obeyed right away, as if he wanted nothing more. He started rocking, sliding his cock against Chaos's palm, the last two beads sticking out of him like his own little tail. It was captivating to watch—made heat curl in Chaos's belly the way Cooper's back and ass muscles flexed and writhed. Cooper seemed so soft at first glance, but there was strength there.

Judging by his sounds, and by the amount of precum coating Chaos's hand, the beads were making him feel very good.

Very, very good.

"Puppy."

It took Cooper a moment to speak. "Y-Yeah?"

"I was right." Chaos shuffled even closer, slapping his hard cock against Cooper's ass cheek, right next to the remaining beads. "I'm getting jealous," he whined. "I want in. Let me in."

"Oh. *Oh.* Shit, okay." It seemed to take Cooper a considerable amount of effort to still his rocking hips. "You'll need to—to take those out first."

"Yes," Chaos hissed, still rubbing himself against Cooper's fleshy cheek, his viscous precum thick and sticky against Cooper's skin. "We'll take them out. Just me inside you. Only me."

"Right. I'm, um— Well, I'm probably going to come when you take those out. I'm too close." Cooper sounded apologetic, like he thought he was disappointing Chaos.

But Chaos thought that was a wonderful idea. "And then you'll come again. With me. Just me."

Cooper let out a weak laugh. "Well, I'll try."

"No," Chaos decided. "You definitely will."

Cooper let out another laugh, like Chaos was being ridiculous. "Okay, so don't completely yank them, but you can take them out kind of quick. It feels good that way. Can I, um, keep rubbing against your hand?"

Chaos was feeling very gracious, now that he knew he was going to be filling Cooper soon. "You may," he said magnanimously. "You may rub against me and come all over the bed. And then you may turn over and let me mount you."

Chaos needed that, actually. It almost hurt now, his need to be inside Cooper. He'd never felt desire like this before. He couldn't decide if he loved it or hated it. It was strange to be ruled by something other than his usual thirst for mayhem.

Cooper started rolling his hips again, pressing into Chaos's hold, that charred caramel arousal scent thick in the air. Chaos waited until he could feel Cooper's cock jerk and swell and then he pulled steadily on the beads as Cooper moaned desperately, shooting all over Chaos's hand.

Yes.

Chaos tossed the beads somewhere or other and flipped Cooper over, pushing his legs back as far as they could go.

"Inside, inside, inside," he muttered, feeling almost feverish now. Maybe he was coming down with something. Could demons get sick? "My turn inside now."

He notched the tapered head of his cock against the hole his tongue and the beads had loosened so wonderfully, and slid right in, while Cooper was still trembling from his orgasm. Yes, yes, yes. This was right and good. Tight and warm and perfect.

Cooper cried out, his back arching off the bed.

Chaos stilled with considerable effort. "Too rough?"

"No," Cooper told him in between openmouthed panting. "Just...sensitive. Just—just came." But he wrapped his legs around Chaos's hips, his calves sliding against Chaos's tail. "It's fine. Keep —keep going."

Chaos didn't ask twice. He moved, a rumbling purr leaving his throat at the feel of Cooper around him. Even with Chaos's natural heat, Cooper's insides were warm, and wet—Chaos really had used quite a bit of lube—and absolutely divine. Chaos slid in easily with each thrust of his hips, but then the muscles gripped him so tightly every time he retreated, like they were eager to keep him inside.

And the *noises*.

Cooper must have still been feeling oversensitive, because he was gasping and whining and mewling, his fingers clenched tightly around the bedcovers. Much louder than he'd been even with the beads.

Oversensitive but letting Chaos do what he wanted anyway.

"So good for me, puppy," Chaos praised. His wings were tucked tight against his back, rigid with the tension of his pleasure.

Cooper's sweaty face flushed an even brighter pink at the praise. "Does it—does it feel good? Inside me?"

"Mm." Chaos leaned back, stroking over Cooper's belly and hips and thighs. "I was right to be jealous of your beads. There's nothing like it. So welcoming. So cozy. I might just live here now. Inside you. What do you think?"

Cooper laughed, then moaned as the movement made his walls tighten around Chaos. "I think—oh fuck!" he yelled as Chaos started stroking his cock again. He was half-hard, either in spite of or because of Chaos overwhelming his senses. "Think it might be, um, hard to get anything done."

As if Chaos cared for anything as insipid as productivity.

"You're hard again," he said approvingly after another minute of stroking.

Cooper groaned, covering his face with his hands, but Chaos tugged his arms back down. He wanted to see. Cooper looked so interesting right now, all flushed and sweaty and openmouthed. So undone. So wrecked.

"Can't help it," Cooper told him when Chaos wouldn't let him cover himself again. "Those bumps of yours. They're pressing—"

"You like my nodules?" Chaos preened, releasing his hold on

Cooper's cock and placing his hands by his head, leaning over him fully. "They get bigger right before I come, did you notice? You'll see again soon."

He dropped his body on top of Cooper's, pressing them together skin to skin. Ohh yes, this was nice. Chaos always like being naked with Cooper—Cooper might not have had any lovely fur, but his skin was always soft and cool.

Chaos started moving again, the call of Cooper's tight walls too strong to ignore.

"Puppy?" he asked, licking a strip of sweat off Cooper's cheek.

"Y-Yeah?"

"Kiss me now."

Cooper did as he asked, his kiss all distracted and sloppy, like he was too overwhelmed to do it properly, grunting into Chaos's mouth with each thrust.

Chaos enjoyed that immensely.

"It's time to come again, puppy," he murmured against Cooper's lips as he felt himself getting close, the base of his tail hot and tight.

Cooper shook his head furiously. "I—I can't. Too soon."

"You can," Chaos insisted, clasping Cooper's hands with his own as he fucked into him furiously. "Whatever I want. Whenever I want. Come for me, and I'll fill you up so nicely."

He put his lips to Cooper's neck, then pressed his sharp teeth in—not enough to break the skin but a threat all the same.

That did it.

Cooper yelled out, his whole body trembling as his release shot between them, coating their stomachs.

"Yes," Chaos breathed, his tail stiffening as his nodules swelled and then emptied into his shaft, shooting all his spend into Cooper. "Yes, yes, yes."

He ground against Cooper's hips, shuddering against him. Breeding his perfect, loyal summoner.

Not truly, sad as it was. There could be no hatchlings between human males and demon males, not even chaos demons. But it was fun to tease anyway. Cooper liked it, Chaos had learned—to be a little frightened when he was aroused.

And Chaos was very good at being a little frightening.

When Cooper's shaking and trembling and little gasping sounds eased, Chaos withdrew, rising onto his hands and grinning down at him. "How was that?"

Cooper slung an arm over his eyes, as if to escape Chaos's gaze. Chaos let him this time. "I can't answer," Cooper groaned. "I'm dead. You killed me with your demon dick."

"Is that human speak for a very good job? Very good, very gentle, very human sex?"

"Sure. We'll go with that."

Chaos got to his knees, sitting back and spreading Cooper's thighs so he could watch his spend trickle out of that poor, puffy hole.

Cooper didn't even try to fight it. He just relaxed his legs into Chaos's hold and let him do what he wanted.

Chaos grinned. Yes, he was growing *very* fond of mating.

13

Cooper

There were feathers on Cooper's pillow. Two of them, to be exact. Shiny and black and soft-looking.

He blinked, trying to clear the bleariness from his vision. Actually, now that he was seeing them up close, the feathers weren't pure black like he'd thought before. There were threads of iridescent blue and purple weaving through them, glimmering in the morning light.

Huh. Cooper hadn't known Chaos could shed his feathers at all. Maybe it only happened when he was...excited. Which he certainly had been last night. Excited and enthusiastic and about a thousand miles out of Cooper's league, sexually.

After fucking Cooper into the most powerful orgasm of his life so far, Chaos had allowed him to recover—lulled him into a false sense of security, really—only to pull out Cooper's Fleshlight and gleefully use it on Cooper's cock until Chaos suddenly frowned, told Cooper that his mouth was "much too jealous" of the toy, and then proceeded to blow Cooper into a third orgasm so overwhelming Cooper had almost been in physical pain.

So yeah. Sex with Chaos was certainly...something, feathers or no. The intensity of his attention, the ferocity of his touch, the way he acted like Cooper's body was a playground he'd never tire of exploring.

It was addictive, basically. Cooper could admit it now—he was in serious fucking trouble. It was going to hurt like hell when Chaos finally left.

But maybe Cooper needed that, even if it felt like the worst thing that could happen. He'd become so accustomed to loneliness, to the certainty that he'd never find a companion of his own, that he'd forgotten *why* people wanted them so badly in the first place.

He was remembering now what the appeal was, to have someone of his own. Someone who was a friend he could laugh and game with, someone who would push him out of the comfort zone he'd kept so small these past years, someone who would hold him and fuck him and love him just as he was...

Cooper slid a finger along one of the fallen feathers—it *was* soft, after all—only to have a whole-ass wing tip suddenly brushing across his cheek.

"You're awake, puppy?"

Cooper craned his neck to look over his shoulder, where Chaos was lying on his side behind him, his chest to Cooper's back with a few inches of bed in between them. They were both still very naked.

Cooper smiled shyly at him as Chaos folded his wing back. Although, it was ridiculous to be shy, wasn't it, when Chaos had turned him inside out in a hundred different ways the night before? "I'm awake."

"I'm glad." Chaos scooted closer until they were touching, his soft fur brushing against the skin of Cooper's lower back and his cock—Jesus, was that thing really hard again?—pressing against Cooper's crease. "Puppy?"

"Yeah?" Cooper asked, the word coming out hoarse.

"I'm cold."

Cooper huffed a laugh. "Liar. You're a furnace." He really was. Cooper could feel the heat of Chaos against his back, prickles of sweat already forming where they touched.

Chaos tucked his chin against Cooper's shoulder. "But I'd be so much warmer inside of you," he whined.

Jesus. Cooper had created a monster. Or he'd let one through the proverbial door, at the very least.

But for all that Cooper was a little sore in some delicate places, he also felt pretty fucking good. Worn out in a satisfying way, his muscles loose and his brain quiet like it almost never was first thing in the morning. He wasn't even spiraling about the meeting they had to attend later today. At least not yet.

So he hiked his leg up, twisting his lower body in a way that exposed him for Chaos's attentions. "All right, menace." He let out a breath, already shivery with anticipation. "Come inside, then."

"Really?" Chaos brushed a finger against Cooper's crease, dipping into the furrow to circle his hole. Probably noting Cooper's slight grimace, he reassured him, "I'll be so gentle. So—so *slow*. You won't be sorry."

Then there was more lube at Cooper's entrance—an absurd amount, once again. And hardly a minute later, Chaos was slipping inside him, nice and easy, just as he'd promised.

Cooper let out another breath, his body sinking into the bed as his muscles relaxed. Besides a little pinch at his rim, it felt really, really good. The tapered tip of Chaos's cock came in handy, sliding in so easily like it did, and with those nodules...

Well, Chaos didn't have to do much for those to hit all the right places.

Chaos's arm slipped around Cooper's belly, pulling him more

firmly against him as he just barely pulled out before pressing in again slowly. "Mm," he hummed. "So much better, puppy. So warm and cozy."

Cooper's cheeks heated. His ears too. He'd never been called warm and cozy in the context of being a receptacle for dick before, but he kind of liked it. It was strangely flattering and weirdly endearing, like pretty much everything Chaos did.

Chaos went slow, just as promised, grinding their lower halves together. Somehow his restraint only seemed to highlight the bumps of those nodules, the way they pressed and massaged against Cooper's inner walls. Cooper was hard in no time at all, and Chaos was instantly gleeful, pressing his hand against Cooper so that the slow drag of his hips rubbed Cooper's cock between his body and Chaos's palm.

It shouldn't have been enough; it really shouldn't have. But it would be, wouldn't it? Cooper would come, just as Chaos wanted. Last night he'd managed it even when he'd been overstimulated and so, so sensitive, but this morning he felt loose and pliant and... cozy. And it just felt so fucking good. Especially with Chaos murmuring in his ear the way he was. "So perfect, puppy. Mm. Yes. Yes, yes, yes."

Cooper's orgasm crested in a quiet wave, no less intense for the way it sneaked up on him. His whole body shuddered, his toes curling, and Chaos's praise intensified, a long, steady stream of adulation. Just a few pumps of his hips later and he was half-draped over Cooper, his arm digging into Cooper's belly as he quivered against him, that otherworldly heat filling Cooper just like it had the night before.

Cooper cupped a hand to his lower belly as he shook and shattered in Chaos's arms. No one had ever come inside him unprotected before. Not until Chaos.

Chaos spent a long few minutes pressing kisses to Cooper's shoulder, letting them both come down from their peaks, and then abruptly pulled out before bounding off the bed to who knew where, yelling, "Be right back!"

Cooper didn't have the energy to follow, but Chaos returned before he knew it anyway, and Cooper gasped at the extremely rough, extremely cold, wet washcloth that was pressed against his ass.

"See?" Chaos asked as he cleaned Cooper with a less-than-delicate bedside manner. "I was so gentle, wasn't I?"

Jarring clean-up aside, he had been, in his way. Just like he had been every time they'd hooked up. But was gentle really what Chaos enjoyed?

Cooper gathered his strength, propping up onto his arm to look at Chaos over his shoulder. "It's still...good for you like that?" he asked hesitantly. "Even though you're used to rough and wild?"

Chaos frowned at him, tossing the washcloth on the floor without looking where it landed. "Of course. I'm not some single-minded brute like Kaisyir—I can like more than one thing. And just because something is soft doesn't mean it isn't strong too. And...appealing." He gave Cooper a sly look. "I still filled you with my seed, didn't I? Planted my hatchlings inside you."

Cooper rolled his eyes. He was 90 percent certain now that Chaos was just fucking with him about the hatchlings thing. Or... 80 percent?

He'd still ask Nix later, just in case.

Chaos hopped onto his feet, clapping his hands. "Now. What does one wear to a Mafia meeting? A tracksuit? A tuxedo? Chain-mail armor?"

Cooper laughed, rising from the bed on shaky legs.

He was growing far too fond of this demon menace. He was totally screwed; he knew that now.

And maybe he should feel bad that he'd sort of just...fallen into being Chaos's human source for sexual experimentation. His fake boyfriend, almost.

But Cooper had been lonely for so long. And honestly, even if this wasn't real, it was a better situation than he'd hoped for in a long time. It was hard to find someone who could handle Cooper's dangerous connections and also didn't mind that he was a shy, nerdy shut-in. He'd had exactly one boyfriend, the one who'd been mean as hell, and Cooper had been too much of a pushover to stand up to him.

Chaos may have been a bit of a bulldozer when it came to what he wanted, but he wasn't mean. He was even sweet, in his way. And interesting and silly and beautiful.

Cooper had never stood a chance.

Plus, it was kind of a nerd's wet dream, wasn't it, to have an otherworldly creature actually want to hop into bed with you?

And going into this meeting of Ivan's, Cooper would have someone at his back for the first time in...well, maybe his whole life. Cooper would be protected by someone who cared enough to make sure he wasn't hurt, who wasn't so lost to his own inner demons that he forgot Cooper existed.

Even if that someone wasn't staying, Cooper was going to enjoy it while he could.

———

COOPER THANKED the driver as he and Chaos got out of the car Ivan had sent for them. They were at a familiar side door entrance of a faded brick building.

"Where are we?" Chaos asked, eyeing the peeling red paint of the door as he sniffed the air. "It doesn't smell like blood or carnage. It smells like...food." He sounded disappointed by that fact.

"It's a restaurant," Cooper explained. "Ivan's father liked to do business here."

Cooper could still remember his own father kneeling in front of one of the red booths inside, begging for Dimitri to take him on. Could still remember Dimitri's cold eyes looking to Cooper instead, sizing him up, calculating whether he'd be useful or if he and his father were just one more bag of trash to dispose of.

Cooper suppressed a shiver—he'd just add the queasy feeling thinking of Dimitri gave him to the nerves already roiling in his stomach—and grabbed Chaos's hand. "Come on, then."

He poked his head inside the door. Ivan and Nix were at a booth with Sascha and a big, burly man with long black hair Cooper hadn't met before. There was another unfamiliar couple at the table, a nervous-looking blond man and his severe-looking partner, who was wearing an unusually ostentatious suit for a Mafia meetup.

Ivan was, of course, pointing a gun at Cooper. It was how he usually greeted unexpected visitors (never mind that he'd sent the car for them). Cooper just nodded at him. He didn't like violence, but Ivan had a steady hand—he wouldn't shoot Cooper by accident.

Cooper led Chaos through the door, and Chaos immediately hissed at Ivan, apparently not liking the weapon aimed in Cooper's direction.

Instead of shooting Chaos for his insolence, Ivan put his gun back in its holster.

There were definitely benefits to being a scary little demon fiend or being a scary little demon fiend's companion.

When he caught sight of Chaos, the big guy next to Sascha growled, turning to Nix for some reason. "What did you do, incubus?"

"Me?" Nix asked innocently.

Chaos grinned at the massive stranger. He was in his human form, but even with his little dimple, his smile looked kind of evil. "Hello, Kaisyir."

Oh, right. The warrior demon who'd been in the Void with

Chaos and Nix—Chaos had told Cooper about him. With the way Kai tugged Sascha to his side protectively—and the way Sascha gave him an adoring, dreamy little smile in return—it seemed like he was more than just Sascha's summoned muscle.

It looked like Cooper's cousin had a demon boyfriend.

That was three of them in the same family shacked up with demons. Jesus. Did they have some sort of blood-borne condition that predisposed them? Or was it just...generally contagious?

Ivan looked weirdly pleased by the ragtag group they all made, his eyes gleaming under the restaurant lights. He was almost *smiling*, which was unnatural enough to give Cooper the shivers. "Cooper, this is Kai, Sascha's...partner. Chaos, this is my younger brother, Sascha, Cooper's other cousin. We also have Eric and Wolfe here with us. Friends of Alexei's."

Cooper barely hid his gasp of surprise, masking it with an awkward cough. As far as he knew, Ivan and Alexei—the middle brother between Ivan and Sascha, and Cooper's other cousin— were still on bad terms. Murderous terms, to be exact.

What the hell were Alexei's friends doing helping Ivan out?

Chaos sniffed the air, pointing to the blond, Eric, and his partner, Wolfe. "Why do you two smell so strange?"

"Vampires," Kai growled in explanation.

Huh. Well, then. Cooper hadn't known those existed. He'd have to muster up the proper shock later, when he wasn't about to pass out from anxiety.

No one else seemed surprised by the news, however. And Chaos looked positively delighted. "*Wonderful*," he crowed.

He tugged Cooper down at the booth with the others, with Cooper next to Nix and Chaos at the end. The arrangement placed them across from Sascha and Kai.

Chaos only sniffed haughtily when Sascha smiled at him—not showing an ounce of his usual chaotic charm—and Cooper nudged him discreetly.

"Yes, puppy?" Chaos asked loudly.

Cooper ignored the muffled coughs of the others at the nickname. "Sascha's cool," he whispered.

Chaos scowled, but he lowered his voice to match Cooper's. "If your cousin is so *cool*, why were you so lonely? He's not doing his job as your kin."

"His job isn't to—" Cooper broke off when he saw both Kai and Eric eyeing him, Eric not even trying to hide his look of sympathy. Right. There was inhuman hearing at this table.

Cooper shook his head. "Never mind."

Ivan cleared his throat, gathering their communal attention, and started talking about what to expect next. The family's lieutenants and their main men, about thirty men in total, would all be here for the meeting. Ivan already had Sergei in the kitchen, bound and subdued and "only missing a little blood."

Kai had given Ivan a bloodthirsty grin at that last bit, and Cooper eyed the demon with new wariness. He seemed so gentle with Sascha, but he clearly wasn't opposed to the sort of violence this kind of meeting entailed.

Cooper's belly was churning already with the news that Sergei was here. Cooper had played his own part in that terrifying man's downfall, and he wasn't looking forward to facing him.

Not that Cooper would have to deal with Sergei directly. The plan was for the demons to transform at the right moment, making a show of paranormal force in Ivan's favor. Demonstrating in whatever way necessary that the family was not to be fucked with.

That was the gist of it, at least. Cooper only half listened— paying too close attention to any of it would only make his anxiety worse. He wasn't going to be doing much of anything, anyway. Just standing there in solidarity while their paranormal counterparts did their thing. Trying not to get shot while he was at it.

He let out a harsh breath at the thought of guns firing around him, and Nix nudged him gently. "You okay, cutie?"

Cooper glanced up, realizing belatedly that Ivan had finished his speech and was now conferring quietly with Eric and Wolfe. Kai and Chaos were in a weird stare-off, Kai grimacing and Chaos grinning way too gleefully.

"Yeah," Cooper told Nix quietly. "Just nerves."

"We won't let anything happen to you," Nix reassured him. "I'll be protecting you and Ivan during the...turmoil."

Cooper glanced at him in surprise. He hadn't realized it wouldn't be only Chaos watching his back. He worked up the nerve to give Nix a small smile and then glanced around again. Everyone was occupied.

"Hey, Nix," he whispered.

"Yes?" Nix whispered back, leaning in conspiratorially.

"Male demons can't...impregnate human men, right? No...no hatchlings? That's not a real thing, right?"

Nix was silent for a long moment, and then he burst into delighted laughter, looking over Cooper's head to Chaos. "Bracchus," he chastised, although he sounded fond. "What trouble have you been getting into?"

"Don't you think we'd make adorable hatchlings though?" Chaos asked, his dimple flashing.

Cooper rolled his eyes. Of course Chaos had heard Cooper's question.

Eavesdropping little imp.

Whatever Nix's thoughts might have been on their hypothetical adorable hatchlings was lost in the shuffle as Jace and Tag and Ivan's driver, Oleg, came in, indicating to Ivan that they were all set to go.

Nix leaned in one last time. "Don't worry, *puppy*. He's just teasing you."

"I figured." That didn't stop Cooper's cheeks from feeling like they were on literal fire though. Why had he even asked? He'd already known Chaos was only messing with him.

"You're...okay though?" Nix asked, almost too softly for Cooper to hear. "Chaos can be hard to manage."

Cooper frowned, his immense embarrassment momentarily forgotten. "That's the thing though," he mused, pushing his glasses up and giving Nix a sidelong glance. "I don't try to manage him." At Nix's questioning look, Cooper explained, "If you let Chaos be who he is—if you don't try to control him—he appreciates it. He pays attention to where the boundaries are. He manages himself."

As Nix seemed to process his words, Cooper wondered if he was about to be told off. Nix had known Chaos much, much longer than Cooper had. What right did Cooper have to tell him how Chaos's mind worked? But at the same time...Cooper just didn't like that phrase *hard to manage* when it came to Chaos. Like he was an unruly child and not a fully grown demon with centuries of life experience.

He'd had to say *something*.

But after a moment, Nix gave him a slow smile. "You two are a good match after all," he murmured. "How unexpected."

Cooper didn't have it in him to explain to Nix that they weren't any sort of match at all. He was just practice, wasn't he? So he twisted his lips in some semblance of a smile, and that was that.

Now it was only a matter of waiting for the meeting to begin.

14

Chaos

C haos was feeling absolutely wonderful.

He was at a strange meeting that was sure to end in glorious mayhem and bloodshed, Cooper was at his side, and Chaos's loyal summoner had somehow just received Nix's tentative approval for their future bond (not that Cooper knew a future bond was coming their way, but still).

Chaos didn't *need* Nix's approval, of course, but it would make things easier if the incubus wasn't trying to save Cooper from Chaos's clutches. It was far too late for any nonsense like that, anyway. Chaos may have originally decided to keep Cooper on a whim, and weren't whims just the *best*? But the decision was burned into his very bones now. Cooper was his. They would bond. They would be happy. They would make adorable—

Well, they couldn't *actually* make adorable hatchlings—as Cooper had found out today—but they would definitely put in the effort over and over and over again.

The big double doors at the front of the restaurant opened,

and Chaos craned his neck to see who was coming in. He was curious about these traitorous mobsters Ivan was trying to weed out. Would they be wearing tracksuits and gold chains like in the movies? Maybe Chaos could start a little jewelry collection with the accessories of whoever they took out during this meeting.

But the duo that entered didn't look anything like that. Instead, there was a big blond guy dressed in black and a little dark-haired man—Chaos sniffed the air and corrected himself: *dark-haired vampire*—at his side. He seemed at first to be dressed in an equally subdued way, but when he turned to glance behind him, Chaos saw there was a very large bright-pink kitten embroidered on the back of his gray sweater.

Ivan nodded at the newcomers. "Alexei," he said shortly, addressing the burly blond.

So. The other cousin. Chaos frowned at him, unimpressed. All these blood relations, and Cooper had still ended up lonely and neglected. So what use were they, really? Cooper didn't need them; that was for certain. He had Chaos now.

Alexei nodded back at Ivan without saying anything. Maybe he was mute or had lost his tongue somewhere exciting .And the little vampire pressed into his partner's side, waving at the table before telling them his name was Johann, "or Jay, if you like."

Cute, Chaos decided. Not as cute as Cooper, but certainly cuter than the other vampire duo at the table. The Wolfe fellow got Chaos's hackles up, his energy weird in a way that was maybe exciting or maybe terrible, Chaos hadn't decided yet.

The front door opened again, and the regular mobsters started coming in, all of them nodding respectfully at Ivan, looking in surprise at Alexei, and in general avoiding their table warily, congregating on the other side of the restaurant instead. There were only a few tracksuits, but there *were* some chunky gold rings on pinky fingers Chaos wouldn't mind stealing, just to see how they'd look on Cooper's elegant digits.

He'd be sure to wipe the blood off first.

Eventually their party stood, getting ready to gather at the front area so the meeting could begin, and Chaos glanced to the side and found that Jay had sidled up to him at some point.

"Are you a demon?" the little vampire asked, his voice bright but quiet enough that none of the humans around them could hear.

Chaos pointed at his chest. "Who, me?" he asked innocently as Cooper walked ahead.

Jay narrowed his gray eyes, but a smile played at his lips, like he was in on the joke. "You are, aren't you?" he pressed. "And do you have a tail?"

"What do you think?"

Jay bent backward to look at Chaos's rear, then nodded once, decisively. "I'd like to see it, please. Nix already promised to show me his."

Chaos cocked his head, pretending to consider. "Nix is nicer than I am though."

Jay's smile fell the tiniest bit. But he didn't argue or try to order Chaos around, so Chaos leaned in, murmuring, "If you look over during the big reveal, you'll see it. *And* my wings."

"Ohhh." Jay's eyes lit up with delight. "Kai has wings too." He nibbled on his lower lip. "His are a little scary though."

Chaos shrugged. "Mine are cute. That's what Nix says, at least." Should Chaos ask Cooper to confirm? Probably yes. Chaos would like to hear it from Cooper's lips, that he was cute. That his wings were fetching.

Jay grinned at him. "And if *you* look over, you can see my fangs."

Psh. Fangs were boring, but Chaos did kind of like the idea of this little guy being a bloodthirsty monster underneath the cute packaging, so he nodded anyway. "Deal."

They all gathered in the big, open area at the front of the

restaurant, facing the men. Cooper and Chaos were on the far left, next to Sascha and Kai, with Ivan and Nix in the middle. Alexei and Jay were on the other side with Wolfe and Eric. They were like a panel of judges on some reality talent show, except without the podiums or cameras or fame or general sense of entertainment.

So maybe not like that at all.

Chaos made sure he was standing slightly in front of Cooper, in case any of these men decided they wanted to start shooting early. The humans they were facing were all feeling very nervous, their anxiety wafting off them in bitter, sour tendrils, which Chaos enjoyed. Of course, Cooper had nerves enough to fill the whole room with, but Chaos felt a bit guilty about liking those particular tendrils. It meant his puppy was suffering while he was enjoying himself.

In the future, once they were bonded, Chaos would handle all these Mafia meetings. There was no reason for Cooper to distress himself with business nonsense when Chaos would be there to do it for him. Cooper could stay home, hacking or gaming or even napping, if he wanted. And then Chaos would return, triumphant and maybe even a little bloody, and they would mate ferociously and make pretend hatchlings together.

Marvelous.

Ivan started his speech, some boring number about business and family and betrayal and *blah, blah, blah*. It was annoying to listen to, but it was easy to ignore the meat of it and focus on the anticipation of bloodshed, and the ease with which all this tension could dissolve into pandemonium.

Chaos was going to leave this meeting stuffed full of delicious mayhem; that much was for sure.

He perked up when some of Ivan's lieutenants brought out a bruised and battered man tied to a chair, the men muttering among themselves at his arrival. This was Sergei. The one who frightened Cooper so much. Chaos eyed him skeptically. Underneath his bravado, he looked...broken. And tired. Just any other human man who'd reached too far and come up short.

Who was *he* to frighten Chaos's beloved puppy?

Well, no more. With Chaos at his side, Cooper wouldn't have to fear judgment or violence or anything else from these silly mortals. Chaos would be his protector, his vengeance seeker, his hand-holder extraordinaire.

Chaos was so caught up in plotting his delectable future that he only barely heard Ivan say the words "—we've gathered new allies, ones I doubt any of you have the gall to cross."

Oops! Chaos had almost missed the signal. Wouldn't that have been hilarious?

The others were already transforming, so Chaos let his demon form erupt, tail and wings and horns sprouting from his body. He caught Jay's gaze—oooh, the little vampire's eyes had turned all black; that was cool—and winked at him, grinning when Jay flashed his little fangs at him.

Men started screaming, and ohhh yes, that was the beginnings of mayhem in the air, thick and smoky and twisted. Chaos drank it in, greedily inhaling the swirly, salty, sweet, bitter, sour mixture.

Several of the men in the crowd drew their guns, and one of them yelled out, "What the fuck is this, Ivan?"

"Why, Gregor," Ivan purred, sounding almost as sultry as Nix for a moment, "what the fuck does it look like?"

"It looks like fucking—fucking Halloween tricks. A smoke screen. You think this is enough to scare us off?"

Maybe this Gregor fellow was trying to sound angry and intimidating, but he only sounded panicked. Chaos grinned.

"Oh for fuck's sake," Wolfe sighed, and then he was off the stage, tearing the man's throat out with his teeth, doing the same to Sergei in the next moment.

Just like that, two men were dead.

Chaos took back his previous indecision—Wolfe was *great.*

He'd started the bloodshed early and taken out that jerk Sergei while he was at it. Good stuff, there.

Ivan and Alexei and Kai seemed less pleased, all three of them frowning like Wolfe had made some sort of social faux pas, possibly because the surprise fountain of blood had led to Sascha fainting on the stage.

Kai was picking up the blond human now, glaring at everything and everyone.

Wolfe—his fancy suit absolutely covered in blood—cocked a brow. "Wasn't that the point of identifying the traitors?" he asked coolly. "So we could do away with them? Eric and I have places to be."

That *had* been the gist of Ivan's plan, Chaos was pretty sure. Maximal pizzazz and a little bit of blood spillage now, and less general warfare to keep his position later.

There was a flash of movement in the crowd. Another one of the traitors Chaos had seen Nix eyeing was trying to run.

No. Nope. Not allowed.

Chaos dove after him, talons extended, their sharp points slicing into the man's chest as easy as breathing. Hot blood sprayed into the air, and Chaos heard Cooper yelp behind him. Was his puppy worried about him? He needn't be. Chaos was fine. He was *wonderful*, actually. Had Cooper really wanted to miss this?

It was fun. Fun, fun, fun, fun.

And now those beginnings of mayhem turned into a proper frenzy, all the humans yelling and some of them shooting. The supernaturals of their party—except Kai, who had hold of Sascha, and Nix, who was guarding Ivan and Cooper—started corralling humans, flicking or kicking guns out of hands. Chaos cackled in delight as men screamed at the sight of him up close.

Maybe he wasn't as cute as he'd thought. He'd definitely have to double-check with Cooper later.

He flashed his fire for show but didn't kill anyone else, as tempting as it was. The blood was fun and all, but it was the anarchy of it all that really fed him.

Although, one man did try to crawl under a table to the exit, so Chaos set the leg of his tracksuit alight just long enough to drag him out screaming.

So silly.

Chaos drank it up while he could, all the noise and fear and bedlam. But sooner than he would have liked, it took a boring turn. The shooting stopped, the men were subdued, and Nix began using his energy-reading skills to sort through them, deciding who could stay in the organization, who could go freely, and who would have to be taken out completely, too much of a risk to let live.

Chaos sighed loudly. When no one paid him any more attention—other than a few cowardly humans giving him nervous looks—he made his way back to Cooper, who was now sitting on the carpeted floor with his back to the wall, far away from everyone else. His muscles were clenched stiffly, and up close, Chaos could see he was trembling.

He smelled like fear.

Chaos crouched and reached out a hand to soothe him, but Cooper shook his head, halting Chaos's gesture in midair. "I need—need to hold it together until the end." He gave Chaos a brittle smile, nodding his chin to where everyone else was gathered. "You have fun, okay? I'll just...decompress here until it's all over."

Chaos frowned. He didn't like that. He wanted to whisk Cooper away, to hold him close and keep Cooper pressed against him until his trembling eased. He could do that. He could take Cooper away from here and demand he feel better.

But he *shouldn't* do that, right? This was Cooper's business, all part of the life he'd been living before Chaos came along, and it wasn't up to Chaos to make decisions for him.

(Unless the decision was about who he was going to bond with, in which case Chaos was definitely in charge.)

Maybe later, after they'd discussed it and Cooper had agreed. Maybe *then* Chaos could take over all this messy stuff for him. But Cooper had told Nix he wasn't going to try to manage Chaos, so Chaos would try to give his summoner the same courtesy. When it was just the two of them, it was whatever Chaos wanted, whenever he wanted. But that only worked if Chaos—how had Cooper put it?—paid attention to the boundaries.

So he didn't scoop his human up. Didn't steal him away from what was scaring him. But he did ask, "You're sure you're okay?"

Cooper gave him a jerky nod, his glasses sliding down his nose. He didn't correct their position. "Mm-hmm."

Chaos cocked his head, unconvinced. "You're not afraid of me again, are you?"

Cooper gave him another one of those smiles that wasn't a real smile. "I'm a little afraid of everything right now. I just need a minute."

It wasn't the most satisfactory answer, but it would have to do.

Chaos left Cooper's side reluctantly and circled the restaurant instead, sticking his face and his talons into the group of men to frighten them every now and again. He let Jay study his tail for a while. He made faces at Ivan that only Nix could see as Ivan led this second—and much, much more boring—meeting with the men who were staying.

In the end, four traitors were set aside for execution, and Ivan asked Chaos to burn the bodies afterward. It wasn't as exciting as setting someone on fire when they were alive and kicking, but it was still a little novel, so Chaos agreed, bounding out to the back alley with Jace and Tag.

Four gunshots from those two, a quick use of Chaos's powers, and it was done. No more traitors.

Which meant Ivan's business was taken care of, which meant

Cooper's immediate obligations were over, right? It was time for Chaos to take Cooper away from this mess, maybe tuck him into bed with one of his video games until he felt better.

Except when Chaos returned to the main room of the restaurant with Tag and Jace—a room that now smelled like food *and* blood—there was only Ivan, neither Cooper nor Nix anywhere to be seen.

Cooper's cousin was staring into the distance, his energy muddled and unreadable, his mouth slack and his eyes dazed.

"Boss?" Jace asked, having to stand directly in front of Ivan to get his attention. "Things have been...dealt with. You need anything else here before we head out?"

And then Ivan was pulling a gun on Jace, holding it to his forehead. He didn't seem to be aware of anyone else in the room. He didn't seem to be aware of much, really. "I do need one more thing from you, Jace," he murmured, his voice strangely robotic. "And I'm afraid refusal isn't an option. I need you to summon a demon."

Oh. Nix was gone, then. Really gone. Like, back to the Void. This meeting must have completed whatever his contract with Ivan had been.

Chaos felt a twinge of sympathy for his friend. Nix had seemed very fond of his human summoner. But Ivan also seemed to have it handled, what with the gun and the threats and the Book in his hand. It was almost enough to make Chaos like the man. Ivan wasn't going to leave Nix in the Void for long. He was going to summon him again, and then he was probably going to bond with him for good right after.

How sweet.

But Chaos didn't need to be here to bear witness to any of that. Not when Cooper was still so distressed. He sidled around the wall instead, making his way to the entrance to the kitchens, following the tug of the soul piece in his chest to where Cooper was. He must have joined Kai and Sascha there before Nix got pulled away.

Chaos would take this as a reminder not to make Nix's mistake. Cooper was too sweet to pull a gun on someone to summon Chaos a second time. Chaos needed to fetch his human and complete his wily seduction so Cooper would never be in that position. He needed to get to the point where he could tell Cooper they were bonding and not have Cooper run away in fright.

He needed to tell Cooper what was what, and then he needed to make it so.

15

Cooper

Cooper leaned against the restaurant's kitchen counter, willing his weak knees to keep him standing.

The kitchen was several noticeable degrees colder than the main dining area, and the cool feel of the stainless steel was a refreshing contrast to his overheated back. He'd gotten weirdly sweaty during the mayhem, considering he hadn't been doing any of the heavy lifting—sweaty but shivery at the same time.

Shock, probably.

Cooper had watched Chaos slice through a man's chest today. Chaos had cackled afterward, delighted with himself. He was outside now, setting corpses on fire per Ivan's orders.

You're not afraid of me again, are you? he'd asked Cooper, the question sweetly hesitant.

Cooper should be. He definitely should be; he knew that much. He was used to violent men at this point—although they still made him nervous as hell—but the bloodshed today had been a little out of his league, hadn't it? He'd seen someone shot before, but he'd never seen anyone rip a man's throat out with his teeth.

Plus, after he'd seen that guy shot, Cooper had hidden in his house for a week, barely getting out of bed to use the bathroom.

So why wasn't he running in the other direction right now?

A sudden silence had Cooper looking around the kitchen. Sascha and Kai were on a folding chair at the other end of the counter, Sascha curled up in Kai's lap. Cooper wasn't sure how the flimsy thing was holding both their weight—Kai alone was a massive dude. They'd been murmuring together quietly, but they'd stopped now. They were looking at him.

On a normal day, Cooper would have felt awkward as hell intruding on their moment, even if he hadn't meant to at the time. But he'd needed to get away from the smell of smoke and blood, and he frankly didn't have the energy to care about whether they minded his presence here.

"Coop?" Sascha asked, his pretty face scrunched in something that might have been concern. Funny, seeing as how he'd been the one who'd fainted.

"Yeah?" Cooper had to clear his throat when that one word came out thready and strange. He tried again. "Yes?"

"You're shaking."

"Oh." Cooper shrugged. He'd already known that. "It'll pass."

Sascha's frown deepened, but he didn't push. Kai wasn't looking at Cooper at all, too focused on Sascha in his lap. Kai looked human again now, but Cooper had seen his demon form earlier. He was giant. And blue. And he had tall horns and these wings that were nothing like the small, cute feathery ones Chaos had. Kai's were big and leathery and...bat-like. Frightening.

But he looked at Sascha like he was some precious creature. One that needed to be cared for and tended to. It was similar to the way Chaos had looked at Cooper earlier when he'd tried to...

comfort him? Was that what he'd been doing? Cooper had been too out of it at the time to register much. He'd only been able to think that, if Chaos touched him, he'd have broken down. Not because he was afraid of him, but because somehow, that manic little demon had become Cooper's place of comfort. A safe place to fall apart.

Cooper took his glasses off while he thought, cleaning them against his shirt and replacing them to find Sascha still staring at him.

He tried to think of something to say. He settled on, "You never did like blood much."

Sascha gave him a small, strained smile. "No."

Kai let out a frustrated growl, the sound echoing through the kitchen as he smoothed Sascha's pale hair away from his face. "We will *not* be doing this again. Ivan can handle his own messes from now on."

Sascha let out a sigh, slumping against him. "No arguments from me, big guy."

"You're a...warrior demon?" Cooper found himself asking.

Kai finally deigned to look at him, nodding once. "I am."

"You've spilled blood, then."

Kai hadn't spilled any at the meeting, too busy taking care of Sascha. But that didn't mean his talons were exactly clean, not after what Ivan had said about Sergei.

Kai's blue eyes gleamed. "Rivers of it."

Cooper looked between the two of them—Sascha and Kai, human and demon. "I don't get it."

He really didn't. What was a warrior demon doing with a human who fainted at the sight of blood? Cooper poked his fingers under his glasses to rub at his eyes as he asked his cousin, "You didn't get enough of violent men already? The life you've led?"

Sascha straightened in Kai's lap, as if affronted. "Kai isn't some 'violent man,'" he argued, shaping his fingers into air quotes. "He's a...protector. *My* protector. He takes the violence for me, lets me close my eyes to it while he keeps me safe. At least until we can leave it behind for good."

Well, yeah, that sort of sounded like a good deal. Cooper looked to Kai. "And what does Sascha give you, then?"

It was definitely the shock making Cooper open his mouth again and again. He would never normally pry into another couple's life like this. By all rights, Kai should be telling him to shut the hell up and mind his own business.

But Kai answered, his voice a deep rumble, "Sascha gives me a reason. A purpose. He...anchors me."

From what Chaos had said, that was what the mate bond was, in a way. A person becoming a demon's anchor to the human realm. But Kai clearly didn't mean it literally, judging by the look in his eyes. He meant something romantic. Soulful.

Was that what Chaos was looking for? His soul's anchor, in more ways than one? Cooper couldn't picture it. Chaos was wild and silly and sweet. What if he picked the wrong anchor? What if they tried to ground him too much, and they snuffed out what made him such a perfect menace?

As if reading Cooper's mind, Sascha spoke again. "You summoned a demon too, didn't you, Coop?"

"Yes."

"Did you mean to?"

"No."

Sascha gave him another smile, this one less strained. "Me neither."

Cooper didn't know what to say to that. It had obviously worked out well enough for Sascha. He hadn't been left alone in the end.

Sascha frowned off into the distance. "Although, yours doesn't seem to like me much."

Kai growled again. "Ignore Chaos. He's a brat."

Defensiveness had Cooper narrowing his eyes at the demon. "He's not," he protested, even though Chaos kind of was. "He's just protective."

Kai cocked a brow. "He thinks Sascha would harm you?" he asked, making it clear how unlikely he found the concept.

"No. He's just—I was just—" Cooper searched his brain for a way to talk about it without embarrassing himself and failed. He let out a breath, admitting, "I was lonely. He wants to blame someone. My family gets the short stick, I guess."

Instead of seeming offended, Sascha gave Cooper a knowing, rueful look.

The thing was, other than being gay and adjacent to the Mafia, the two of them had nothing in common. Sascha had always like clubbing and shopping and reality TV. He'd been young enough when his mother had died that he barely remembered her, and he often seemed to forget exactly how Cooper was related to him, calling him a distant cousin. He wasn't cruel, but whether he felt like acting charming or sullen seemed to turn on a dime.

Cooper was his nerdy, antisocial relative but definitely not a friend.

"You never liked blood much either," Sascha eventually said.

Was he trying to get to an area of common interest? Not wanting to watch men get dismembered wasn't the most solid basis for friendship Cooper had ever heard.

But Sascha continued, "You know, if you wanted to get away to, like, recover from the shock of all this, we have a place in Maine with extra rooms. Our housemate, Matty—I think you'd get along. He's...quiet also."

Kai made a vague, affirmative sound. "Leave Chaos here."

Sascha swatted lightly at the big guy's arm. "He can bring Chaos if he wants to." He cast Cooper a sidelong look. "If— Are you—? You're...together?"

"He's my friend," Cooper said simply. Then immediately complicated it by explaining, "He's, um, trying to find the right human to bond with. Down the line. He's with me until then." He left it vague as to what being "with him" entailed, and Sascha and Kai exchanged an indecipherable glance.

"Well, either way, then," Sascha eventually said. "Come visit. Stay a while. I didn't mean to neglect you."

Before Cooper could protest that Sascha wasn't at fault, Chaos's voice rang through the kitchen. "We'll consider it," he declared loudly, sounding all kinds of haughty but maybe slightly less acerbic toward Sascha than before.

He'd come in through the swinging door leading to the main room of the restaurant, and then suddenly he was right in front of Cooper.

"Come, puppy," he said at a much quieter volume, his golden-yellow eyes boring into Cooper, their noses almost touching. As always, he smelled faintly of smoke, but it didn't turn Cooper's stomach the way the scent of the restaurant had. "Time to go home."

"You're done with..." Cooper trailed off, reluctant to finish his own sentence. "You're done?"

"All done." Chaos's brow dropped into a scowl. "You're still shivering." He made it sound like an accusation, zipping up Cooper's sweatshirt for him and pulling the hoodie over his head aggressively.

He grabbed Cooper's hand, tugging him to the back exit, then stopped, looking over his shoulder at Sascha and Kai. "Your brother's about to lose it," he told Sascha. "Should be fun to watch, if you're interested."

Sascha heaved a sigh, rising from Kai's lap. "What's happened now?"

"Nix was sent back to the Void."

Kai stood in a flash. "*What?*"

Chaos waved a hand, dismissing Kai's shock. "Ivan's getting him back already. Get out there if you want to see the show." He turned, dragging Cooper behind him. "Puppy and I have places to be."

———

PLACES TO BE APPARENTLY MEANT in Cooper's bed, with Cooper tucked under a million blankets—more than he'd known he owned—sweating his balls off while Chaos insisted they all stay on until he'd "made a full recovery."

Cooper wasn't sure what Chaos's version of a full recovery even was—it seemed to involve Cooper taking a nap. But that was kind of hard to do when Chaos was hovering over him, his fox eyes wide and unblinking.

"You didn't like that," Chaos finally said, after making Cooper finish yet another water bottle. It was the third one. At this rate, Cooper was going to have to get out of bed to pee long before he fell asleep.

Cooper licked the last drops from his lips, cheeks warming when Chaos's eyes tracked the movement. "No. I told you I wouldn't."

Cooper had been to meetings before where men ended up dead. They were nothing like what had just happened in that restaurant—the abject terror and frantic chaos. But that was probably the thing about the supernatural and why Ivan had wanted a show of more than just the usual guns and muscle. It provoked a deeper, weirder kind of fear than what Mafia men were used to.

Cooper should have been paralyzed by it, that fear. More than he had been, at least. He should have tried to run from Chaos the moment he'd seen his demon slice through a man's chest. But maybe Cooper's history—the constant thrum of anxiety that already ran beneath his skin—had broken him in some way.

He still liked Chaos just fine. So what if he was a little scary? So was going to the grocery store.

Chaos nodded thoughtfully. "I'll handle any meetings from now on. You'll stay home and manage your computer work. There's no need for you to do both."

Should Cooper be offended that Chaos was declaring him unfit for duty? He was acting like it was a sure thing too, like he'd be around to handle the unpleasant side of Cooper's work for the foreseeable future.

It was an odd echo of what Sascha had said about Kai, the way he used his naturally violent nature to protect Sascha from more of the same. But Kai was Sascha's mate. And Chaos was...not that for Cooper.

Still, Cooper was too worn out to let the comparison hurt. He let it warm his chest instead. His demon did care for him, in his way. "Okay," he said easily. "I'd rather stay home, anyway."

Chaos continued to stare at him. Cooper stared back. Chaos finally spoke again. "Nix was taken back to the Void."

Cooper blinked at him, his eyelids heavy. "So you said." Should he be comforting Chaos? Was that why Chaos was acting a little strange, even for him? His friend *had* been taken away. That had to be painful.

But Chaos spoke again before Cooper could think of what to say. "It's because he completed his contract before he could bond."

He looked expectantly at Cooper, like that was a revelation.

Cooper let the words penetrate his tired and fuzzy brain. Oh. Chaos didn't want to go back to the Void. And...he thought the same thing could happen to him? He was worried?

Cooper closed his eyes. Opened them again. "And you're worried about that?" He tried to think of what would end their contract and came up blank. "What were our terms again?"

Chaos answered immediately, "I'm to be your friend until you no longer need one."

"Oh." Cooper let his muscles relax, settling him deeper into the mattress. He was still too hot, but it was kind of soothing now. He wasn't sure if he was falling asleep or passing out, but he also wasn't sure if it mattered—Chaos would watch over him either way. "Well, that's no problem, then. I'm probably always going to need you to be my friend." He gave Chaos a loopy grin. "I think maybe you made a bad deal, Bracchus."

If Chaos felt that way, it didn't show on his face. He only grinned back at Cooper, his sweet dimple flashing, and then settled next to him on the bed, on top of the covers. He laid his head on Cooper's shoulder, a wonderful, warm weight. "Sleep, puppy. We'll talk more after you've rested."

Cooper let himself drift into oblivion.

He was safe here, with his demon.

16

Cooper

Seventeen-year-old Cooper sighed as he locked the apartment door behind him, turning to find his dad exactly where Cooper had left him—slumped over on the couch.

Napping? Passed out? But no, his dad opened one eye to peer out at him blearily. "Umnitsa," he said, the word slurred with either sleep or booze or both. "Back so soon?"

Cooper repressed another sigh. "It's been hours, Pop."

"Has it?" His dad sat up, kicking over the bottle at his feet with the effort. It was empty, at least, so no vodka spilled on the carpet this time.

"I thought you were going to get groceries." Cooper didn't know why he said it. Chastising his dad never worked—it only ever made him more maudlin.

"Was I?" When Cooper didn't take the bait, his dad tilted his head, a sad smile playing at his lips. "You look so much like your mother when you get disappointed in me like that. She made that exact same face when I forgot the milk."

There was nothing to say to that, so Cooper kicked off his shoes before coming to sit beside his dad on the couch, ignoring the sharp smell of vodka as his dad threw an arm around him.

"How was it?"

"Fine." Cooper shrugged. "An errand."

Cooper had been delivering a package to Sergei. He hadn't known what was in it—hadn't wanted to know—but his knowledge of its contents wasn't required to complete the task.

He wasn't exactly lying to his father. It hadn't quite been fine, but it hadn't been awful either. Sergei just fucking hated Cooper for some reason. Probably because Cooper was so scared of him, or maybe because of his youth. Either way, he always referred to Cooper as "that drunk's son," making his men laugh by mimicking Cooper's father's swaying walk.

He was an asshole, basically, but there was nothing Cooper could do about it. Not if he didn't want to end up bleeding out in some alley.

His dad let out a gusty breath, leaning his cheek against the top of Cooper's head. "This was supposed to be a fresh start, a new country. But we ended up right back here, mixed up with gangsters. Just like home." He chuckled, but it was a sad sound. "At least we have a nice apartment now, yes?"

"Yeah," Cooper agreed dully.

The truth was Cooper missed the shithole he'd grown up in. At least there, no one had cared what they did. No one had cared that his dad was a mess, that he smelled like liquor or swayed when he walked, or forgot his keys and phone and had to yell at Cooper to let him in the door. Their neighbors had all had their own issues to deal with. Some of the moms had even made them plates of food when they'd had extra, dropping them off and not accepting a word of thanks for it, just reminding them to return the dishes when they were done.

But here, in their richer digs, people noticed. They cared, and not in a good way. Cooper had become aware now, every time he and his dad left the apartment. Aware of the looks they were given. Aware of the judgmental murmurs between neighbors.

He'd started to become anxious leaving the apartment, hypervigilant in a way that couldn't be healthy.

What if one of them got sick of his dad making a mess of things, and tried to get him arrested for drunk and disorderly conduct? Would someone come and take Cooper away? He still had a year until he turned eighteen. Or what if enough people complained to Dimitri, and he decided that Cooper and his father weren't worth the trouble and finally put them down like dogs?

"Should've protected you better, huh? Should've—should've done it differently."

As his dad lurched off the couch, shuffling to the bathroom, Cooper let the anger run through him.

His dad had been doing that a lot lately—going on about his failures in protecting Cooper. All the ways he'd let him down. But he never actually did anything differently, did he?

After Cooper had signed on with Dimitri, his dad had been horrified. But he hadn't decided to suddenly pull himself together. He'd gone on a two-week bender instead. Left Cooper alone and frightened as he entered a world he'd never wanted to be in.

So Cooper let the anger run through him—let it burn in his veins just for one blissful moment—and then he let it all go.

His dad was sick. It was an illness. That was what they'd said in health class, what all the online forums agreed on. Maybe without Cooper to care for him, his father would hit some sort of rock bottom, some new low that would force him to seek help. But Cooper couldn't bear it, to think of his dad out on the street, all alone. And he wasn't convinced it would happen at all. There was a deep, overwhelming sorrow in his father, ever since the death of Cooper's mom. Nothing Cooper did could touch that sorrow. Only vodka seemed to help.

Who was Cooper to take that from him? He'd only turned seventeen last month. He might have graduated from high school early, thanks to skipping a grade, but what did he know about fixing something like that?

And he didn't want to lose his father. The only person left who really loved him.

The man in question shuffled back out of the bathroom, scratching at his chest. It looked like he'd splashed some water on his face. He still looked like crap, his nose red and splotchy and the bags under his eyes bigger than ever. He needed some real sleep, not just naps caught on the couch. Maybe if Cooper got some food in him, he'd go to bed for real.

Cooper would stay up, maybe work on coding. He was getting pretty good with computers, courtesy of hardly ever leaving the house. What did he need to leave for, anyway? He was done with school, and he didn't have any friends to speak of. Before, he'd had neighborhood kids he'd been friendly with, but when Cooper and his father had moved, those relationships had fizzled.

It was just him and his father, for better or for worse.

His dad wiped a hand over his face before approaching the couch. He did look a little more alert. Maybe he hadn't had as much to drink as Cooper had thought. "Should we watch something together, umnitsa? One of your mysteries?"

It was something they'd done together since Cooper was a preteen. They would watch a murder mystery, and Cooper would try to figure out the culprit before the big reveal. His dad would clap and cheer whenever he succeeded, like he'd won a game show instead of guessed at some subpar plot point.

Cooper leaned his head back against the couch with a sigh. "Sure, Pop. And I'll order some food, yeah?"

"Sure," *his dad agreed, not sounding like he cared either way. He shot Cooper a wink.* "Who needs groceries, huh?"

He sat down, ruffled Cooper's hair, then slumped back and reached for the remote. "So good to me, umnitsa. I love you so much."

The words sounded heavy. Like the love he had for Cooper was painful to him. Maybe it was. Maybe that was why it could never be enough.

There was nothing to say except "I love you too, Pop. So much."

So what if his father couldn't protect him or care for him the way other parents did for their children? They'd managed just fine so far. They'd keep managing, just the two of them.

What other choice was there?

————

COOPER WAS WOKEN up by the need to pee.

He grabbed his glasses and hurried to the bathroom before Chaos could see that his eyes were wet.

Fuck, it had been a long time since he'd dreamed about his dad. It was like a knife to the chest—his feelings about his father might have been complicated, but he still missed him. Every day. So damn much.

He took a quick shower while he was in there, washing off the sweat that coated him, leftover from the meeting and by sleeping with too many blankets.

When he came out into the bedroom, his glasses back on and a towel wrapped around his middle, Chaos was sitting cross-legged on the bed, kind of bouncing in place, looking almost maniacally happy.

Cooper couldn't help smiling at him. "You look cheerful. Is it because you're all full from the meeting?"

Chaos gave him a smug look, waving his finger in the air, his tail swishing wildly. "You'll always need me to be your friend. That's what you said."

"Oh. Yeah." Cooper's cheeks warmed. He'd been loopy as hell when they'd been talking before, and he was a little embarrassed by the admission now. He wasn't sure why—it wasn't like Chaos had cared about Cooper's lack of social life before now. He shifted on his feet, running his hand through his wet hair. "But I won't stand in the way either," he reassured Chaos. "When you find your bondmate, I mean. Just—just so you know." Cooper cleared his throat. Why was this so hard to say? "And I should be thanking you too. For helping me realize."

Chaos had paused his bouncing midway through Cooper's little speech, and now he cocked his head, his tail in an arc behind him. "Realize what?"

"You've made me realize... Well, I guess that I don't want to be alone. That I need to—to look beyond casual hookups. To find someone who's both lover and friend. I—I like that, with you. I want to find that again."

Now Chaos was not only *not* bouncing, but he was holding himself with that unnatural, predatory stillness that Cooper still found so eerie. "You wish to mate with other humans?" he asked, his voice deadly soft.

"I mean—" Cooper suddenly wished he was wearing real clothes. Why was he having this conversation in his fucking towel? "Isn't that—aren't *you* going to find another human? Someone to bond with?"

Cooper yelped as Chaos went from frozen on the bed to standing mere inches away from him in a flash.

"*You* are my human," Chaos hissed, literal flames dancing in his eyes. "I found you, fair and square. I'm being patient and gentle and tricky as a fox to keep you close, but if that's not working, I can be much—" He looked around the room, as if trying to find an answer there, then settled his gaze back on Cooper. "Much *scarier* about it."

"I—I don't understand." Had Cooper hit his head at the restaurant? What was happening right now? Why was Chaos so pissed off?

Chaos pressed a taloned finger to Cooper's chest. It maybe should have frightened Cooper, now that he knew what those talons could do, but he was too confused by the turn this conversation had taken. He'd been so sure they were on the same page.

"*We* are bonding," Chaos declared, haughty as anything. "You and I. No other humans. Not for you, not for me."

"We are?" Cooper asked. He didn't add the obvious question: Since fucking *when*?

Chaos nodded decisively, his talon digging into Cooper's skin. "Yes. We are."

Cooper tightened his towel, which had begun to slip. "Do I get a say?"

Chaos's lips turned down into a pathetic pout. "No."

Cooper almost laughed. What right did Chaos have to be pouting right now? Kai had been right—he was such a brat sometimes. "You'd force me into it?"

Chaos growled, releasing Cooper so he could throw his hands into the air. "Who said anything about forcing? But if you refuse, you—you'd be choosing *wrong*! And you shouldn't be allowed to choose wrong. It's very frustrating." He began pacing in front of Cooper, tossing him belligerent looks with every turn of his heel. "Why are you being so *frustrating*?"

Cooper had a better question. "Why do you even want me?"

"Because," Chaos said and left it at that. When Cooper raised his brows at him—was that really it?—he let out a heavy breath, as if Cooper was being ridiculous. "You want reasons?"

Cooper nodded.

Chaos huffed, crossing his arms over his chest as he told Cooper grudgingly, "I'm tolerated by some. Feared by many. But no one...cares for me, not like you do. You care about my feelings and making sure I get to do the things I want to do. You care about my friendship. And I do the same for you, don't I? I think about how to please you, how to make you happy. I've never done that before." He frowned down at Cooper's bedroom floor. "I should hate it," he muttered. "I wanted freedom, and instead I'm tied to you. But I find I don't mind being grounded, if I'm grounded with you, Cooper."

"Oh." It was a strange sort of confession, but then, Chaos was strange. Cooper pushed his glasses up his nose. "That's kind of romantic, actually."

"Yes." Chaos preened, dropping his arms. "I'm very romantic. I've shown you, haven't I? How I can be so sweet and so gentle." He drifted closer to Cooper, his intensity ratcheting up with every inch he closed between them. "I can be everything you need. So you needn't worry any longer, Cooper. Not with me here."

Cooper was finding it hard to blink, staring into Chaos's fire-filled eyes.

Was Chaos really trying to convince Cooper to keep him? That was almost funny. It should have been the other way around. It should have been Cooper on his knees, trying to show Chaos he was good enough, interesting enough, *brave* enough to be a demon's mate.

Holy shit. Cooper's stomach bottomed out with the realization. *Chaos wants to keep me.*

The knowledge felt like free-falling. It wasn't a sensation Cooper normally liked. But unlike Cooper's father, or his cousins, or his past failed attempt at romance, Chaos could actually catch him, couldn't he? Chaos might not have been the most stable being, but he was strong. He'd just sliced a man in half a few hours ago. And yes, that maybe should have made Cooper hesitate more instead of less, but...maybe Cooper had been around violent men too long after all. All it seemed to tell him was that, for once in his life, someone could back up what they were putting down.

Someone would catch him before he hit the ground.

They might be a strange pair in other people's eyes, but what did it matter what the rest of the world thought? Chaos was beyond this world. Above it. Better and stronger and weirder than anything else in it.

And he'd chosen Cooper.

"Okay," Cooper breathed. He felt...free, all of a sudden. Weightless. "Okay. We'll bond. You and me."

"Really?" The flames in Chaos's eyes went out in an instant, replaced by a soft golden gleam. He grabbed Cooper's shoulders tightly. "No take backs," he said quickly. "We bond. You and I." His lips twitched into a sly smile. "I'll need to get the Book from Ivan, of course."

"I can ask," Cooper offered.

"No." Chaos grinned widely now. "I want to steal it from him. It'll be hilarious."

The idea of stealing anything from Ivan was terrifying, but Cooper kept his mouth shut. This was what a future with Chaos would be like—a little terror with the comfort of his presence.

Cooper would take it. He'd take all of it. He still wasn't sure why Chaos would possibly want him so badly. Weren't there other humans that could care for him the way Cooper did? But he wasn't going to argue. He didn't want Chaos to leave him for someone else. Not ever.

"What does it all entail?" he asked instead of arguing over things like petty theft. "Like, how do we do it?"

"First, we get the Book." Chaos started stroking his fingers lightly down Cooper's bare arms. "There's a passage at the end—a sacred vow. I take a little nip of blood from you, you take a little nip of blood from me." He ran his tongue over his sharp teeth. "And then we consummate."

"Oh." Cooper choked on a breath. "Sounds simple enough."

"So simple," Chaos agreed, his hands trailing down to Cooper's wrists, stroking his pulse points. "So easy. But maybe—" He stepped closer, close enough for his shirt to brush against Cooper's bare chest. "Maybe we should still practice."

"Biting each other?" Cooper asked, his brain going a little fuzzy with the warmth of Chaos's touch.

Chaos grinned, flashing his fangs. "If you like. But I meant we should practice consummating."

"We've done it before." Quite thoroughly, if Cooper remembered correctly. Which he definitely did.

"Not enough," Chaos insisted. He pulled at Cooper's arms until Cooper was pressed fully against him, rubbing his nose along Cooper's neck and shoulder, his wily fingers dipping under Cooper's towel. "Don't you want to, puppy? Don't you want to practice with me?"

As if he couldn't feel Cooper's hard dick tenting his towel. As if Cooper had ever said no to more "practice."

"Hey," Cooper said suddenly.

Chaos's wandering fingers paused against Cooper's skin.

"Was all that 'practice' talk just a way of getting into my pants?"

"Yes," Chaos told him gleefully, throwing his head back in a throaty laugh. "Wasn't that clever of me?" He beamed at Cooper. "I've wanted to keep you from the start."

"Shouldn't you have told me that?" Cooper asked, wondering if he should be angry for the deception. He didn't feel like getting angry though. He felt like spreading his legs and getting Chaos inside him. To be wanted like that was kind of...heady. More warmth pooled in his belly at the thought of it.

"I'm telling you now," Chaos said, as cocky as if he were reading Cooper's thoughts. "Because you like me. Because I'm lover and friend both. And a gentle, skilled bed partner. And handsome. And my wings and tail are adorable. You think so, right?" he asked suddenly, the tail in question wrapping around Cooper's thigh.

"They are pretty cute," Cooper admitted.

"I knew you'd agree." Chaos backed Cooper up to the bed and pressed him down onto his back, whisking the towel off him in the process. His own clothes disappeared in a flash as he knelt between Cooper's legs. "I'm going to breed you now, puppy," he purred. "To practice. For later."

"Okay," Cooper agreed easily, his cock heavy and full against his hip.

Chaos began kissing along Cooper's inner thighs, nibbling gently, managing not to break the skin even with his fangs. Teasing, in his way.

Cooper spread his legs wider, willing to let Chaos tend to him however he wanted.

And then Chaos's hands were in Cooper's hair, stroking gently. Except...

Except Chaos was down between Cooper's legs.

Cooper jolted. "What the fuck?" But the hands in his hair tightened their hold, and he couldn't lift his head to look properly.

Chaos rose from his kneeling position, looming over Cooper with a sly smile. "Puppy," he crooned. "Did I ever tell you one of my special powers? How I can duplicate my form?"

"Um. No." Cooper tried to calm his breaths as he tried to understand what Chaos was saying. "Is that— Are those *your* hands in my hair?" Maybe that was why it had taken him a moment to react in the first place—the touch had been familiar.

"Yes." Chaos grinned at him, his hands running up Cooper's sides. "So smart, my delectable little summoner. And I'm clever too, aren't I? You're intrigued by group sex, but you're shy, and also I would slice out the organs of any human who dared to touch you. But you don't need other humans to try it," he said with the air of someone imparting a delightful surprise. "You have me."

And then Cooper was being tugged into a kiss. Not by the Chaos looming over him, but by the Chaos above him, the one with his hands in Cooper's hair. An exact duplicate. He kissed the same too, eager and aggressive, his tongue claiming Cooper's mouth like he had a right to it.

Cooper moaned into it, the fear that had gripped him when

he'd thought a stranger was in his room melting into a desire so hot he thought he might combust. This was weird and kind of scary.

And Cooper was definitely broken inside, because he fucking loved it.

The other Chaos giggled, his hands sliding from Cooper's sides to his belly, to his hips, and then a hot mouth was engulfing Cooper's cock.

Cooper gasped into the duplicate Chaos's mouth. "Oh my God."

"Yes," the Chaos at his head crooned, releasing Cooper's lips to gaze down at him. He looked just the same, his eyes yellow and gleaming. "I will be your lover and friend and family and god and anything else you need."

That was an insane thing to say, and Cooper should definitely tell him that, but then out of nowhere there was a third Chaos lying at his side, grinning at Cooper before sucking Cooper's nipple into his mouth.

Cooper barely had time to process that before there was a lubed finger at his hole, and then the Chaos at his side was grabbing Cooper's cock, stroking as he sucked and bit at Cooper's nipple. Cooper's mouth was claimed again, the kiss kind of upside down and sloppy but no less devastating for it.

He could hardly breathe. Hardly think. There were more fingers inside him, stretching and crooking and making him see stars. There were hands everywhere. Three pairs? More than three? He couldn't open his eyes to see, too lost in sensation.

It was so much. Too much. Perfectly, horribly, wonderfully too much.

"Chaos," Cooper warned in the spare second the Chaos at his lips allowed him to breathe. Cooper's back was arched so high he couldn't lift his head from the mattress. "Gonna come."

"Yes," all three Chaoses crooned at once. "Come for us, puppy."

The hand on his cock started stroking faster, twisting around the head of his cock with every pass. Cooper's balls tightened, his muscles spasmed, and then he was coming with a hoarse yell, shaking and shivering and maybe crying too. There were murmurings of praise, from one or maybe all the Chaoses, and then three pairs of hands were turning Cooper over, rolling him onto his belly.

The one at Cooper's head started stroking his hair again as someone's cock pressed into him. Cooper keened, his overworked body opening at Chaos's insistence.

"That's it, puppy. Let me in."

As if Cooper had ever been capable of anything else.

17

Chaos

Chaos sighed his pleasure as he filled his puppy, gripping hard with his talons at Cooper's raised hips. There was nothing better than the feel of Cooper when he'd just experienced release, his body both lax and tensed at the same time, his overworked inner muscles fluttering around Chaos's cock like frantic little bird wings.

Chaos's other self was still stroking Cooper's hair, and his other *other* self was contemplating taking a bite out of Cooper's side. But as Chaos bottomed out, Cooper groaning like he was being murdered, Chaos called his duplicates back into himself. They were fun and all, and hadn't Cooper been so delightfully surprised? Still, splitting himself dulled external sensation, and Chaos wanted to feel every bit of ecstasy.

Although, if Cooper wanted it one day—if he asked so very nicely to have Chaos's cocks in two holes at once—Chaos would of course oblige.

He was generous that way.

Chaos stayed exactly where he was for a long, blissful moment, his hips pressed flush against Cooper's ass, Cooper's channel clamping down on him. Cooper had gone kind of slack against the mattress, too overwhelmed to hold himself up, so Chaos lowered himself fully against Cooper's back, rubbing his fur against Cooper's soft skin and nuzzling his head into the tender crook of Cooper's neck.

"You feel so good, puppy," he murmured. "Did you like my special trick?"

Cooper groaned again. Or perhaps it was more of a whimper.

Chaos grinned, raising his hips and fucking into his puppy with an easy glide. When Cooper was this boneless, Chaos could be a little fierce. A little less...gentle. He was still mindful of Cooper's fragile human frame, of course. But he could give in a little to this boundless enthusiasm inside him, this biting need to fill Cooper up again and again with all his seed.

Cooper had accepted Chaos as a mate.

He'd seen Chaos at—well, not his worst, but definitely not at his most gentle—and he wanted to let Chaos keep him anyway. An eternity of companionship, of Cooper's wonderful weight in Chaos's chest, of getting to claim Cooper's beautiful human body over and over again.

Cooper had said it. Out loud. He'd voiced his permission.

Chaos wanted to hear it again.

"Puppy," he urged, using the grip of his hands on the mattress to drive into Cooper in a way that made his human keen. "Tell me you want me."

Cooper flopped his head to the side, stammering out, "I want —oh fuck—I want you."

"Only me," Chaos pressed.

"O-Only you."

Oh, this was lovely.

"Tell me I'm an excellent lover," Chaos urged, driving in again to the hilt and grinding there, rubbing his nodules against Cooper's prostate as he waited for his answer.

"Oh my God," Cooper said—not the words Chaos had asked for at all—and tucked his forehead back against the covers, as if hiding himself.

Chaos waited.

"You're the best sex I've ever had," Cooper eventually choked out, his whole body shaking, the words muffled by bunched fabric.

Chaos cackled. Yes, of course he was. This feral need couldn't belong to Chaos alone. It was mutual, this desire between them.

Chaos picked up the pace again. It was burning inside him once more, this need to fill Cooper up. His body was so perfectly tight and warm, sucking Chaos in again and again, and Chaos needed to—to *claim* it.

His rhythm grew sloppy as blood roared in his ears, and he urged Cooper again, "Tell me you love feeling my spend inside you."

Cooper's neck turned a lovely shade of red as the words spilled out of him. "I love when you come inside me. I love when you fill me. I love when you can't—can't get enough of it."

The words were faint—more pained panting than clear speech —but Chaos heard it all. His nodules grew stiff and swollen, and his hips stuttered, the world narrowing down to him and his puppy, to that perfect heat, to the way Cooper cried out as Chaos filled him.

Perfect. Perfect, perfect, perfect.

Afterward, Chaos turned Cooper on his side, pushing his thigh forward to better watch his spend trickle out. He peered over Cooper's hip curiously.

"Oh no," Chaos tutted, the perfect picture of a concerned partner. He cupped Cooper between his legs. "Your poor cock's hard again." He clucked his tongue. "That won't do."

Cooper's arm flopped over, landing weakly on Chaos's side. Was he trying to smack at him? "Your fault," he mumbled.

"Should we go again?" Chaos asked, running a finger along Cooper's silken length. "We should, shouldn't we?"

They could do it just like this, with Cooper turned halfway onto his front, his leg hitched up. They'd done it in this position before, and Chaos had been very fond of it. It had been just like cuddling, only with his cock nestled inside his puppy, so safe and warm.

Cooper let out a harsh breath but nodded his agreement, shifting his leg even further forward. Chaos pressed an approving kiss to Cooper's shoulder and rolled his hips, rubbing himself against the soft skin of Cooper's bottom until Chaos was hard again too, and then he slipped right in, hissing at the tight fit.

He was gentler this time, some of the ferocity of his need assuaged by his first claiming. He stroked Cooper's cock steadily as he rocked into him, mindful of his puppy's pleasure.

Cooper seemed to be having quite a lot of it—pleasure. He kept chanting, "Oh God. Oh God," over and over. It was repetitive but oddly stimulating at the same time.

"Come for me again, puppy," Chaos urged when the chanting took on a particularly frantic edge. "I want to lick it off my hand."

That earned him another "Oh God," and then Cooper was coming over Chaos's hand again, just as Chaos had asked, Cooper's muscles trembling with the effort. Chaos loved the way he did that, the way Cooper's entire body was involved in his release.

Chaos let go of Cooper's cock and swiped at his own hand with his tongue, messy and sloppy and missing half of what he aimed for as he kept driving into his puppy, rocking until he felt the familiar tightness in his spine. "I'm going to fill you up again," he warned. "Double the hatchlings."

"Jesus."

Afterward—after he'd focused properly and cleaned every

drop of Cooper's cum off his hand—Chaos couldn't resist pressing his finger against Cooper's hole, pushing his spend back where it belonged over and over again. He watched eagerly as Cooper's cock valiantly try to fill again.

"I think we'll do very well with the consummation," he murmured, his chin hooked over Cooper's shoulder, laughing as Cooper batted Chaos's other hand away from his cock. "Don't you?"

"You're a menace."

"Yes," Chaos agreed cheerfully. "And soon you'll be stuck with me for always."

———

IT SEEMED Cooper needed more rest after all that.

It was possible Chaos *maybe* should have taken it easier on him, right after the shock of the meeting. Maybe he should have kept it to those two rounds and not pressed for a third. And maybe also not used his mouth on Cooper in the shower.

Maybe.

Chaos had been trying to be gentle—he really had—but he was still learning.

It was cozy in bed, anyway, the two of them tucked under the covers, both of them on their own laptops.

Cooper was exuding happiness and contentment in a new, fascinating way. Chaos hadn't realized the weight it had held over Cooper, thinking Chaos was going to leave. But now that it was gone, Cooper's soul piece tasted different. Sweeter, with a delicate hint of hopeful lemon.

What a silly puppy he'd been, to think Chaos would really leave him behind.

Or maybe Chaos was just very *extra* good at being sneaky.

Yes, that was probably it.

Now Cooper was doing some hacking thing ("just for fun, to cleanse my brain a bit"), and he'd taught Chaos how to do something he called "trolling." From what he'd explained, acting like a troll mainly involved entering internet forums where people were particularly passionate and commenting something incorrect or absurd, and then watching the comments roll in, all of them fighting with either Chaos or each other.

"I haven't experienced it personally, but I'm told parenting forums are particularly hostile," Cooper had told him. "Same with anything involving dog training."

And then he'd lectured Chaos on only using his trolling powers for good and not harassing anyone who seemed sincere or kind or truly sad. It had been a Cooper version of a lecture—more of a strong suggestion than a command—but he seemed to really feel something about it, so Chaos would be good.

Probably.

Mostly.

Really, Chaos had been skeptical about the whole thing, but the absurd ways humans interacted online was *fascinating*. He was all full from the meeting already—chaotic energy buzzing in his veins—but he could see this becoming a solid source of food down the line. A bit strange maybe, with the fuzzy-edged electronic taste to it, but it would still be filling enough.

He'd just posted in a forum called NYParentsOfLittles: *I don't believe in bike helmets. We have skulls around our brains for a reason. To wear a helmet is an affront to our Maker.*

Chaos was cackling quietly to himself as the replies came in— a weird number of which seemed to agree with him—when Cooper let out a small, triumphant, "I did it."

Chaos added a few exclamation points to his latest comment (*Well I think* YOU'RE *stupid!!!!*) as he asked, "What did you do, puppy?"

Cooper startled, like he'd forgotten Chaos was there for a

moment, even though Chaos was pressed against him, arm to arm and hip to hip. "Oh." He pushed his glasses up. "Um, just a side project I've been working on for a friend. A proving-my-mettle type of thing. But it's done now."

Chaos looked up from his trolling. "Friend? What friend?"

"An internet friend. I haven't met him in person."

Chaos hooked his chin over Cooper's shoulder, peering at Cooper's laptop instead of his own. Cooper was messaging with someone named RedRabbit.

It's done, Cooper had typed. *Good challenge, by the way. I enjoyed myself.*

Chaos didn't know how to feel about this. He supposed it was a good thing that Cooper had an internet friend—Chaos didn't like that his puppy was so lonely—but Chaos also didn't like that he hadn't met them himself and scoped them out for Cooper ahead of time. It made his talons itchy.

What if this friend was tactless and hurt Cooper's feelings? His puppy's feelings were tender, like his fragile human body. This RedRabbit person needed to be made aware.

"Tell them your feelings are very tender," Chaos commanded.

Cooper blinked, his lovely fingers poised on his laptop keys. "Um. What?"

Chaos sighed, his gusty breath making Cooper's ear twitch. "Never mind."

Chaos would just have to deal with it himself, if it came down to it.

He watched as RedRabbit replied, *Knew you'd get it. You're the first. Probably the only.*

Well, that seemed all right. This person appreciated Cooper's fine mind, at least.

Still...

Chaos dug his chin more firmly into Cooper's shoulder,

ignoring his wince. "Tell them they're *only* a friend. Not a lover or family or god of intercourse."

"So, um..." Cooper cleared his throat. "No. I'm not going to do that."

Chaos let out another sigh. Was this what it was like when one's mate was being unreasonable? It was so rare for Cooper to be stubborn like this.

But then Cooper twisted his torso to pat at Chaos's head. "They don't want to be my lover, Bracchus, I promise. They haven't even ever suggested meeting in person."

The patting was nice—Chaos butted his head into the touch—but Chaos remained skeptical. "What if they want to cybersex you?"

Cooper let out a strange, choked noise, cleared his throat, then answered, "I'll politely decline."

"Rudely decline," Chaos corrected.

"Okay, I'll rudely decline."

"All right." Placated, Chaos shuffled back into position—arm to arm and hip to hip—and went back to his laptop, typing out a statement about helmets being the leading source of microplastics in the water supply.

"When should I steal the Book back from Ivan?" he asked after having received many, many wonderfully rude replies. "I don't want to leave you alone yet. You're still recovering."

Both from the meeting and from Chaos's enthusiastic demonstration of consummation, but Chaos kept that last bit to himself.

Cooper was still typing away to his internet friend, but he furrowed his brow in thought. "You could go Friday. I have to go out, anyway. It's time to pick up the fake passports for Nix and Kai." He paused his messaging, looking to Chaos with wide eyes. "You're going to need the same, aren't you?" He shook his head. "Back to square one, then. But I do need to pick up these first to get Ivan off my back."

Chaos cocked his head. "But I should accompany you, if it's a Mafia errand. What if someone needs slicing?" He held up his talons to demonstrate.

"No one is going to need slicing," Cooper told him, suddenly looking a little pale. "My contact is super chill. He only deals in fake documentation—passports and IDs and stuff. So he's only Mafia-adjacent. I've met with him tons of times."

Tons of times?

Chaos narrowed his eyes. "Is he handsome?"

He didn't really know why he was asking, except that Chaos had never really had cause to feel jealous before, and it was a fun feeling to play with. Jealousy was the root of much chaos in the romantic realm—Chaos appreciated its power.

"Um." Cooper scrunched his nose, his glasses rising a bit with the motion. "Could be? If you like scraggly beards and kind of not-great hygiene and men in their sixties?"

"*Do* you like those things?" Chaos had never asked about Cooper's preferences. Perhaps he'd been remiss.

Cooper bit at his lip, as if hiding a smile. "Not particularly."

"Good." Chaos gave a decisive nod. "All right, puppy. We'll both run our errands. A real power couple, as they say."

Cooper let the smile he'd been battling grace his lips. "Who says that?" he asked, sounding amused.

Chaos waved a hand. "Some human somewhere." Although, now that he thought about it, it may have been Nix. "It's hard to keep track. Humans are always saying all sorts of nonsense."

18

Cooper

"And you're sure you'll remember how to get there?" Cooper asked for maybe the second or third time; he couldn't be sure.

"Puppyyy," Chaos chastised, drawing out the word with a sly smile. "What a silly question."

Cooper could only stand there, staring at him doubtfully. He was vaguely aware he was acting like a mother hen, but he couldn't help it. He'd given Chaos directions to Ivan's apartment—and then to his office, in case the Book was stashed there instead—but how much experience did Chaos really have navigating human cities?

Basically none, was the answer—at least not without Cooper at his side. Because, frankly, Chaos just wandering around the blocks, circling Cooper's apartment for funsies, didn't really count.

And now he was being stubborn and refusing to let Cooper order a car for him. When Cooper had suggested it, he'd wrinkled his nose and whined, "How will I enjoy the delicious disorder of the city from inside a vehicle?"

Cooper wished he'd thought to get Chaos a phone before now. He'd feel better with something connecting the two of them while they were apart. Obviously Chaos could handle himself when it came to any physical threats or danger, but there were just so many damn *people* in this city. Cooper couldn't shake the nagging feeling that Chaos was going to disappear like smoke out of Cooper's life the second he let him out of his sight.

It was a terrifying thought. Cooper had only just found out he got to keep Chaos—he couldn't go losing him now. And he couldn't give Chaos his own phone and have him contact the apartment security desk if he got into any trouble, because Cooper needed the damn thing to connect with *his* contact, who still hadn't told him the meeting location for the day.

The nerves and panic started growing, churning in Cooper's gut, and then Chaos's hot hands were on Cooper's cheeks, his eyes boring into his very soul. Their yellow-gold color clashed with Chaos's hair today, which was a bright tennis-ball green. It had made Cooper smile when he'd seen it upon waking up—at least Chaos would be easy to find in a crowd.

"Listen to me, puppy," Chaos said, firm and clear, all his slyness tucked away for the moment. "I'm very clever, aren't I? And strong. And not afraid of any of the silly threats of your realm. Your worries are sweet, and quite tasty on the air, but they're foolish. Even if I got lost, I would track your soul via our contract." He released one hand from Cooper's cheek to tap at his chest, over his heart. Was that where he was holding a piece of Cooper's soul? "You can never, ever hide from me, even if you want to."

For something that sounded like it should be a threat, it was surprisingly reassuring. "Oh." Cooper let out a breath as Chaos poked at his cheeks, as if to encourage him. "That's good, then. Cool. Freaky but cool."

"Yes." Chaos nodded seriously, his fox eyes unblinking. "I am both those things." He cocked his head, stroking his thumb along Cooper's cheekbone. "But as for you, sweet summoner." He tapped his thumb, the talon poking sharply at Cooper's skin. "If you feel any distress on your errand—if anyone is unkind to you in any way—you'll phone Ivan, and he'll have Nix come get you."

"He will?" Cooper asked, doubtful once again. That didn't sound like Ivan. He was more likely to hang up on Cooper and then later fire him for the inconvenience of his interruption.

"He'd better," Chaos said ominously. "Tell him I said so. Remind him of my teeth." He grinned, displaying his fangs. "And my claws." He tapped Cooper's cheekbone again. "And fire."

Cooper let out another breath. It would be a last resort for sure, but that was better than no resort at all. "Okay," he agreed. "I'll call him if I need to."

"Good, obedient puppy." Chaos pressed a surprisingly chaste kiss to Cooper's lips, then both his cheeks, and then finally his nose. He grinned impishly, his horns, wings, and tail disappearing and his eyes returning to an oddly dull brown, though his hair remained the same bright green.

"Time for thievery!" he cried and turned on his heel to bound out the front door, which opened for him as if Cooper didn't have ten different locks engaged. The door slammed behind him, the locks somehow still in place.

And just like that, he was gone.

He'll be back, Cooper reminded himself immediately when his stomach started turning over again. *He might even finish his errand before I do. He could be waiting here when I return. Either way, he'll be back.*

He told himself the same thing over and over, breathing in and out slowly, until his phone finally dinged at him. It was a message from Smith—his contact for fake identification—with the address for the day. It was unfamiliar to Cooper, but that was normal.

Smith switched offices regularly, sending Cooper a different address almost every time they met. He was a chill guy in the sense that he wasn't a murderous mafioso, but he was pretty paranoid.

Cooper felt practically well adjusted in comparison.

He left his apartment building, wincing as the frozen outdoor air hit his face. Good thing he'd finally put a coat on over his sweatshirt. It had been a mild, dry winter so far, but the mornings were finally starting to turn bitterly cold.

Yet, coat or no coat, Cooper missed Chaos's warmth already. If they'd been together right now, Chaos would be holding Cooper's hand, swinging their arms between them, his skin burning hot against Cooper's. He'd probably also be making a spectacle of them in some way, but Cooper wouldn't mind—getting noticed by people wasn't so scary when Chaos was around.

Because Cooper might be going unnoticed right now—walking alone by himself, his hood up and his head down—but somehow he felt more vulnerable than ever.

He'd gotten used to the comfort of his demon beside him.

Still, he took the subway rather than use any of Ivan's drivers. Smith didn't like any more outsiders than necessary to know his location. The station and the subway cars were as crowded as ever, but everyone was minding their own business, so Cooper did his best to breathe out his anxiety.

He distracted himself by trying to figure out which of humanity's little quirks on display would tickle Chaos the most. After three stops, he gave the honor to a guy carrying a dog that looked like some sort of husky mix in an oversize tote, technically in compliance with the rule that all dogs be contained in carriers on the subway. The massive dog was absurdly calm and well behaved, clearly used to this method of transport.

Yeah, Chaos would definitely get a kick out of that. Although, he'd probably like it even more if there was another, rival dog—

maybe a really tiny one—and the two dogs started barking at each other and then leaped out of their respective carriers, jumping all over each other and all over the passengers and generally causing a terrible commotion.

Yeah. Cooper smiled to himself. Chaos would probably like that best.

He got off at the stop closest to his destination and walked the last block, his head down and his gaze focused on his feet once more, the nerves from being away from Chaos giving way to a new sense of anticipation. This meeting would be quick enough, and then...

Then they were going to bond. Today. As soon as Chaos could get back with the Book.

Chaos had told Cooper he didn't want to wait. "No take backs," he'd reminded him as soon as Cooper had opened his eyes that morning, as if Cooper being a flight risk was a real possibility.

Maybe it should have been. This was the kind of life-altering decision that Cooper would normally think and rethink and rethink again until he'd talked himself out of any course of action.

Instead, this would be the second time in his life he'd acted completely on impulse. The first had been offering himself up to Dimitri in place of his father. Maybe not the smartest thing he'd ever done. But if he hadn't done it—if he hadn't inserted himself into the Mafia world—he never would have come across that Book in Ivan's office, would he?

The rough, lonely road he'd traveled had led him to Chaos.

It was a comforting thought. Cooper didn't believe in fate—if it existed, it was a real bitch for taking away his mother the way it had and leaving his dad in such despair—but he could pretend, for just a moment, that he'd always been meant to belong to Chaos. To be his friend. His anchor. His human mate.

And that would mean Chaos, in turn, had always been meant

to be Cooper's. To be *his* friend. His lover. His wily, tricky, wonderful demon.

Cooper stopped in front of the address that matched the message on his phone. It was a narrow, nondescript building, with little placards at the entrance for each office inside. A good number of them seemed to be empty, but there was one for a lawyer and one for a personal accountant. The office number Cooper had been given didn't have a business name next to it, but then, Cooper wouldn't expect it to.

The main door was unlocked, no buzzer needed for entry, and Cooper walked down the narrow, dimly lit hallway until he came to the last office on the first floor. He knocked, but there was no answer. He tried the handle—unlocked.

He walked inside to find himself in what seemed to be an abandoned waiting area, with a few busted chairs and an open doorway leading to some sort of inner office.

"Smith?" he called out.

Silence.

The door to the back room was open, though, and Smith liked to use noise-canceling headphones while he worked sometimes. He never sat with his back to the door, but it wouldn't be the first time he hadn't heard Cooper come in.

Cooper tried again anyway. "Smith?"

Nothing.

He approached the open doorway, looking through to a small, windowless office with an empty desk and no chair. There were a few boxes with the lids half off, filled with what looked to be old paperwork. There were none of Smith's usual accessories. There wasn't even a computer.

Cooper checked his phone again. He had the right address and the right office number. And Smith was meticulous with communication—it would be unlike him to give Cooper the wrong information.

Hey, Cooper texted. *Any chance you changed locations?*

Maybe Smith had given him an old address after all. Unlikely didn't mean impossible.

He saw the three little dots that meant Smith was typing out a response, but then the softest whisper of a footstep had Cooper raising his head, ready to turn.

Before he could, something sharp jabbed into his neck. He lifted his hand to swat at it—had he just been bitten by something?—but his arm flopped only halfway up, heavy and useless.

Cooper's head swam. He tried again to turn, but he couldn't get his feet to cooperate. He couldn't get his knees to lock either. He was falling, the floor rising up to meet him.

And then nothing. Only darkness.

19

Chaos

Ivan's apartment had a man protecting the front entrance. A man at the door. A *door*man.

So literal sometimes, these humans. Chaos giggled from his spot on the sidewalk, but no one walking by glanced his way. They were all too focused on staring straight ahead as they marched toward their various destinations.

No matter. Chaos had something more entertaining for them than a little quiet cackling. There were a few trees lining the edge of the sidewalk in front of the apartment. Their leaves were gone, but the branches were all spiny and twisty. Very pretty.

Chaos lit one ablaze.

One of the passersby let out a yelp, and the doorman looked up from where he'd been surreptitiously glancing at his phone. "Holy *shit*."

Some cool-headed human who'd stopped at the flaming sight turned to snap at him. "Hey. You got a fire extinguisher in there?"

"Shit. Um, yes. Shit."

The doorman ran inside the apartment building, and Chaos slipped in after him, keeping his giggles to himself now. He'd already put the fire out the moment the man's back was turned. The doorman would come back out to nothing at all—a perfectly intact, leafless tree. Maybe he'd think he was losing his mind, if no one else stuck around to confirm what he'd seen.

Very funny, but not Chaos's concern anymore.

He sneaked past the doorman fumbling with the fire extinguisher, down the hallway, around to the elevators. Once inside the little moving carriage, he hit the button for the very top floor, sticking his tongue out at his reflection.

At the top, the elevator opened directly into an apartment, and Chaos waltzed right in, calling out, "Helloooo?"

It probably wasn't very burglar-y of him, but if Ivan and Nix were home, Chaos would just pretend he was here for a little visit and then sneak the Book out when they were distracted.

No one answered his call though. There was no sign of Ivan or Nix, other than their mingled scents threading through the apartment.

Well, goodness, that was easy.

A little disappointing, since Chaos might have liked to see his friend. But Nix would no doubt track Chaos down soon enough. He wouldn't be able to help himself, all sentimental like he was.

Chaos poked around the place for a minute. It was much more modern than Cooper's, all straight lines and boring noncolors. Although there were already little touches from Nix —throw pillows, art on the walls, a few pieces of furniture that weren't beige or white. He could scent Nix's demonic signature on them. Apparently, he was making himself right at home with his human. Should Chaos be doing the same for Cooper? He wasn't really one for decorating though. Perhaps Chaos would ask Nix to help him pick out a...rug? Something soft that wouldn't irritate Cooper's knees if a situation were to occur where he might be on all fours. Perhaps with Chaos on top of him.

Just in case.

Chaos could scent the demonic signature of the Book as well. He followed it to what was clearly Ivan and Nix's bedroom. Clear because of the giant bed and Nix's magical signature but also because the place reeked of incubus sex magic, the kind that leaked out of Nix when he was all worked up. The whole apartment did, really, but this room in particular was stuffed full of it.

Nix and Ivan obviously hadn't had any trouble consummating the bond and then some.

Chaos ignored the sex magic puddles and tracked the Book to a little bedside table. There was a lock on the drawer, which Chaos exploded with relish. He scooped the Book out with one of Cooper's cloth bags he'd borrowed. Demons couldn't touch a Book with their own contract page in it, but that was easy enough to work around. It was a stupid rule, anyway, to have such a simple solution.

Chaos peered down at the thing, secure at the bottom of his bag. He could feel the telltale magic of the bonding page, weighty and a teensy bit intimidating. He could feel the messy signature of his own contract page as well. Nix's contract page was inactive now, bonded as he was. Same with Kai's.

But that was it.

Huh. Chaos hadn't noticed before—he hadn't been thinking of it *to* notice—but Nightmare's page just...wasn't there. Where could it have gone? The Book was supposed to be indestructible.

Chaos clucked his tongue. Ohh, tricky, tricky, Nightmare. Had he found a way to get himself summoned, to arrange it even from inside the Void? Chaos wouldn't put it past him. Once he'd seen Nightmare sitting in his cave, eyes closed, shadows swirling around him. Chaos had crept in to see if he could give him a scare, but when Nightmare had opened his eyes, they'd been a swirling, cloudy gray instead of his usual glowing white. Chaos knew what that color meant—Nightmare had been feeding somehow. Feeding *in* the Void.

But when Chaos had asked him about it—maybe pestered him a bit, if one considered asking the same question over and over a hundred times *pestering*—Nightmare had sicced his shadows on Chaos, chasing him out of the cave.

Funny but a little rude.

So maybe Nightmare had already been summoned into this realm, even with Ivan hoarding the Book. Maybe he'd even found himself a bondmate. Wouldn't that be hilarious? All four of them stuck together again, not in the Void but in the human realm. They could have dinner parties. Nix would host.

It would be like...like *fate*. That was what the vampire kind thought about their own mates. That fate chose them, the perfect humans to anchor their vampiric souls and stop their demonic corruption.

What would Cooper think about that? Fate throwing him and Chaos together. Too practical for it?

No, Chaos decided immediately. *Too hurt*. By what had happened with his parents, by the loneliness of his life so far.

Still, it was a fun idea to play with. It made Chaos feel positively smug, to think that Cooper had been waiting just for him. It was a self-centered idea maybe, but Chaos had never claimed to be anything else. What was better to center his thoughts on than his own self?

Only Chaos's self now included Cooper. His soul piece was in Chaos's chest, and soon enough their souls would be locked together in a more permanent bond.

Who would Nightmare end up with, if he were fated to be with a human? A gothic crypt keeper, perhaps? Or a serial killer, one who used paralytics on his victims? Chaos smirked, wrapping the bag around the Book and placing the little bundle in his sweatshirt pocket. Yeah, a gothic, crypt-keeping serial killer. They would stare moodily into each other's eyes, reliving their glorious torments together.

Chaos cackled out loud at the thought, jumping onto Ivan and Nix's bed and bouncing around until their neatly made covers were mussed. Then he wandered around the apartment again, just for a minute. He couldn't leave without messing with the place at least a little bit. Nix would scent that he'd been there, and he'd think Chaos hadn't cared enough to cause mischief.

It would be so terribly rude.

So Chaos headed to the kitchen and mixed up the drawers and cabinets until nothing was where it had started. He switched around the art on the wall. He tossed the extra linens around, arranging them artfully on the floor. All of it was silly, impish stuff —beneath him, really, considering his powers. But anything bigger—an apartment fire, flooding the place entirely—would ruin the home Nix was making with his human. And wouldn't that be beneath Chaos in a different way, to be so mean to his friend?

Plus, this way, Chaos could tell Cooper about his restraint, and then Cooper would be all quietly proud of him.

And really, Nix *had* been a very good friend. He was deserving of a little bit of consideration. Once Cooper and Chaos were fully bonded to each other, Chaos would go searching Nix out himself, let the other demon dish about his relationship, as Nix was no doubt dying to do.

Nix had always wanted to stay in the human realm, after all. Humans were his food, like any other demon, but also his passion. He liked them, really and truly. Chaos had been more...diffident about it, he supposed—staying in the human realm. He'd wanted out of the Void, sure, but the demon realm would have been fine too. Stirring up trouble between demons was easy, hot-blooded as they were. There was plenty of mayhem to go around.

And with his contracts completed, Chaos would have returned

all powerful and revered. That would have been *hilarious*. Other demons were already a little bit wary of his kind, unpredictable as they could be.

Would Chaos have found himself a demon mate, someone to make hatchlings with for real? He wrinkled his nose at the thought. Whoever it would have been, their hatchlings wouldn't have been nearly as adorable as his imaginary ones with Cooper. Chaos pictured them coming out of their shells with little glasses already on their tiny faces.

Cute. Cute, cute, cute.

Chaos wouldn't have stayed with his hatchlings, anyway. He and this stranger demon would have raised them to self-sufficiency, and then they'd have been on their own. It was the demon way.

Cooper would raise his own hatchlings though. Chaos was sure of it. He wouldn't be able to help himself. He'd care about their thoughts and feelings, and he'd lecture them too mildly about following the rules. Chaos would have to be the disciplinarian.

That seemed unlikely, actually. Maybe they'd just have to be spoiled, like Chaos.

Just thinking about it was making Chaos restless. He needed to get back to Cooper. To tell him all about their imaginary future with their imaginary, bespectacled hatchlings. His puppy would get all horrified but also red and pleasantly embarrassed. It would be wonderful.

Chaos saluted the empty apartment, went back down the elevator, and walked outside, nodding to the doorman. The man gave Chaos a confused stare, looking back to the apartment Chaos had just walked out of.

Chaos grinned at him. "Lovely day, isn't it?"

"Whose guest—"

Chaos didn't get a chance to hear the rest of the question.

Because Cooper's soul piece, which had been thrumming with nerves and worry in a steady, reassuring way that meant he was overthinking but not in danger, suddenly gave a strange, painful clench inside Chaos's chest.

And then it went quiet.

Chaos tapped at his chest, frowning down at his sternum. The piece was dormant in the way that usually meant Cooper was sleeping.

But why would Cooper be asleep?

"I *said*—" the doorman repeated, raising his voice and coming to stand directly in front of Chaos.

"Quiet," Chaos commanded, slapping a hand to the man's mouth. The doorman tried to pry him off, but he wasn't nearly strong enough, and Chaos simply used his grip on the man's jaw to lift him off the ground, removing some of his leverage.

Now the people passing by were giving Chaos looks, their attention no doubt drawn by the muffled, panicked yelling coming from the doorman as he thrashed his arms and legs around, trying to dislodge Chaos's hand.

But Chaos couldn't enjoy the attention. He was too focused inward. Yes, the soul piece was very, very quiet. Maybe Cooper had finished his task and was taking a nap?

But Chaos had felt pain there, for just a moment, hadn't he? He hadn't imagined that.

Something is wrong. Something has happened.

Something had happened to his puppy.

Icy fingers trailed down his spine, and the heaviness in Chaos's chest was nothing like the comforting weight of Cooper's soul. It wasn't an anchor but an anvil, dragging him down, making it hard to gather his fuzzy thoughts.

Chaos had told Cooper he didn't fear anything in this realm. But he'd have to come clean when he saw him next. Because this was fear, wasn't it? Panic, even. Dread.

Chaos dropped the doorman on the ground, ignoring the man's frantic gasps as he turned on his heel. He needed to find his puppy right now.

And if anything or anyone had hurt him in any way...

Then this realm would find out just how dangerous an unleashed chaos demon could be.

20

Cooper

I t was the pain that woke Cooper, a dull throbbing at the back of his skull, like someone was drumming on the bone from the inside.

Drumming, drumming, drumming.

Had he hit his head? But when? How?

He tried to reach up a hand to feel it out, but he couldn't move his arm.

He couldn't move either of his arms.

Cooper blinked his eyes open. If he'd hit his head, it hadn't dislodged his glasses, because he could still see clearly. And he was looking at a...gaming setup?

It certainly looked like one. There was a massive U-shaped desk with multiple computers and different-sized monitors. There was various other tech he was too dazed to categorize properly too. Cooper winced at the blinking lights, which were intensifying that horrible drumming in his skull.

He didn't inspect it for long. It hurt too much, plus he was a little distracted by his restricted movements. His gaze dropped to his uncooperative arms. He was tied to a chair, thick rope wound around his chest and limbs.

Fuck. *Fuck.*

Sergei. Tied to a chair. Bruised and beaten, with a bloody bandage around his arm.

Was the same fate about to befall Cooper? He didn't handle pain well. And torture...

Panic set in, swift and vicious. Cooper tried to shake himself out of the rope, tried to kick his legs for leverage. It was futile. His limbs were tied too tight, the rope was too thick, and he just wasn't that strong. But the fear didn't let him stop trying. It was choking him, insisting that if he thrashed long enough—hard enough—*something* had to give. There was no other option. If he stayed here, he was going to die. His heart would stop if nothing else.

He didn't know how long he struggled.

Long enough for his muscles to start trembling, for that horrible, suffocating panic to give way to a strange, dark numbness. Cooper realized with a start that he wasn't gagged. He hadn't even thought to try screaming.

He didn't try now. If someone had left him tied to a chair like this without a gag, that meant there was no one to hear him scream, was there?

At least, no one who would help him.

Instead he called out softly, "Hello?"

There was no answer, but one of the blinking red lights in front of him flashed to green. Was there someone watching him? Recording him? Who the hell had Cooper pissed off enough to be in this situation?

He looked around the room again, this time ignoring the tech. There were no windows, no natural light. Just an orange-yellow overhead that buzzed and flickered in a way that indicated it was on its last legs.

It wasn't the same office he'd been knocked out in, then. It was somewhere new. Somewhere unknown.

The light that had turned green before flashed suddenly to red, and then Cooper heard the sound of a door opening behind him. The panic returned, tightening his chest and closing his throat. He didn't breathe—couldn't—and he was too frightened to look over his shoulder and find out what he was dealing with.

But he didn't need to. His captor came around to the front of his chair.

The man was lanky, practically rail thin, with a receding hairline that had been buzzed to the scalp. He was wearing glasses—small, wire-rimmed rectangles. No mask or hat or any attempt to hide his identity.

Cooper didn't recognize him, anyway. He'd never seen him before in his life.

"You're awake," the stranger said, his voice reedy in a way that matched his stature.

"Who are you?" Cooper asked.

He jerked back in his seat—as much as he was able, with the ropes tied around his chest—when a penlight was suddenly shined into his eyes.

"Your pupils are even, equal, and reactive. That's good. Although, those eyes of yours are a bit unsettling." The man lowered the penlight, rising from the crouch he'd dropped into for his inspection. "I didn't mean for you to hit your head," he explained, although he didn't sound apologetic. "You went down faster than I expected."

"Who are you?" Cooper asked again. Then, in case he'd have better luck with it, "Where are we?"

"I'm a friend," the man told him, answering the first question and ignoring the second.

A sharp little burst of indignation cut through Cooper's panic. This guy wasn't a friend. Cooper had exactly one of those these days—a perfect, wild, menacing demon—and this stranger wasn't it.

The indignation made him stupid. "Friends don't tie their friends to chairs," he said, shaking his restrained arms as best he could in some sort of demonstration. "Or kidnap them."

"When you run in the circles we do, little wasp, friends do all kinds of things, don't they?"

Cooper froze. AtomicW4sp. It was the screen name he used in hacker forums. A silly thing he'd come up with as a teen. A protected identity.

And this man claimed he was a friend.

Cooper hazarded a guess. "RedRabbit?"

"You can call me Red." There was a small smile on the man's thin lips, one that didn't show his teeth, but his eyes were strangely flat, void of all emotion. "You did very well on your task, Cooper."

"And this—this is my reward?" When RedRabbit—Red—didn't answer, Cooper tried a different tack. "What happened to Smith?"

"Oh, he's just fine." Red pulled a chair away from the desk, some cheap folding one, and set it in front of Cooper before sitting down across from him. "He was instructed on what to do, and he followed his instructions. There was no need to harm him."

Smith had given Cooper up, then. Cooper couldn't muster up any anger over it. Smith had either been threatened or tricked, and they weren't close enough for Cooper to expect him to make some sacrifice of himself on principle alone.

Or maybe the anger would come later, when Cooper had room for something other than confusion and fear.

None of that gave Cooper any better idea of what was happening right now. "Why didn't you message me yourself?" he asked. "You know how to contact me."

Those flat eyes studied him. "You likely would have refused.

Other hackers have tried to meet you in person. You're notoriously shy."

"I don't think I'm notoriously anything."

"You underestimate yourself."

He really didn't. Cooper was skilled enough, but there were more talented people out there than him. "Are you going to tell me what I'm doing here?"

"You're joining my team. You passed the initiation already." Red gave him the same strange, dead-eyed smile. "Congratulations."

"I already have a job, thank you."

"Yes, I know all about your little Russian family business." Red leaned forward, invading Cooper's space. He smelled like menthol but not of smoke, as if maybe he'd been sucking on medicated cough drops before he'd come in. "Aren't you tired of managing small tasks for petty gangsters? What you do now is small potatoes. What I'll be using you for will make us millions upon millions upon millions."

A chill ran down Cooper's spine. It was never good when that much money was on the table. He'd learned that over the years. He started subtly testing the restraints again, even though he knew it was a lost cause. "How do you know so much about me?"

"We have a mutual friend. Said he had a little hacker, talented but meddlesome." That smile of Red's was really beginning to creep Cooper out. "You must have really pissed Sergei off."

Cold dread sank in Cooper's gut. Sergei. Here it was, then. His retaliation from beyond the fucking grave.

"Sergei's dead," Cooper said with a calmness he didn't feel. He didn't like thinking about how Sergei had died. If he thought about it, he could see it, and it hadn't been a pretty sight. A bit anticlimactic, though, for all that there'd been fountains of blood spraying everywhere. Sergei hadn't even had to beg Ivan for his life.

Would Cooper beg Red? Probably. His pride wasn't stronger than his survival instinct, he didn't think.

Red didn't even flinch at the news. "What a shame," he said dryly.

"You're still not going to let me go?" Cooper asked, already knowing the answer.

"No."

Cooper sat with it all for a moment, considering the computers in front of him, the Mafia background this man must have had to have been in Sergei's circle of communication. He thought of what he knew of RedRabbit, before he'd known him to be Red.

Cooper knew this type.

"You want me for what? Data breaches? Ransomware? Siphoning off bank accounts?"

Red shrugged a shoulder. "How about all of the above?"

"Why do you need *me* specifically?"

Another shrug, although it was belied by the intensity of Red's gaze. "You dropped into my lap. And I meant it before—you're good. You have a reputation, even among those who don't know the gangsters you play with. And if this goes south—and it's more likely a matter of when, isn't it, in this day and age?—then you're the perfect scapegoat, given your background." He gave a little smile, like he was confiding in a friend. "I wouldn't do well in prison, I'm afraid."

Cooper swallowed. "And if I refuse?"

The smile dropped. "I kill you and find someone else."

Well, cool. There was the panic again. "Why don't you just send me home?" Cooper asked, hoping he sounded less frantic than he felt. "No harm, no foul."

Oh God. Panic was making him talk like a frat boy.

Red shook his head. "Oh, but I made a gentleman's agreement, you see. Sergei wanted you gone, one way or another."

"Sergei's dead," Cooper repeated.

"I believe you. But the family he was working his way into are still around, even if your boss...wounded them. I'm not planning on making enemies this early by reneging. On top of that, you've seen my face. You know one of my handles. I don't trust you on your own."

"You *chose* to show me your face though. It didn't happen by accident."

Red shrugged again. Unapologetic. Unbothered.

"That's...pretty ruthless."

Red cocked his head. "Given our mutual connection, you must realize you and I have similar business backgrounds. We've worked for similar men. You can't be around people like that for long without catching a little ruthlessness."

Except that was bullshit. Cooper had been around those same men, and it hadn't made him fucking evil. He wasn't kidnapping semi-innocent hackers and threatening their lives for no good reason.

He frowned. "I think maybe you're just a little psychotic."

Red gave him a full smile now, although it still didn't reach his eyes. His teeth were too white and too square, like maybe they were veneers. "You're braver than Sergei said you'd be. From the way he described you, I was expecting a cowering little worm."

It was true that Cooper was acting braver than he had any right to. It wasn't because he wasn't scared. He was fucking petrified.

It was because he knew Chaos was coming for him.

The realization swept through him, warming him to the tips of his fingers. Chaos had told Cooper he couldn't run or hide. He'd told Cooper he would find him no matter what.

Cooper's taut muscles relaxed their tension, just a little. "You really think you can kill me? Have you ever even shot a man before?"

Red's lips twitched, like he was amused with something. "I'm not a fan of guns, actually. So noisy." He reached an arm out and dragged over a rolling stand Cooper hadn't noticed before. It had a small metal tray, like the kind a dentist used to lay out their instruments. There were different syringes on it, and the sight of them chased away any warmth Cooper had gained. "But see, Cooper, I don't need a gun."

"Is that what you used to knock me out?" Cooper asked. There'd been a sting at his neck, he remembered now.

Red picked up one of the syringes, holding it in front of his eyes. "This one, yes." He placed it back down, spreading his hand over three others. "But these three? These are the cocktail for a lethal injection. If I managed the dosage right, it should be relatively painless." He cocked a brow. "Let's hope I did, hm?"

And just like that, Cooper was shaking again.

Time. He needed time.

"How long do I have to decide?"

Red glanced at his phone. "Thirty minutes. We need to be leaving town soon, I'm afraid. I've been hearing some nasty rumors about your employer these past few days. New York suddenly feels much too small. You and I will be taking this show international." He rose from his cheap metal chair, pushing the tray of lethal drugs off to the side again. "I'll leave you alone with your thoughts, shall I?"

21

Cooper

The kidnapping and the threats of murder weren't great, but leaving Cooper alone with his thoughts? That was truly evil.

His thoughts were...not good. Not good at all.

As soon as Red had walked out of sight, the sound of the door closing reverberating behind him, whatever bravery Cooper had gathered from thoughts of Chaos fled.

Chaos would come for him. Cooper knew that.

But would he get there in time?

Chaos claimed he could track Cooper down wherever he was, and knowing him, he probably could, at least with enough time on his side. But Red was taking Cooper away. Out of the city, on a plane, most likely. International—that was what he'd said.

And while Chaos might have figured out navigating a human city—and Cooper still wasn't certain of even that much—he definitely didn't know anything about modern air travel.

If Red took Cooper away, he would be well and truly lost.

And if he refused, he'd be dead.

And if Cooper really wanted to face the truth, he was going to be dead either way. Red seemed like exactly the kind of cold fish who'd do away with Cooper once he was even the slightest bit less than useful.

And just like that, anger reared its head, rising through the fog of fear and despair. This was just so...fucking *pointless*. Pathetic, really. All of Cooper's struggle to survive, to try to make some sort of life out of the shit hand he and his father had been dealt, and now it was all going away because some hacker wanted lots of *money*? Handed over like a trading card because Sergei had wanted revenge for getting caught doing something he shouldn't have been doing? Maybe Sergei could have tried not betraying his own mob boss! How about that? Cooper had been doing it for years. It wasn't that fucking hard.

When would these greedy, shitty men stop pulling Cooper into their stupid games? And for what? Dimitri had been just the same —power-hungry and ruthless. And where had it gotten him? Death by an aneurysm before he could even enjoy any of that money he'd killed so many men for. Unmourned by the sons who hated him, and definitely unmourned by the wife it was rumored he'd had murdered.

Pointless, pathetic games.

Chaos would agree; Cooper knew it. Chaos had more power in his cute little wing tip than any of these narcissists, and he cared about it only so much as it made him laugh. He used it to amuse himself, to make life fun. And now he used it to make *Cooper's* life fun. To try to make him a little less anxious, a little less lonely. To protect him and make him happy.

I love him, Cooper thought. *I love that demon menace, and I might never get to tell him.*

He allowed himself a moment—one moment to let the sorrow fill him—and then he let it go.

This whole stupid kidnapping had clearly been in the works for some time. RedRabbit had approached him months ago, before Cooper had even started looking into Sergei's finances. So this all would have gone down no matter what. But at least Cooper had gotten to meet Chaos first. He'd gotten to remember what it felt like to care for someone and have that care returned. He'd had his small, contained life blown up, if only for a little while.

Cooper still didn't know what drew Chaos to him, but he was grateful for it, whatever it was. And if Cooper died, Chaos would at least get summoned again. Cooper knew Nix and Kai would make sure of it. And hopefully they'd find another summoner who'd allow Chaos to be who he was. Maybe even someone who was a better match than Cooper.

His heart clenched painfully at the thought. Fuck, that hurt. He wished he could rub at his chest to ease it, but his arms were still tied down.

He missed his friend.

The door behind him opened again, and Cooper pushed the pain away. He needed to focus on the anger now. He wanted to be more than his usual scared, trembling self. He wanted to be brave for Chaos. Cooper owed it to him to keep himself alive for as long as possible. Even if Chaos couldn't find him, he could at least stay in the human realm as long as Cooper was living and still in need of a friend.

Because Cooper would always need Chaos—that wouldn't change just because he was under some madman's thumb.

Red circled around, one thin brow arched over his glasses. "Well?"

Time was up. Cooper cleared his throat. "I'd like to live."

Red's lip curled in satisfaction. "Then you won't do anything stupid, will you?"

"You're going to hold me hostage by syringe all the way to the airport?"

"I have some hired muscle coming, and a private plane waiting. Money leads to such convenience, doesn't it?"

Cooper scoffed. "Money's empty."

"*People* are empty," Red hissed. "They're common, and they're disappointing. Hard data? Cold cash? *Those* are reliable." He leaned in, his hands gripping the armrests of Cooper's chair. The scent of menthol crept into Cooper's nose again, and he had to hold back a sneeze. "You know what I'm talking about, don't you? Sergei told me your sob story. People have let you down your whole life."

It wasn't a very convincing supervillain speech, in Cooper's humble opinion. His life had certainly had its lows but no more than any other person's. It didn't mean there was no good in the world. It didn't mean people and connections and love weren't worth it.

But he wasn't going to waste his breath on this guy. He would have shrugged if he could have managed it. "People have disappointed me, maybe," he conceded. "But demons? Never."

Because even if Chaos wasn't going to find him in time, Cooper knew in his bones that his demon would try. And that? That was enough.

Red looked at him in confusion and then cocked his head. Some sort of door or window or something had slammed overhead. The sound was muffled, like maybe they were underground. A basement, perhaps.

"My muscle," Red murmured. Then he frowned as something slammed again. "I'll have to teach them how to be more discreet."

And then there was a garbled scream, louder than the muffled slamming. Closer.

Cooper grinned, the relief so sweet it was almost painful. He knew a certain creature who could invoke that kind of terror.

Red seemed to realize at the same moment that his hired muscle might have come with company. He swiped a hand out, grabbing a syringe from the medical tray. And then he was behind Cooper, his arm around Cooper's clavicle. He rocked Cooper's chair, turning them both to face the door, and Cooper felt the sharp pinch of a needle poking at his skin.

The door flew off its hinges. Smoke filled the room.

And then there was Chaos, his feathered wings spread wide, fire racing along his arms, his horns, his tail. There was blood on his clothes. Cooper's clothes, actually, since Chaos was still wearing his hoodie.

"Puppy," Chaos greeted lowly, though his eyes were locked on Red. "I'm sorry it took me so long. You were right. I got a little lost."

In contrast to his cool tone, Chaos's flames were flaring out in bursts, lighting up his eyes and even his hair. Almost like he couldn't control them.

Cooper winced as the needle jabbed deeper into his skin.

"I don't know what or who the fuck you are," Red said, sounding about a thousand times calmer than Cooper would have been in his position. "But don't come any closer, or this goes right into his veins and he dies."

The scent of harsh campfire smoke filled the room, thick enough to choke them, but it wasn't visible in the air anymore. They still had a clear line of sight to Chaos, his flames flickering in and out as he held himself perfectly still. "I'll stay right here."

And then Chaos's voice was behind them, even as they could still see him in front of them. "And I'll be right *here*."

There was a choked scream from behind Cooper. Something hot and wet landed on the back of his neck, and the needle pressing against his skin fell away.

Then there were two Chaoses in front of him, melding into one as Cooper blinked in shock.

He tried to smile, the gesture faltering as he heard pained gurgling behind him. It sounded like someone had their throat cut but was still trying to speak. Cooper hated that he knew what that sounded like. "You came for me," he said, soft as a whisper.

Chaos glared at the ropes tying Cooper down, at the spots along his wrists where they'd rubbed Cooper's skin raw. "You're hurt."

Chaos jerked his head, and there was another scream, and then the gurgling stopped, the smell of burned flesh filling the room. Cooper gagged, glancing out the corner of his eye before he could help himself. There was...a lot of blood. He looked away again.

Flames flared on the thick ropes around him, and they fell away. Cooper wanted to leap up, to hug his menace, but fire was still flickering along Chaos's skin, and he was still frowning horribly.

"Bracchus," Cooper soothed. "I'm okay."

"You're *not*," Chaos told him, uncharacteristically cold. He wasn't even pouting, which was alarming. "You have rope burns, and you smell like stale fear."

"But I'm okay."

Cooper didn't exactly understand what was happening. He had known Chaos would come for him, that Chaos didn't want him hurt, but also...shouldn't this have been a little fun for the demon? He'd killed some men—*don't think about it, don't look behind you*—and he'd gotten to hunt Cooper down through the city.

Wasn't this his idea of a good time?

"You're so upset," Cooper found himself saying.

"Yes!" Chaos's wings flared, and flames shot up to the ceiling. This time, the fire caught. Cooper watched in horror as it began spreading down the walls, faster than it should have been able to. "Yes, I'm upset!" Chaos cried, ignoring the fire that was circling around them, heating the room. "He *hurt* you. He told me he'd *kill* you. You. My mate. My friend. My puppy. My Cooper." He glared over Cooper's shoulder. "I let him die much too quickly. I should have made it *hurt*."

Smoke was filling the room now but not the yellow campfire smoke of Chaos's magic. Just ordinary, life-extinguishing smoke. Cooper coughed, gesturing to the flames. "How about you put out the fire?"

Chaos crossed his arms. "No."

"If it spreads, someone else could get hurt."

"*Let them.*"

"You don't mean that."

The flames reached the computers and tech behind them. Sparks began showering as Chaos narrowed his fire-filled eyes. "If I killed every human in this realm, there would be no one left to hurt you."

Holy shit. Cooper's kidnapping had broken his demon.

Cooper coughed again, his eyes watering. "That would be... extreme, Bracchus."

"Everyone in the city, then," Chaos offered, almost flippant. "We could keep Ivan and Nix."

"That would still be *extreme*," Cooper told him, getting desperate now. "And unwelcome. People aren't too bad. You like them, remember?"

"I like you more."

Cooper still didn't know exactly what was happening, but he was getting some idea. He gathered his courage and grabbed Chaos's fiery hand, trying to exude a calm he wasn't sure he felt.

"Do you love me, Bracchus?"

Chaos frowned, like Cooper's question had caught him off guard. The flames on his hand trailed over to Cooper's skin, but they didn't burn. They only tingled, a warm caress.

"Love," Chaos mused, still frowning. "It's a stupid, human word. A nonsense word. I'm *yours*. You're mine."

"But why?"

"Is it normal to give reasons for these things?" Chaos shook off Cooper's hold. "I want you because of this." He flung out a hand, and the fire on the walls and ceiling went out. "I love you because of that." He flung out his other hand, and the tech stopped sparking. He pressed both hands to his chest, over his heart. "Isn't the whole point of emotions that they're *feelings*?"

"Well, feelings can sometimes be based on reason."

"Fine." Chaos glared at Cooper like he was being unreasonable. "I want you because you're lovely and special and bright, even when you're sad. Because even when you're scared or nervous, you carry on. Because you're brave, though you don't see it. I love you because you're not the strongest or the fiercest or the wildest, and yet somehow you're still perfect. It doesn't make sense, and that's the best part."

Cooper grinned, so wide it hurt his cheeks. The room was still smoky, but some of the furor around them had quelled. "I love you too, Bracchus."

Chaos stared at him, the flames on his skin dampening slowly until they extinguished completely. His eyes returned to their fox-like yellow as he pushed his lower lip out into a pout. "Stupid, human word," he griped.

And without another word of warning, he scooped Cooper out of the chair, holding him bridal-style tight to his chest. Cooper closed his eyes so he wouldn't see anything he didn't have the stomach to see. He'd have to be careful with himself from now on, for the sake of the humans around him. Red had been a jerk—and he'd definitely intended to kill Cooper if he'd needed to—but did that mean he'd deserved to die?

A suspiciously Chaos-sounding voice in Cooper's head let out a resounding, *Yes. He did.*

Still. Cooper should try to limit bloodshed in the future. He knew he was lucky Chaos had been willing to put the flames out.

Lucky he'd had the trump card of an ill-timed conversation about feelings in his pocket.

"I'm taking you out of this dungeon, and we're going to bond now," Chaos told him, and Cooper could still hear the pout in his voice.

Cooper wrapped his arms around Chaos's neck, resting his head against his demon's shoulder. "Okay. Whatever you want."

He could feel some of the tension ease in Chaos's frame. "Yes. Whatever I want."

"I knew you were coming for me, you know."

Chaos scoffed. "Of course I was. I always will."

Cooper smiled, letting Chaos's warmth surround him. He kept his eyes shut as Chaos took him out of the building he'd thought he might die in.

Always. Always sounded good.

22

———

Chaos

Chaos burst into the hotel room, some of the wood of the doorjamb shattering around them with the force of his entrance.

"You could have used the key," Cooper told him mildly, the words slightly muffled against Chaos's neck.

Chaos sneered. "Human locks are inconsequential."

But Cooper liked his privacy, so Chaos turned and shut the door behind them, sliding the dead bolt into place. It still fit where it should, so he hadn't broken the door too badly, anyway. He managed it all without lowering Cooper to the floor.

He wasn't willing to release him. Not yet. Not so soon.

Chaos had needed to walk many city blocks to find this place, and he'd held Cooper close to his chest the whole way. They'd gotten strange looks from some humans too stupid to realize their lives were in danger, but Cooper hadn't noticed the attention, too busy tucking his face into Chaos's neck. So Chaos had let the humans keep their snooping eyeballs in their heads.

For now.

He could acknowledge that the tether of his self-control was maybe a teensy bit frayed. He was just so *angry*. Angry at the man who lay dead on a cement floor some blocks away—his throat cut and his flesh charred, a fate too merciful by half—angry at this city for trying to keep Cooper from him with its traffic and its nonsense, and angry at himself for having let Cooper face an enemy all alone.

Normally Chaos would let that anger burn, dispensing it with a rush of power until he was settled again. But Cooper wouldn't like the resulting carnage, so Chaos was trying his best to be good.

Cooper asked me not to kill everyone, he reminded himself for the hundredth time. *He set a boundary, as he says. I will respect it.*

It had been more difficult than Chaos would have guessed, to follow the tug of Cooper's soul piece through such a busy city. The man who'd taken Cooper had brought him to a neighborhood far from Cooper's home and Ivan's apartment. Chaos had tried a taxi —threatening the driver with his talons when the man had asked for money—but the other cars had repeatedly trapped them in place on the street.

He, a great and powerful chaos demon, subjected to the mercy of *traffic*.

So Chaos had run. He'd run and run and run, faster than any human could. There were definitely human bystanders who'd seen something they shouldn't have, but what did Chaos care? It was a good thing he'd pressed his limits, because when he'd gotten to the building where Cooper's soul was waiting, there had been two large human men entering, and they'd been discussing something about a plane.

An aircraft. To take Cooper far, far away from him.

Chaos had seen red. He'd been moving before he'd known it, sliced through one's neck, incinerated the other after he'd run, cutting off the man's terrified scream. He'd raced down to Cooper only to see some *weasel* threatening his puppy with deadly human medicine. Cooper had been hurt and scared and—and—

And it's all okay now, Chaos tried to tell himself before the anger could get away from him and he burned through the hotel room they'd only just found. He had to remember. Remember that he had his puppy safe in his arms. No one was going to part them now.

Cooper lifted his head, peering around the room, the skin of his face creased from where it had been pressing into Chaos's sweatshirt for so long.

It was nowhere near as nice as the hotel they'd squirreled away in when they'd been hiding from Ivan, but it was private, and it was here, so it would have to do.

"Are we going to bond now?" Cooper asked after he'd made his perusal.

Chaos took a moment so that his words would come out soft and sweet and not in the harsh growl he could feel burning his throat. "After I bathe you. You have blood on you." *Weasel blood.* It was all over Cooper's neck and the back of his lovely tawny hair. "It smells disgusting."

"I thought you liked the smell of blood."

"Not on you." Chaos considered, then amended, "Not unless it's mine."

Cooper scrunched his nose. "Gross."

"Romantic," Chaos corrected.

Cooper was always getting mixed up about that.

"A shower would be good," Cooper said, ignoring Chaos's correction. "I probably smell like flop sweat."

"Mm," Chaos agreed. Although, Cooper's *soul* didn't taste fearful anymore. It hadn't emitted any fresh terror since Chaos had arrived in that basement doorway, flickering with flames. Even with a syringe of death held at his neck, Cooper had kept faith that Chaos would save him.

Chaos would make sure Cooper never regretted such faith in him. Never ever, *ever*.

He took Cooper into the bathroom. It was small, just a toilet and a bathtub/shower combination. But that was fine—neither of them was overly large.

Chaos set Cooper down gently on the floor and began removing his human's clothes. The hooded sweatshirt Cooper was wearing had weasel blood on it, so Chaos incinerated it, then disappeared his own. He turned the knobs on the shower, feeling the water. The shower pressure was good, at least.

"Tell me if it's too hot."

Cooper held a hand under the spray, then yelped, jerking it back. "Fuck! It's scalding."

It had barely been warm to Chaos. He sparked out a flame before he could help it, annoyed with himself.

Stupid shower. Chaos would burn it down if he didn't need it to wash off the weasel blood.

Cooper started patting Chaos's back. "I'm fine. Let me try." He fiddled with the knobs, waited a moment, and then tested it again, letting out a relieved sigh. "That's better."

It was still a stupid shower.

Chaos removed Cooper's glasses and lifted him over the edge of the tub, then followed him in. He made a note of the temperature while he was in there so he wouldn't accidentally scald his puppy again.

Cooper gave him a sweet, tired smile, tawny strands plastering to his face under the spray. "Are you going to wash my hair for me, menace?"

"Yes," Chaos told him, reaching for the hotel's miniature bottles of cleansing agents.

Cooper eyed him, not yet turning around to let Chaos get at his hair. "*Your* hair's black," he said after a moment. "And so are your eyes. I can barely see the whites around them."

"I'm having dark feelings," Chaos admitted.

"Because I was hurt."

"Because you were almost taken from me."

"I'm sorry," Cooper said softly, like it was his fault. He turned around, letting out a little groan when Chaos massaged shampoo into his hair.

It *wasn't* Cooper's fault, but Chaos didn't mind a little bargaining power. "From now on, wherever you go, I go." He tugged Cooper's head until Cooper tilted it back for rinsing, then poured more shampoo on it.

"Won't I be stronger after the bond? You won't have to worry so much."

"Don't care," Chaos said shortly.

Cooper let out a resigned sigh. "Okay, menace. Wherever I go, you follow."

It was the exact opposite of what Chaos had wanted, back in the Void. It was essentially a leash of his own making, when all he'd wanted was to be free. And he didn't care. Not at all. He'd take that leash and wrap it round and round and round himself until no one and nothing could ever take it off. He'd tie himself so tightly to Cooper no one could ever take him away.

Chaos washed Cooper's hair and skin until his puppy no longer smelled like weasel blood. He now smelled like fake flowers instead, and it made Chaos's nose itch, but it was better than the alternative. He turned Cooper to face him. "You're shaking again."

Cooper shrugged his trembling shoulders. "Shock, I guess. That was all a bit scary."

"Are you—" Chaos tried to make himself say the words. They didn't want to come out, but he made them. "Do you need to wait? To rest before bonding?" Despite his best efforts, the question still came out as a whine.

But really, how far did Chaos being gentle and patient have to go? He was a demon, not a saint. And he was ready *now*.

Before he could get too worked up about it, Cooper smiled softly, pressing a finger to Chaos's lower lip, which had jutted out into a pout at some point. "No, Bracchus. I won't make you wait. I'm ready now."

"Good." That was a relief—it was so tiring being good when he didn't want to be.

Chaos lifted Cooper out of the shower, locating his glasses and pushing them onto Cooper's nose. He dried him, sizzling the water off his own skin as he switched back to his demon form, and then took Cooper out to the bedroom, where the Book lay in its bag on the floor.

Cooper eyed the book-shaped bag. "Is that it? Can I see your mark again, the one I summoned you with?"

When Chaos nodded, Cooper removed the Book from the bag, turning it to Chaos's page without having to search for it. He traced one of his lovely fingers over the yellow markings. "Your symbol is so beautiful," he murmured. "So wild."

Chaos turned for him, parting his wings to display the markings on his back. "It matches my tattoo. You see?"

Cooper grinned at him. "I know."

"So you think my back is beautiful too," Chaos pointed out, wanting them on the same page about this.

"I do."

"Come, puppy." Chaos bounded onto the bed and took a seat, cross-legged with his wings against the headboard. Cooper clambered a little more slowly after him, mirroring his position, with the Book between them.

They were both still naked, which was lovely but maybe not good for Cooper's shivers. His shaking had quelled, but Chaos summoned his sweatshirt back anyway, draping it over Cooper's shoulders before settling back into position.

"Okay, puppy. Turn the Book to the last page and repeat after me."

Chaos said the bonding words, each one deliberate, and Cooper repeated them obediently. He didn't ask what they meant —didn't question any of it—but Chaos wanted him to know. He didn't need to be tricky, not about this.

He gave Cooper his version of the binding spell's human translation. "We bind ourselves together, form, spirit, and heart. To be taken from each other only by death, and even then only for a little, itty bit. My soul for my mate, and my mate's soul all for me."

Cooper grinned at him, and Chaos held a finger to his lips. "Hold out your hand now, puppy."

Cooper held out his hand.

"Which one is the human marriage finger?" Chaos asked.

Cooper wiggled the fourth finger of his left hand, and Chaos grasped it oh so gently. He brought it to his lips and sucked it into his mouth, pressing sharp teeth at the base in a perfect ring. He bit down until blood filled his lips, then bit down a touch harder.

Cooper winced, but he didn't draw back, and he didn't start smelling of fear again.

Good puppy.

Chaos sucked the blood into his mouth, swallowed, and released the finger. Cooper drew his hand to his chest, cupping his fingers together to catch the remaining blood. Chaos could heal it, but he wouldn't. It would scar.

Chaos wanted it to.

"I didn't bite it off," he told Cooper proudly.

Cooper arched his brows, still cupping his hand to his chest. "Was there a risk of that?"

"There's always a risk of that. You have lovely hands."

"Your version of cuteness aggression is alarming."

But Cooper didn't smell alarmed at all. He smelled peaceful. Happy. Safe.

Chaos bit his own finger—the fourth on his left hand—letting the blood well for a moment before he held it out to Cooper.

Cooper winced again, but he took it obediently into his mouth, swallowing once.

"Good puppy." Chaos withdrew his finger, shifting in position. He was getting hard now. He couldn't help it. Cooper wasn't—not yet—but that would change soon.

Sure enough, as the blood hit his system, Cooper immediately started shaking violently, the sweatshirt draping his shoulders sliding off onto the covers. Chaos was trembling now too, and yellow smoke began filling the room, until it looked like the bed they were sitting on was a boat in a river of golden fog.

"I f-feel weird," Cooper stuttered, staring out at the smoke. His pretty penis was filling rapidly, rising out of his lap.

"Yes, puppy," Chaos said. He started grasping his own cock, unable to resist. "It's the bond magic."

Cooper's gaze fell to Chaos's hand. "C-Consummation time?"

"Yes, puppy," Chaos crooned. So smart, his Cooper.

"L-Lube?"

Chaos had been carrying some in his pants pocket, so he summoned them to the bed and dug it out. He ripped open the packet and coated his cock quickly. "Come here."

Cooper shuffled over on his knees and clambered onto Chaos's lap. Chaos swiped off some of the excess lube onto his fingers. He parted Cooper's cheeks. "Let's open you up."

Cooper shook his head. "No fingers. It's too—I need—" He laid his trembling hands on Chaos's arms. "Just go slow."

Chaos knew what Cooper meant. He needed too. It was the magic of the bond urging for them to be joined in body as their souls took root in each other. He lined his tapered tip up with Cooper's entrance. Despite the near-painful urge to *take*, he left it at that for the moment, sliding his hands down Cooper's shivery sides to soothe them both. He let Cooper shift himself down inch by inch until he was seated to the hilt, and their shaking instantly eased.

Cooper was filled with Chaos, and Chaos...Chaos was filled by Cooper. His human's soul was no longer a little piece in Chaos's chest. It *filled* his chest, expanding until there was room for nothing else. As if Chaos's soul hadn't just merged with Cooper's but he'd given his away, given it all to his sweet summoner.

Chaos liked that idea. What did he need with his soul? It already belonged to Cooper.

"Oh my God." Cooper leaned back, his rump resting on Chaos's thighs, his beautiful mismatched eyes wide with wonder. "I can feel you." He tapped his chest. "So wild. And joyful. Brave."

Chaos lifted his fingers to Cooper's cheeks. They were wet. "You're crying."

Cooper blinked, and more tears fell from beneath his glasses. "It feels so good, to have you here. I think—I think I missed you. I've been missing you my whole life, and I didn't even know."

Chaos shifted them, lowering Cooper onto his back on the bed without dislodging himself, Cooper's knees bent and spread wide around Chaos's own. Chaos pulled back his hips, then slid back into him in a tight, tortured thrust. "You'll never be alone again," he promised. "Never, ever."

Cooper moaned and arched his back, encouraging Chaos to move again. "Love you."

It was a silly, nonsense human word, but Chaos liked hearing it come from Cooper's lips. It meant something to Cooper. It meant he'd missed Chaos's soul, before he'd even known who Chaos was. Chaos felt that too. It made no sense at all, and that was a wonderful thing.

Wonderful, wonderful, wonderful.

Chaos wiggled and petted and cajoled until Cooper's body was taking him easily, and then he bred his puppy with slow, smooth rolls of his hips, for once happy to be steady and contained. They had their whole existence for wild and unrestrained. Chaos had an eternity to tease Cooper now.

"Stroke yourself, puppy," he murmured. "Slow for me."

Cooper's breath hitched, and his hand drifted to his weeping cock, stroking almost languidly as they rocked together. He wasn't crying anymore, but his gaze never left Chaos's eyes, even as his breaths grew ragged and his moans desperate.

"That's it, puppy," Chaos crooned when Cooper was right at his edge, his legs shaking desperately as Chaos drove into him. "Come for me. Only for me."

Cooper's hand stilled, cupping the head of his cock, and he hunched with a cry. Chaos bent his head, capturing Cooper's mouth to drink in the sound. That cry was for him. Only for him.

He licked and nipped lazily at Cooper's mouth as his mate whimpered and moaned, and then he let time stop and splinter around them, the fire that had pooled in his belly rushing out to flood his human with his spend.

He came back to himself to find that he was still sucking on Cooper's tongue, his cock still nestled deep and warm within him. Chaos drew back slowly—regretfully—and his perfect Cooper grunted at the loss.

"It's done," Chaos told him, giddy and gleeful.

Cooper touched Chaos's cheek with a smile. "I hope our imaginary hatchlings have your eyes."

Chaos grinned. All the panic and rage of the day had been washed away, and there was only his Cooper, beautiful and generous and so much braver than he knew. "Half will have yours, and half will have mine. How does that sound?"

Cooper pressed a kiss to his lips. "It sounds perfect."

23

Cooper

Flames running along the walls. A strangled scream. Chaos, beautiful and fierce and full of rage, all of it for Cooper.

Cooper woke up with the words already on his lips. "Let's get out of here."

Chaos jolted upright in the hotel bed, although Cooper didn't think he'd been asleep. "Out of the hotel?"

Cooper shook his head. "Out of the city. Let's just...go."

He'd had enough of this place. The people it housed. The men in it who kept creating trouble for him and the people he cared for.

Chaos flopped to his side, setting his head on his hand as he peered at Cooper. "To your cousin?"

Right. Sascha had offered them a place to rest in Maine, if they wanted it. Cooper shrugged. "Sure. As long as it's away."

Cooper needed it. He was pretty sure Chaos did too. Cooper hadn't forgotten Chaos offering—or threatening, really—to take the whole city down for what had been done to Cooper. His demon's rage might have cooled with the sweetness of their bonding, but Cooper didn't want to push it. They could use a little space. Not from each other—Cooper wasn't ready to let Chaos out of his sight anytime soon—but from everything that had happened.

And for once, Cooper was excited to venture out and away. He could feel Chaos through the bond, that bit of him that was supposedly his soul in Cooper's chest, and it was...exciting. Like a new kind of buzzing energy, something Cooper had never experienced before. A new kind of bravery, almost. It wasn't exactly like Cooper had changed overnight but more that he could finally see it. Feel it. The joy Chaos had in exploring the world, in making messes, in being unapologetically himself at every turn.

A little extra courage Cooper could borrow when he needed it.

Cooper might anchor Chaos with this bond, but Chaos...*lifted* Cooper.

He laughed, suddenly overwhelmingly pleased with everything. "Let's get the fuck *out of here*!" he crowed.

Chaos cackled, jumping onto his knees in excitement, bouncing on the bed. "Yes, puppy! Let's go play."

———

THE SEAT BELT sign flashed on with a ding, and Cooper belted his obediently, then leaned over to do the same for Chaos, since the demon was busy making "scary" faces at an older toddler who'd been bawling uncontrollably five minutes ago.

Bawling and throwing things and kicking Cooper's seat. Cooper had been worried, when Chaos turned around and peered over the back of their chairs, that he was going to scold the kid or threaten him with fire or something. But Chaos had been grinning at the overwhelmed child, ignoring the frantic apologies of the parents.

"Aren't *you* a wild one?" he'd asked gleefully, and the little kid had been so shocked by Chaos's approval that he'd stopped crying immediately.

And now he and Chaos were apparently the best of friends. They were taking turns making strange faces and even stranger sounds, and each time Chaos switched it up, it sent the kid into manic giggle fits.

The parents, who had another baby they'd been trying to contend with when their older child was losing it, were looking at Chaos like he was a saint from above.

If only they knew.

Cooper was glad he hadn't splurged for business class this time. He'd had a feeling Chaos would enjoy the close-quartered jumble of coach, and he'd been right. Plus, with the season approaching midwinter the way it was, the flight was only half-full. He and Chaos could have had a seat between them if they'd wanted, but Chaos had insisted on taking the middle seat, pressing himself against Cooper's side.

It had been easy to get tickets. After a quick call with Sascha, Cooper had gotten them onto the next direct flight to Portland, Maine. Sascha and Kai would pick them up from there and drive them the three extra hours to Seacliff, since Cooper didn't have a license.

He'd need to remedy that, if they were going to start leaving the city regularly. He couldn't imagine letting Chaos behind a wheel. Cooper might have access to a little more bravery than before, but he hadn't *completely* gone off the deep end.

Chaos had been pleased when Cooper had suggested flying. "Yes, yes," he'd muttered. "It's time to get familiar with air travel. Just in case."

Chaos's concern had solidified Cooper's decision to get out of town, at least for a bit. They needed to go somewhere where there were no threats, no Mafia business to get tangled up in. Leaving danger behind was why Sascha had gone to Maine in the first place—why he'd stayed—so maybe it was fitting that it was the reason Cooper was visiting.

They landed, everyone started deplaning, and Cooper and Chaos waved goodbye to Chaos's new little friend. They hadn't checked any baggage, seeing as how they only had a computer bag and one backpack between them, since Chaos could summon his own clothes (when he wasn't stealing Cooper's).

They found Sascha and Kai waiting at the curb, Sascha looking tiny next to his massive demon mate. Sascha waved brightly as soon as he caught sight of them. "Welcome, welcome!"

Kai was...glaring? Or maybe that was just his face, even in human form—Cooper didn't know him well enough to know yet. Either way, he eyed them for only a moment before letting out a resigned huff. "You bonded?"

"You did?" Sascha asked in surprise, wide eyes darting between them. "Congrats!"

Kai was still maybe scowling at Chaos. "I suppose I'm stuck with you again."

Cooper stepped in front of his demon, his hackles raised by Kai's attitude. As if it was some burden to have Chaos in the same realm. "You don't need to be around us if you don't want," he told the other demon. "We can find another place to stay."

Sascha made as if to get between them and start offering apologies, but Kai held out a hand, cocking his head. "Are you... defending him from me, little hacker?"

Cooper squared his shoulders, even though the move put him nowhere near Kai's absurd height. "Yes. I am."

Weirdly, Kai grinned at him. He may have been a bit of a jerk, but he was beautiful when he smiled. Even Cooper could admit that. "Very good," the big demon said in approval. "But there's no need. I don't mind Chaos's presence on occasion. I became used to his chatter centuries ago."

Cooper glanced over his shoulder to check with Chaos. He didn't look the least bit offended by anything Kai had said. Instead, he started petting at Cooper's shoulders, gazing at him adoringly like Cooper had just declared his undying love.

"What a good puppy," he crooned, nuzzling his cheek.

And now Cooper's cheeks were hot, and not just from Chaos's touch. It was time to change the subject. "Where's your, um, roommate?"

"Oh. He's super shy about leaving the house. Worse than you." Sascha winced at his own words, laughing awkwardly. "No offense."

Kai pressed a kiss to Sascha's pale hair. "No one is offended, *zaychik*." He waved a hand to Cooper and Chaos. "Into the car with you. It's a long drive in a tiny vehicle."

———

THE HOUSE they pulled up to was big but a little run-down, with peeling paint and a porch that had seen better days. Cute though. Cooper could see the potential.

They made their way inside, and Sascha showed them to the spare bedroom they'd be staying in, then shepherded them back down to the living room. It didn't seem like Sascha's style —not nearly chic enough, compared to his New York apartment—but maybe it had been furnished by the previous owners.

Chaos cocked his head, peering intensely at the bookshelf against the wall, muttering something that sounded like, "So *that's* where it is."

Before Cooper could ask him what he was talking about, a short, young-looking guy with enormous brown eyes and dark hair shorn close to his head poked his head out of the hallway. He kept it at that, the rest of his body hidden away by the wall. Those big eyes darted between them, and it looked as if maybe he was trying to place their faces.

"Matty!" Sascha greeted. "Come meet our guests. This is my cousin, Cooper, and his partner, Chaos. Guys, this is Matteo."

Matteo kept eyeing them warily, not making any more headway out of the hallway.

Cooper stayed still, letting the other man—boy, maybe?—decide for himself whether to face them or flee. Sascha might have decided to lump Cooper and Matteo together as two shy introverts, but this...this didn't seem like what Cooper dealt with at all. It didn't read to him like general anxiety. It seemed more like fear. Specific and overwhelming.

Out the corner of his eye, Cooper caught Kai switching to demon form, tall and blue and horned. After a moment, Chaos followed suit, stretching his wings out as much as the little space allowed.

For some reason, that had Matteo's hunched shoulders lowering. He crept forward until he was framed in the doorway. He was wearing sweatpants and a hooded sweatshirt at least three sizes too big. "Another demon?" he asked quietly, eyeing Chaos's wings and tucking his hands into his sleeves. "And you're...together?" His cheeks went dark pink at his own question, but he didn't backtrack. He just waited patiently for an answer.

Chaos wrapped a proud arm around Cooper. "He's my puppy."

"They're bonded," Kai informed Matteo, which was probably a more helpful explanation.

Matteo gave them a shy smile. "Oh. Okay."

He turned around and disappeared again.

Yeah, he and Cooper were bound to be the best of friends.

Cooper cleared his throat in the resulting silence. "If it's all right, I was thinking I'd show Chaos the beach before it gets dark."

"Of course!" Sascha told him, making a little "shoo" gesture with his hands. "Go explore. The town's pretty small. You're not going to get lost."

Cooper reached into his back pocket. "I brought you something," he said, his throat suddenly tight with nerves. "As a thank-you for having us."

"Oh!" Sascha's eyes widened in surprise. "You didn't have to—"

"I meant to get you a copy a long time ago."

Cooper held out his offering—the two photos he had of his father and Sascha's mother together. In one, they were laughing quietly together, looking like they were sharing a secret. In the other, they were standing side by side, staring solemnly at the camera.

"Oh." To Cooper's immense alarm, Sascha's eyes immediately watered, tears spilling over. "Oh, Cooper. My father didn't—I don't have any—"

"I have duplicates," Cooper said quickly, hoping to stave off any full-out sobbing. "So you can keep these."

And then he was being pulled into the tightest hug of his life. "*Thank* you."

Sascha released him quickly, possibly because Chaos was sparking little flames next to them. Sascha waved his hands toward the door again, sniffing back more tears. "Go. Enjoy the walk. It'll be cold but—but gorgeous."

Kai and Chaos switched back to human form, and Kai walked them out the door, giving Cooper an alarming, forceful clap on the back that was maybe supposed to be his version of gratitude. He pointed them to a path that would lead along the cliffs and down to the beach.

Cooper and Chaos walked along it, hands clasped and arms swinging. Chaos eyed the few people they came across with avid interest, but he didn't start any trouble.

For his part, Cooper ignored everyone, choosing to look at the scenery instead. He breathed in the winter air, noticing that the cold didn't bite into him the way it should have. Maybe that was the demon bond working in his favor, or maybe it was just having Chaos at his side.

Dad would like him, Cooper thought suddenly, and he knew it immediately to be true. Cooper didn't have many memories of his mother, but his dad had told Cooper she was brave and bright and beautiful. Maybe it was the fate of the Zaitsev men, to be drawn to their opposites.

"You're pensive," Chaos finally said, when the path started dipping down toward the shore.

"I was just thinking my dad would like you."

"Really? How odd. Not many do."

Cooper frowned. "That's not true. Your demon friends like you, I can tell. Or the two I've met, at least. Anyone would get sick of each other a little bit, after being stuck together for so long like that. I wouldn't use that as proof of anything."

Chaos was grinning at him. "So protective of me." He kissed Cooper's clasped hand. "My puppy has grown."

Cooper was saved from having to respond by their reaching the beach. It was a small, sandy cove, surrounded by rocky cliffs on either side. The water was dark in the late afternoon but not rough.

It was beautiful.

Next to him, Chaos let out a happy sigh. "Oh, it's lovely. Lovely, lovely, lovely."

"You like it?" Cooper asked, not sure why he was surprised. "The ocean?"

"Mm." Chaos nodded happily. "It's different seeing it in person. I can feel—" He held out a hand toward the water. "There's the rhythm of the waves, so steady. But underneath, in the depths, it's turmoil. Struggles of survival. Storms and massive waves way out deep. A very interesting energy," he said with approval.

"We could see more beaches," Cooper offered. "We could even

do some traveling by boat. Or by plane. Just..." He hesitated but then kept going, spilling out a plan he'd only half come up with. "I can work remotely, you know. We could travel. For the next year, even. Get away. We can come visit regularly so you can see Nix and Kai."

Chaos gave him a look. "And so you can see your kin."

"Yeah, sure. But—would you want to? To do that with me?"

Chaos tugged Cooper into him, back to chest, wrapping his arms around Cooper's waist and tucking his chin over Cooper's shoulder. "Whatever you want, my sweet summoner. Whatever, whenever, wherever. I go where you go."

Cooper laughed, happiness fizzing in his stomach. "But would you enjoy it?"

"I would enjoy it very, very much," Chaos told him with a nuzzle.

Cooper believed him. For whatever reason, this wild, wonderful demon would be happy wherever they went, as long as he was at Cooper's side.

So they'd go. Maybe they'd come back for good at the end. Maybe they'd find somewhere they liked better than the city, only coming back to visit.

Maybe they'd make a little mischief along the way.

But no matter what, they'd be together. Neither of them would be alone. Not anymore.

Cooper leaned his head back, letting his cheek rest against Chaos's. "Me too. I'm going to enjoy it all. Every minute."

EPILOGUE

Chaos

Chaos darted through the apartment, light on his feet. Like a tricky mouse. Or a tricky gazelle. Or maybe just a tricky demon.

He slipped into the steam-filled room, his gaze caught on the silhouette of his prey. He disappeared his clothes and then projected himself into the shower, grabbing onto the warm body in front of him.

"Oh my fucking *God!*" Cooper screamed. He said that phrase a lot when Chaos touched him. Usually when Chaos was inside him, though, and usually with less sheer terror.

Cooper might have slipped and fallen too, but Chaos locked onto him, one arm around his belly and one around his chest. It lined them up perfectly so Chaos's hard cock pressed against the seam of Cooper's bottom.

Lovely.

Cooper realized quickly enough what was happening—Chaos's sweet, intelligent summoner—and relaxed in Chaos's hold. "You scared the life out of me, you know." He craned his neck to peer at Chaos. "I thought you didn't want a shower."

"I got cold."

Cooper chuckled, pressing his delightful bottom back against Chaos's erection. "And what's this you have for me?"

"It's my penis," Chaos told him helpfully. "I'm hoping to place it inside you."

Cooper's chuckle turned into a full laugh. "Dude. I was being coy."

"Ahh. Human games." Chaos nodded in approval, his hands beginning to wander on their own. He enjoyed the way it made goose bumps ripple across Cooper's skin, even with the warmth of the shower. "Then it's a gift," he murmured. "Just for you. Where should I put it?"

Cooper let out a little hum as Chaos's thumb teased his nipple. "You didn't get enough earlier?"

"Never enough." Chaos rocked against Cooper, nestling his hard cock even more firmly into that furrow. "And we'll be apart for hours. I need to stock up."

When Cooper only hummed again, pressing a hand against the shower wall and arching his back, Chaos nipped at his ear in approval. "Good puppy."

He stepped back and spread those lovely cheeks, lining himself up with no hands and—in one perfect, glorious thrust— burying himself where he loved most to be.

Cooper let out a small, punched-out noise. He'd been loosened already from their mating this morning—even lubricated still, since he hadn't gotten to washing himself there yet—but Chaos held himself still anyway, letting his puppy adjust to him. Eventually Cooper shifted, letting out a satisfied moan.

"Stock up," he said, placing his other hand on the wall. "You say it like you're storing it somehow. Sex with me."

"I am," Chaos told him while he let his hands wander again.

He liked touching Cooper while he was nestled inside him, all snug and warm. "In my mind, I have so many beautiful pictures of you, taking me so well like you do. And in my chest, the taste of your soul piece suffused with lust. And in my skin, the feel of you against me. I store it everywhere, my time with you."

Cooper let out a breath, and when he peered over his shoulder at Chaos, his gaze was soft as silk. "Bracchus. That's so—"

"Creepy?"

"Romantic."

Ah yes. Chaos *was* a wonderful romantic. Just look at him, breeding his puppy before their time apart.

Speaking of.

Chaos withdrew to the very tip and then sank back into Cooper with a growl. The way Cooper's tight insides welcomed him, sucking him in, always made his belly clench, that heat pooling in a way that reminded him of old bloodlust.

"Mm," he crooned. "So nice and warm inside you, puppy."

"Says—" Cooper gasped, the sound trailing off into a broken moan as Chaos repeated his earlier motion. "Says the furnace."

Chaos placed his hands over Cooper's on the shower wall and began rocking into Cooper in earnest. He ran his nose along the soft skin of Cooper's neck, along his jaw, before trailing back up to nip at his ear again. Lovely charred caramel rose in the air.

His good, sweet, perfect puppy let himself be ravaged. Let Chaos take what he wanted from his body. Let Chaos know how much he loved it with his gasps and moans and wonderful little whimpers.

It was Chaos who lost himself first. He set his blunt teeth into Cooper's shoulder and shuddered, filling him up.

For once, he withdrew his cock immediately, shoving his fingers inside instead, feeling his own spend, hot and wet inside his summoner.

Cooper let out a choked "Oh *fuck!*" and Chaos reached his other hand around to stroke Cooper's poor, swollen cock.

"Your turn, puppy," he ordered, scissoring his fingers, pressing his cum all over Cooper's inner walls. He wished he had more to offer, wished he could coat him from the inside out.

Mine. My puppy. My summoner.

Cooper twisted his neck to slam his mouth against Chaos's, kissing him in that openmouthed, sloppy way that meant he was close to his own release. Chaos hummed his pleasure, taking what Cooper offered him, sucking at his tongue and licking all around his mouth.

Cooper came with a sweet, surrendering sob, splatting cum against the shower wall. Chaos soothed him as he trembled and shook, although he left his fingers where they were. "Good puppy," he praised. "There it is. All for me, hm?"

"Fuck," Cooper eventually sighed, slumping back against Chaos's chest. "Fucking fuck."

Chaos nuzzled his cheek. "Shall I leave all this inside you? A little treat for the day?"

Cooper let out a shuddering laugh. "Menace. Clean me up, will you? You can defile me again when I get home, if you really need to."

Ohh yes. Chaos would definitely need to.

Chaos washed them both, and they dressed quickly.

As Cooper was getting his computer bag together, Chaos sneaked his human's phone out of his pocket, sending a text that he immediately deleted before tucking it back where it had been.

His face was perfect innocence when Cooper turned to him. "You sure you don't want to come with me?"

After having spent the last year and a half bouncing around the world, they were planning on returning to the city for the summer—or some time in the city, some time in Maine—and

Cooper was heading to a nearby computer center to ask about volunteering to teach coding to teens.

Chaos knew he'd be amazing at it. His Cooper was so patient. So kind.

Cooper had changed over their year away. Grown into himself. He'd told Chaos that repeated exposure to new people and places and experiences had helped, but Chaos thought it might also have been about getting away from the place where so many of his bad memories resided. He hoped too that he'd helped, in his way.

He adored his puppy just as he was—Chaos wouldn't have been any less devoted to Cooper if he'd remained anxious or a homebody—but Cooper seemed happier this way. More comfortable in his own skin.

And he *was* still a homebody. Even though they'd traveled, they would also spend days inside their rental where they never went out, just had laptop time and sex time and bath time on repeat. Chaos loved those days, snuggled up with his puppy, just as much as he loved exploring the human realm. He'd never thought he could find comfort in peace and calm, but the universe was full of surprises, it seemed.

And sometimes, when Cooper got lost in a hacking project, Chaos would go out and explore and make mischief on his own, coming back at regular intervals to make sure his summoner was eating and sleeping properly.

Now he kissed his puppy goodbye, waving him off, and immediately left the apartment.

Chaos had a mission.

He made his way to the address he'd gotten from Ivan. It hadn't taken much coaxing either. Maybe Ivan was more protective of his hacker cousin than he let on.

Chaos knocked on the run-down office door.

A human answered. He looked to be somewhere in his early sixties, with a scraggly gray beard and the look and scent of someone who hadn't showered in more than a few days. He narrowed his eyes in suspicion, the door held mostly closed in front of him. "You're not who I was expecting."

"No. You were expecting Cooper, weren't you? But that was me, texting from his phone." Chaos grinned. "Wasn't that devious of me?"

There was a flash of fear on the man's face—*Smith's* face—but Chaos was already pushing him inside, locking the door behind them.

"Hello," Chaos said, since Smith had apparently forgotten the niceties when he'd seen Chaos at the door. "I'm Chaos. Cooper's friend. His *best* friend."

Smith held up his hands, as if a silly gesture like that could ward off any of Chaos's ire. "Listen, I'm sorry for what happened. I told Coop so, when he came to pick up the latest papers." He cocked his head, his hands still held in front of him. "That was for you, right? I recognize you from the picture now. Bracchus something or other."

"Yes. Thank you for those." Look at Chaos, being so polite. Cooper would be proud. "But we still have our own business to attend to."

Smith tried to back away, but he only ran into his own desk. "Wh-What kind of business?"

Chaos stepped forward, closing the extra distance Smith had gained. "I've been away, so I apologize for the delay. I usually like my vengeance right up front. Cooper was hurt. You played a part." He grabbed Smith's hand, ignoring the man's efforts to tug it away. "Index, middle, pinky, or ring?"

"Wh-What?"

"Which will you miss the least?" Chaos asked, ever so patient. "I'm being very kind, letting you choose and not even bringing your thumb into it. You probably need that most of all, yes?"

Smith didn't answer.

Chaos switched into his demon form.

Smith screamed.

Chaos growled. "Which finger, human?"

Smith only screamed again, so Chaos chose for him. And in the spirit of Cooper's mercy, Chaos would be generous.

He'd take the littlest.

He bit down on Smith's pinky. There was a crunch. Another scream. The taste of warm copper and old man skin.

Ugh.

Chaos spat out the pinky immediately and cauterized what was left with a flash of fire. He released Smith's hand, not eager to hold it any longer than he needed to.

Smith immediately tucked it into his chest protectively. His screams had died down with the shock of the cauterization.

Chaos made a face at him. "That wasn't very tasty." He looked accusingly at Smith's hand. "Cooper's would have been much more delicious."

"What the *fuck*?"

"Anyway, I must be off. Hurt Cooper again and it'll be your whole hand. Or better yet, your head."

Chaos wouldn't really be able to unhinge his jaw wide enough to bite off a man's head—who was he, Nightmare?—but he thought it was still a very good threat. His talons would do the trick if nothing else.

With another flash of his sharp teeth for good measure, he flounced off, leaving the cowering, whimpering man behind. Chaos needed to hurry if he was going to surprise his puppy at the computer center.

Once there, he caught Cooper on his way out of the building, and the look of pure delight on his human's face made something thump in Chaos's chest. Cooper was always happy to see him. Every single time.

"Perfect timing!" Cooper told him, hitching his computer bag higher onto his shoulder. "Did you get bored all by your lonesome?"

Chaos tugged Cooper into his arms, nuzzling his head against his shoulder. "Yes, puppy. So bored."

Chaos wouldn't tell Cooper about his small piece of vengeance, not unless Cooper asked specifically. His puppy was tenderhearted and wouldn't like to hear about his friend getting hurt.

But that was what Chaos was for. Chaos would protect Cooper no matter what, with or without his explicit knowledge. Cooper hadn't had anyone at his back before, but he had a chaos demon at his disposal now. The fact that Cooper never used that fact to an unfair advantage when it came to all the cruel and annoying humans in the world was a very fortunate thing for them.

Chaos wouldn't lie, though, if Smith ever spilled the beans. He knew Cooper would forgive him instantly. Being tricky and sneaky and a little vicious was part of Chaos's nature, and Cooper understood that. Just like Chaos would have accepted Cooper if he stayed firmly in his shell, Cooper would accept Chaos even if he stayed ferocious and wild.

Luckily for the world, Chaos didn't mind being a little domesticated.

As long as that world left Cooper alone.

He clasped Cooper's hand in his, swinging their arms between them. "You ready, puppy?"

"For what?"

"Anything. Everything."

"Oh, is that all?" Cooper laughed. "I'm ready. Whatever you want."

Chaos kissed Cooper's lovely cheek and started pulling him down the sidewalk. He already had what he wanted, as well as what he needed, right here in his hand. It had all dropped into his lap in an instant, when he'd been summoned by Cooper and his computer.

But while they were out, they might as well have a little fun.

THE END.

AUTHOR'S NOTE

Thank you so much for reading Calling Chaos! I hope you enjoyed your time with this duo as much as I did.

Ohhh Chaos aka Bracchus aka little menace. Sly but sweet, mischievous but willing to be oh so good to keep his puppy happy. I loved writing him so much, and I especially loved getting to pair him with Cooper, who desperately needed a little burst of wild and wily romance in his life. I knew these two would be fun and a little weird, but I was pleasantly surprised by how sweet and tender they ended up being together. They've both come to mean a lot to me, and I hope you feel the same.

What's Next?

Matty and Nightmare, our last couple of the Demon Bound series! You've asked, you've (gently) pestered, you've hyped them up! I've started their story already, and I can tell you it's going to be sooooo very delicious. I can't wait to unleash them on the world!

If you're too impatient to wait, you can read WIP chapters as I write them on Patreon.

If you want to stay in the know, you can sign up for my newsletter for updates and news on upcoming releases. And I can always be reached by email if you just want to say howdy. I love, love, love hearing from my readers!

graebryanauthor@gmail.com

ALSO BY GRAE BRYAN

Vampire's Mate Series

<u>Roman</u> (Book One) – Danny and Roman

<u>Soren</u> (Book Two) – Gabe and Soren

<u>Lucien</u> (Book Three) – Jamie and Lucien

<u>Johann</u> (Book Four) – Alexei and Jay

<u>Wolfgang</u> (Book Five) – Eric and Wolfe

Colin (Book Six) — Colin, Fox, and Dane

<u>Cassian</u> (A Vampire's Mate Novella) – Blake and Cass

Demon Bound Series

Wreaking Havoc (Book One) — Sascha and Kai

Inviting Bedlam (Book Two) — Ivan and Nix

Calling Chaos (Book Three) — Cooper and Chaos

Unleashing Mayhem (Book Four) — Matteo and Nightmare

Novellas

An Unwitting Bargain - Benny and Helio

ABOUT THE AUTHOR

Grae Bryan has been reading romance since she was far too young to know any better. Her love for love stories spans all genres, and while her current series is of the paranormal variety, she knows she'll be exploring other worlds further down the line.

She lives in Arizona with her family, who graciously share space with all the imaginary men in her head. When not writing, she can generally be found reading more than is healthy, walking her monster-dog, or cuddling her demon-cat. She loves anything and everything gothic, strange, lovely, or cozy.

Find her online: graebryan.com
    Patreon: patreon.com/GraeBryan
    Facebook: @GraeBryanAuthor
    Instagram: @authorgraebryan
    Sign up for her newsletter: graebryan.com/contact
    Join her Facebook reader group: Grae Bryan's Reader Den

www.ingramcontent.com/pod-product-compliance
Lightning Source LLC
Chambersburg PA
CBHW050509260626
47157CB00004B/1245